SEDUCING A SPY

EMMALINE WARDEN

EMMALINE WARDEN LLC

ALSO BY EMMALINE WARDEN

Genus of Gentlemen
LOVE AND OTHER PERENNIAL HABITS

Digital Edition ISBN: 979-8-9874003-3-3
Print Edition ISBN: 979-8-9874003-2-6

Cover design by Lily Bear Design Co.

FIRST EDITION
Print Edition

To those who were told they were too strong,
too loud, too much.
You aren't and you never were.
Keep going.

ACKNOWLEDGEMENTS

Putting a book together takes so much more than simply writing it, and I wouldn't have been able to bring this book to life without a group of phenomenal individuals.

Huge thanks to Nicole McCurdy of *Emerald Edits* for helping to make this book stronger and for reminding me that Ronan is a cinnamon roll. Thank you to Catherine Stein for reading through it even as she tackled her own projects. And a big thanks to Raine Lam for fitting me into her schedule and making sure this book is polished. Also, to Lindsey Vandehey of *Lily Bear Designs* for creating another stunning cover.

To the *Let's Get Critical* group: I love you all and adore you more than you know. I'm so grateful to whatever fates put you all into my life. Onto the next chapter!

CHAPTER ONE

October 1815
London

I F THERE WAS one thing Eloise Delacroix abhorred, it was cigar smoke. Unfortunately, that very stench was the exact scent emanating off the body currently pressing down on her. As she attempted to wiggle free, she found that the body's deadweight was pinning down her shoulders. The entire circumstance was laughable. Had Niraj or Sophie been present to witness her predicament, they would no doubt be in peals of laughter. In truth, she still could not understand how it happened, nor why the laudanum had taken so long, but alas, here she was, trapped beneath the Earl of Eastwick without a means of escape.

Eloise dragged in a breath, praying she would not vomit, before placing her feet on the floor and pushing with all her might. The earl rolled off her with a thunderous snort, the sound of his body hitting the floor thankfully muffled in the quiet of his home office. He emitted another deep snore, hinting he would not awaken for some time. She sighed with relief.

Flat on her back, Eloise stared at the ceiling, forcing her breathing to even. Her already tight bodice left little room for each breath and the fresco that decorated the ceiling seemed to spin with each pull of air. Squeezing her eyes closed, she stood, praying her feet would hold her. She had very little time to work given the earl's leisurely consumption of his drink. With a scowl, she looked at the sprawled body of the lord. The man could wax on about himself for a lifetime but could not finish a finger of scotch in thirty minutes. It was, quite frankly, disappointing.

Eloise ripped open the earl's waistcoat and unbuttoned his shirt, smiling at the result of her effort. The Earl of Eastwick was a large man in both height and weight, yet his body seemed more a lump of clay never given the proper form. It was no doubt the reason that, beneath his fine linen shirt and well-tailored vest, he had outfitted himself with a corset in the hopes of appearing more human-shaped.

Eloise rolled her aching shoulders as she scanned the room. The walls were draped in dark silk and decorated with various pictures of fox hunts, each one more grue-some than the next. Her stomach clenched. With a frown, she forced herself back to the matter before her. "If I were a traitor to the crown, where would I hide the proof?"

The earl's desk, an enormous piece, seemed the proper place to start, but each drawer proved fruitless. Eloise glared at the prone figure on the floor, hoping he could feel her disdain. The bastard was not making this easy.

Over the fireplace hung a large oil painting depicting Lucifer's fall from heaven. It was the one work of art in the entire room that did not involve the death of a harmless creature. With a smile, she pulled a chair before it. Rucking up her skirts and tying them to one side, Eloise stepped onto the chair. Her fingertips danced along the frame, and she cursed as she found it attached to the wall. Hands on her hips, she leaned back and inspected it again. The gilded frame fit the portrait almost to perfection, except for the smallest gap of space. Sliding a fingernail between it, she drew back the portrait, revealing a shelf of oddities. A glass eyeball, a shrunken head, and a bottle claiming to be a love potion lined the wooden shelf. Eloise sighed, the effort shifting an errant curl on her forehead as she stared at the space with disdain.

Intriguing design, but useless, nonetheless.

Swinging the portrait back into place, Eloise hopped off the chair and shook out her skirts. Bouncing up and down on the balls of her feet, she wiggled her fingers as she scanned the room. *Think.*

Her gaze landed once more on the desk and a frown pulled at her lips. There was something off about it. *Something...*

She circled it, her finger tapping on her lips as she inspected the massive piece from all angles. A sculpted section took up the place in the center of the desk where a drawer should have been, the unique carvings covering the spot where a handle should be, and a smile took hold as realisation dawned.

Hurrying back, she slid her hand underneath the center of the desk. Her fingers skimmed a latch, and she swallowed her cry of delight as a small shelf dropped open. She withdrew the singular piece of paper inside and closed the drawer.

Eloise set the paper on the desk and scanned the document, her pulse humming in her ears. This was it, the clue she had been looking for. Joy surged through her veins and she tampered the urge to dance a jig. Copying the information on a separate slip of paper, Eloise kissed her copy before stuffing it into her skirt. Returning the original to its hidden location, she smiled.

Tossing the remains of their drinks into a potted palm, Eloise shook her blonde curls free from several of the pins holding it in place. A tug at her bodice left more of her breasts exposed to onlookers, and she shimmied her well-endowed bosom, displacing the fabric a touch more. With a sigh, she pocketed the useless pins, before swallowing a chuckle. This life had its ludicrous moments, for certain, but there was something to be said about her scandalous reputation. It provided the perfect cover. With a pinch to her cheeks, the last piece fell into place and she looked down at herself.

Decidedly tumbled.

After one last glance at the room and the sleeping lord inside it, Eloise took a deep breath and prepared to act out the final part of her charade. The odious earl's ancient butler awaited her exit on the other side of the door, blocking the means to her escape. Opening the door, and lowering her gaze in an attempt to appear demure, Eloise tugged at her neckline enough to draw the man's attention to how far her clothing had shifted.

"The earl was exhausted after our talk," she said to the severe-looking man. "He decided to rest."

"Certainly, Mrs. Delacroix. Would you like me to call for a hack?" the butler asked, his tone disapproving as his eyes drilled into her.

"No, thank you. My conveyance should be right outside."

Alone on the steps of the earl's Grosvenor Square townhouse, Eloise lifted the hood of her crimson cloak before wrapping the dark fabric around her body, more for warmth than cover. The dark, empty streets of London stood before her, having succumbed to the night's tedious embrace. Between the flicker of the lamps lining the street and the stillness before her, she could almost understand the allure of the city. Almost.

Once ensconced in her carriage, Eloise released the breath she had been holding. As they pulled away, she held the paper close to her chest, where it certainly could not disappear. It was the biggest piece of evidence she had uncovered in weeks, and undoubtedly the key to her survival, causing both fear and joy to weave themselves together in a tangled web in her chest.

"I assume you found something," a voice said from the darkness.

Eloise reached for the dagger in her boot, but stopped at the soft chuckle.

"No need for weaponry, El," said the voice.

As the figure leaned forward, the light from the street lamps caught in his blond locks and she scowled. "Bloody hell, Knight. I wouldn't have pinned you as a lurker in women's carriages." Frowning at the man, Eloise sank back into the plush seat.

"There's a lot about me you don't know," her superior said, his tone jolly. Remington Knight was the second son of the previous Duke of Harcourt, but instead of following the usual role of a younger son and enlisting or joining the clergy, Knight had opened the most notorious club in London, The Rogue's Den. The club itself not only provided a decent income for the aristocrat, but was also a magnificent cover for a man who secretly worked for the Foreign Office. Even better, the place ran on secrets. The more you knew, the easier the access to its doors and the delectable extravagance contained inside.

"What did you find?"

"A list of names," Eloise said, handing the scrap of paper to him. "It's not much, but it's a start."

Knight glanced at the sheet and nodded. "Good work. I hope you didn't go to too much trouble to procure it."

Eloise replayed her evening and stifled a laugh. "None at all."

He gazed at the passing streets of London, his silence echoing through the confines of the carriage. Knight was not one to waste words. So, while the muscle of his jaw clenched and his eyes took in the lacklustre scenery, she remained quiet. Sitting back against the seat, she left him to his ghosts.

"There's an event this week which I'm required to attend. You'll accompany me. We should be able to put your list to good use and determine your next target." Tapping on the roof with his walking stick, Knight waited as the conveyance slowed before leaping out. "Eloise, you only have a month to convince the secretary of your usefulness. I don't want to put added pressure on you, but you must resolve this, or I'm afraid your time with the Foreign Office is over."

"I know how much is at stake, Knight."

Knight touched his cap before closing the door and the carriage began to move once more.

The fate of not only her career, but Sophie's, and any

other woman within the Foreign Office, sat upon her shoulders. Immense terror grabbed at her chest, the pressure near unbearable.

In the month since Napoleon's exile to St. Helena, agents within the Foreign Office had gone missing. The few leads they had found pointed to a group of underground revolutionists calling themselves The Fall of Caesar.

Their mysterious leader instructed his followers to do whatever necessary to bring down England and restore Napoleon to power once more, and their criminal connections spanned from Parliament to Bow Street. Drastic measures had been taken by the Foreign Office to fight this new threat, measures they no doubt regretted dearly. They had hired new agents. Female agents.

Eloise could feel the noose tightening as each day passed. The fate of England rode on her reconnaissance, but more importantly, not only her future in espionage, but her future in general. It was her only accomplishment, the one thing she could claim to be good at. With only a month to prove herself, things were looking bleaker by the moment.

The carriage raced towards her townhouse in Marylebone, the streets of London flying by as Eloise forced down her fear, counting her breaths with each clop of the horse's hooves.

Eastwick's butler, like the rest of the ton, accepted her facade. In their eyes, she was a courtesan looking for her next protector, exchanging her body for a refined meal and diamond earbobs. It mattered little that women in this role sold the jewelry when their arrangements ended, using the funds for continued survival. The butler, like everyone else, believed what they saw in front of them and never looked further.

If they did, they would be shocked to find that Eloise Delacroix, one of the most sought-after courtesans in London, was actually a spy.

✧　✧　✧

THE MARQUESS OF Vaughn, Lord Ronan Tomar, sat back in his chair, swirling his second glass of scotch. Staring at the massive fireplace gracing the sitting room of the Rogue's Den, he pondered his current predicament.

The scene for his next chapter had been cast perfectly in his mind. Dark, exotic music played in the background, setting the mood. Candlelight created an ambiance sensual enough to make Aphrodite weep. Luscious fruit lay on silver platters decorating the table. The daughter of the sheik nibbled on a date as she looked across the table at him, contemplating making him her next foray into danger. And then...

His mind drew a blank. What should happen next?

A door opened, drawing him out of his thoughts.

"You're a liar, Wick," a high-pitched voice said.

The Earl of Eastwick and Baron Strauss walked into the elegantly appointed sitting room, their raucous banter filling the quiet space. Rolling his eyes, Ronan returned his attention to the journal upon his lap.

"I'm not, Strauss! I'm telling you, we sealed the deal last night," the earl said, crowing his excitement.

"I find it hard to believe, Wick. I do."

"I invited her to dine at my home and afterward we had a refreshing interlude in my office. She plumb wore me out, the little minx. She was so spectacular I slept like a babe afterward. Luckily, the wife is in Surrey or I would've been in quite a pickle," Eastwick said with a chuckle.

"You're to be Mrs. Delacroix's next protector? You'll be the envy of every man in London." Strauss' voice was filled with wonder.

"Quite right, quite right. I'm having my solicitor draw up the papers this morning. After such a splendid evening, one can bet Mrs. Delacroix will be mine by this afternoon!"

Ronan's hands tightened around his glass at the obnoxious lords' interruption. Releasing a deep breath, he set it down on the mahogany table with a sharp click.

Eloise Delacroix's name graced the lips and bedrooms of every nobleman; widowed, married, or old enough to have found his bollocks. The sought-after female was said to be a rare gem, allowing her protectors to have her in any fashion, as long as they kept her in style. And then, of course, there was what she embodied: the fashion, the drama, the endless uselessness. She was the personification of the breeding grounds the ton had become, an unending society of loveless marriages that left spouses seeking affection from others more willing.

"Lord Vaughn, how are you this wonderful morning?" asked Remington Knight, the Rogue's Den's owner, as he strolled into the room. His overwhelming presence filled up the space as it always did. The large man fit in well with the lavish environment. The dark drapes and plush leather furniture created a stunning backdrop that would have had ladies aflutter, but, alas, since no women were present, the effect was sadly lost.

"Simply delightful, Lord Knight, until graced by your presence. Unfortunately, I have neither the time for idle chatter nor the energy to give you veiled threats, so off you go," Ronan said, shooing off the blond giant. In truth, he had nothing but time, another blinding fault of the aristocracy. But the bastard did not need to know that.

"Yes, I'm sure you have places to be, Ro. Your home must be lonely without you in it, pacing worn spots into the carpet. Drinking from its endless supply of liquor."

"That's enough," Ronan said, his eyes motioning to Eastwick and Strauss, two of the biggest gossips in the aristocracy.

Remy scoffed. "Instead, you're at my establishment, imbibing in my spirits."

Ronan raised an eyebrow at the man before him. "It's funny how you claim this to be your establishment." Running his finger around the rim of his glass of scotch, Ronan smiled. "I could've sworn you used my funds to build this place, which makes me part owner. So, yes, Remy, I will stay here and drink your spirits, considering it's my coin that paid for it."

Remy sighed and took the seat next to Ronan. Ronan could feel the man's dark gaze staring, taking in his disheveled state. "I'm sorry to hear about your father. If there is anything you or Felicity need at all...,"

"It's so sweet of you to worry about us." Ronan touched his chest, forcing a look of gratitude to his face. "In another time, your concern would have been much appreciated, but we're long past that, are we not? Especially with regard to my sister."

"Ronan..."

Ronan shook his hand. "No, no. None of that reminiscent nonsense. I'm sure if you could go back in time, you would do things differently. Be a genuine friend, take care of Felicity and her children, and on and on. I have little interest in hearing your regrets for the millionth time, Remy." His gaze returned to the two lords chatting in the corner. The heavy drapes on the walls created a quiet cavern for their discussion.

"Don't worry yourself over them. Eastwick seems to have won the favor of Mrs. Delacroix. They are much too deep in their excitement to overhear us," Remy said.

"I have not forgotten that the currency of the club is information, the more secret, the better."

"Only the secrets of the people wishing to gain access to the club. Your mysteries are better left alone. Let me have the footman bring you some tea and something to eat. I can have a room set up for you to rest for a bit. You look as if you are going to fall asleep in that chair."

"Instead of mothering me, aren't there other items, other people, you should be seeing to?" Ronan asked, sending a bland smile to the proprietor. "Perhaps you should take care of them before clucking over me." Remy flinched at the words, and it elated Ronan that he had got under his skin.

Shutting his book with a loud snap, Ronan stood and brushed off his trousers. That was certainly enough socializing for one day, and the fact that it involved needling his once closest friend was a fitting win altogether. Doffing a pretend cap and bowing to Remy, he took his leave. The two lords sent him startled looks as he ambled from the room, leaving the club's owner behind. He could feel Remy's weighted stare, and a corner of his mouth lifted with delight.

Inside his carriage, he forced his mind to return to his writing instead of the abject irritation that burned inside him each time he spoke with Remy. The blighter was intent upon repairing their shattered friendship, but only an act of God would make Ronan forget that Remy had abandoned Felicity and her children after the duke's death. The children had needed their uncle, and Felicity had needed her friend. A sharp pain at his jaw sent awareness that he was clenching his teeth and Ronan rubbed at it, willing it to loosen, yet the motion proved useless.

As the grand carriage drew up to his father's Mayfair townhouse, Ronan grimaced. He needed to stop thinking of the large manse as his father's, especially since the man had left this Earth nearly a fortnight ago. Now, the pristine white structure gleaming in the morning sun was his. Ronan withdrew from the carriage, heading up the stairs. He never broke his stride as the front door opened for him.

"Good afternoon, my lord," Jenkins, his butler, said. "The post has arrived. I've placed it in the library."

With a nod to Jenkins, Ronan headed towards the room and shut the door behind him. The room was his sanctuary, the musty smell of the books within like a soothing balm to his broken heart. He conducted estate business within the space, and even planned to have his father's will read here after the wake. He allowed his solicitor to believe it was his eccentricity, but in truth, he could not bring himself to open the doors to his father's office. The old man's desk loomed like a bad omen, a sign he would never measure up to what his predecessor had accomplished. No, the room would remain closed off to preserve what little sanity he had left.

Ronan sighed and paced the worn carpets of the library, praying that the texts within the room would jostle his memory of the previous night. He should never have drowned himself in spirits while writing. His publisher anxiously awaited his next novel, writing to him daily as his deadline loomed, but the words failed him no matter how hard he tried.

Unlike other sons of the aristocracy, Ronan had remained in his father's home, which provided the perfect bachelor residence. After the passing of his mother, and Felicity's marriage, the marquess beseeched Ronan to remain. When his father's illness had begun to leave him weak, Ronan had been glad he had agreed. The enormous expanse of the home ensured they saw very little of each other, their relationship already strained, but Ronan could remain on hand should the marquess have another one of his fainting spells.

For Ronan, the house had provided the perfect place to have all his needs met without having to lift a finger. There was less to worry over and more time for his books.

Retracing his steps, Ronan let his mind wander, in the hopes that the loose threads of the scene would miraculously stitch themselves together. What had he planned to have the woman do? Drug his punch? Lace the food? Tell her father about the affair?

This would be so much simpler if he were like normal heirs of the aristocracy, but no. Instead, he chose to spend his time cavorting within the caverns of his own mind. He could be spending his days traveling the world and dallying with an actual sultan's daughter instead of making it up in his head, and yet, here he was.

Ronan's reflection appeared in the glass of the bookcase, his countenance startling. No wonder Remy had insisted upon his getting some sleep given the haggard appearance of his face. His state of dress was what society required, albeit several seasons outdated. His valet, Turner, eternally griped at the lack of tailors visiting the home, but Ronan could not be bothered.

His sad excuse for a cravat hung limp around his neck, its wrinkled state surely to send Turner into fits. His coat fit a bit too tightly across his shoulders, and his beard created a dark shadow across the lower half of his face. A night of little sleep, and too much drink, only highlighted the carved wrinkles on his face. His dark hair brushed at his collar, a few bits starting to curl at his forehead, and the same blue eyes as his father's stared back at him, although, they had lost most of their luster. It was little wonder Remy had seemed so concerned. If a nearby theater were in need of actors, they could cast him as a macabre villain.

In truth, he had never been this unpolished. He usually tried for a modicum of respectability, but his lack of sleep was beginning to catch up with him. Each time he closed his eyes, he was met with dreams that left him rattled. He would awaken, covered in sweat, certain he was the catalyst of doom that would befall the estate and everything his father worked for. It was this very thing that had driven him to the club in the first place: the temptation of noise and drink that could drive away the demons that loomed in this house.

The anxiety and terror had become unbearable, stealing every bit of light from his world. The pressure of not only his father's legacy, but his own career, had started to mix and churn together until each day became nothing but a constant haze of chaos, a void of joyless black that threatened to suck him in at any given moment. The urge to run away had grown stronger as each day passed.

In any other life, he would be a highly desired lord, the newly-minted marquess. Matchmaking mamas would urge their daughters to pursue him, and widows would beg to be in his bed. In this life, well, he was a reclusive lord with an abnormal obsession for books. If only they knew he was the author behind the novels they consumed with desperation.

Ronan eyed the post, piled high on a silver salver by the door. He rifled through the letters and invitations, pausing at one in particular. The familiar script caused his stomach to drop. Another letter from Felicity, most likely filled with pleas for him to visit her and the children at the duke's townhouse. As much as he longed to see them, sorrow would no doubt hang like a curtain over their time together. Pain from the loss of their father would dim their visit. With their father's wake in the morning, it made little sense for him to waste a day in their company when she would no doubt be arriving for the service.

Ronan tucked the unopened letter into his jacket pocket, patting it as he left the room. He adored Felicity and the children, but the pressure to finish his book was monumental. A trip to their home was out of the question, even if it was only for dinner.

"Jenkins," he called out, "I'll be in my rooms."

"Very good, sir. Shall I have the dining room set for luncheon?"

Ronan paused, his hand gripping the banister, his knuckles turning white from the force. "Not today, no. Have a tray sent up." He stepped back, forcing his hand to release its grip.

He had a scene to remember and a novel to finish. Tomorrow, he would be required to play noble marquess and stoically grieving son, but for now, he would be Ronan Tomar, Gentleman Explorer.

CHAPTER TWO

H IS CRAVAT WAS choking him. Ronan tugged at the silk Turner had tied around his throat, forcing two fingers in the nonexistent space between his skin and the cloth. He wiggled them around, attempting to make more room, but it seemed his valet possessed more skill than expected. The blasted garment would not budge. Fuck.

Ronan ripped the thing from his neck, and Turner's gasp filled the silent room.

"Do it again, less tight this time," Ronan said.

"If you want all of London to think you are plebeian at your father's wake, fine by me. It's only my reputation as a valet you're ruining, but we both know how little you care for that," Turner said as he grabbed another starched cloth and began once more.

Ronan growled as the insipid twit squeezed his Adam's apple under the new cravat, but Turner merely shushed him and continued his work.

"I am forced to dress you in this outdated and ill-fitting garb as you parade about town with your careless attitude towards presenting yourself as a fashionable lord." Turner pointed at the new cloth adorning Ronan's neck. "Remove this one and I'll tender my resignation." With a final brush at his black jacket, the valet took his leave.

"Bloody ingrate. I should fire you for talking to me that way," Ronan called out after Turner had left the room. The closed door ensured the man did not hear him. If the blasted fool had, he would happily leave this post. While Ronan hated being presented as a peacock, it was unfortunately true that the only reason he had clothes that were clean and somewhat decent was due to Turner's unending attention.

Ronan eyed his reflection once more and sighed, turning away from the image. Even with Turner's care, he looked an utter mess. Dark bags hung beneath his eyes from his unending lack of sleep and Turner had given him an aggrieved look when he had refused to let him shave his beard. He looked as he felt, and he felt chaotic. And that was putting it kindly.

He had thrown himself into his work, drowning in the words, praying they would be his salvation. Yet the further he buried himself inside the worlds he created, the more lost he became. His father was gone, and the responsibilities he had hoped to avoid for a few more decades were now resting solely in his hands. The prospect was terrifying.

A soft knock at his door had him straightening to a stiff posture, while a voice in his head called him an imposter. He found Felicity on the other side of the door, her black crepe dress drowning out her already pale complexion.

"People will be arriving soon," she said, her gaze scanning his attire. "Are you ready?"

"As ready as I'll ever be."

She stepped forward and adjusted his cravat. "Father

would be proud of you."

Ronan drew in a hard breath and closed his eyes, the words piercing like an arrow into his chest. "Right then."

Felicity set her hand on his forearm and he led her down the stairs to the front parlour. Inside the room, black baize was draped over the windows and furnishings, and a multitude of candles burned, illuminating the brass lid of the coffin. A scrawny gentleman sat next to the coffin, two legs of his wooden stool in the air as he leaned back against the wall, his cap pulled low over his brow. Ronan cleared his throat, and the man startled, sending the legs forward and nearly tumbling into the coffin in his attempt to catch himself.

"My lord," the bloke said with a stammer, removing his hat and bowing his head.

"You're excused. Thank you for keeping watch," Ronan said, his attention pinned to the ornate lid of the coffin and the smiling angel that adorned the breastplate.

"Yes, my lord. Thank you, my lord." The man slapped his worn cap back on his thinning hair and departed the room, leaving behind the smell of death and flowers.

"This is bleak," Felicity said, unmoving from the doorway. Her eyes were fixed on the coffin as well. Her face seemed to pale further, even taking on a hint of green.

"Lissy, you don't need to be here if it causes you distress."

Felicity seemed to shake out of her daze, and she scowled at Ronan. "Nonsense. I'm no squeamish miss." She clapped her hands together, the slap echoing in the silent room. "Lord Strathmore will be here soon, as will the rest of the mourners. The funeral furnisher has the coach waiting in the mews, and you will need to notify him when you are ready to depart for Heathermore."

"Lissy..."

"The church will ring the bell for Father as the procession is led past. I have written to Mr. Kennings from the parish at the estate and he said he would ring the bell there as well. The children and I will await your return, unless you have changed your mind about us accompanying you to Heathermore for the burial."

"Felicity..."

"I know the ton frowns upon women being involved in the funeral process, but truly, I'm perfectly capable of keeping myself composed for the burial. I'll have the children's nanny come along so that she can occupy George and Beatrice while I accompany you to the family tomb—"

"Confound it, Felicity. Will you stop chattering and let me speak?" His shout echoed in the near empty room.

Felicity's incessant prattling, while completely understandable, drove him to insanity. His nerves were already a wreck since his father's passing, along with the unending planning that took place for a funeral. All of that, in addition to the surety he would defame his family's reputation by becoming the worst marquess in history? He would be utterly shocked if they were not preparing a room for him in Bedlam at that very moment. If she continued with her nonsensical chatter, Ronan was ready to commit himself on his own merit.

Ronan pinched the bridge of his nose and let out a deep sigh. "Forgive me. I don't need you or the children to accompany me to Heathermore, but I appreciate that you are concerned for me. It shall not take more than a week's time. I'll be back before you and the children even know I am gone."

"If you even return."

Ronan stared at Felicity. A petite firebrand, she had never minced words and apparently did not intend to do so now. "What do you mean? Of course, I'm going to come back to London."

A single auburn eyebrow rose as she eyed him. "Do not play me for a fool, Ronan Tomar. I know very well, given the opportunity, you'd disappear from London altogether and become the hermit of Heathermore. Hole away inside that monstrous house with your ink and your paper and never see society again."

Ronan scoffed, and Felicity frowned at him. It was phenomenal to see her old fire back, especially after that devil of a husband of hers put her through such misery, but she could not have chosen a worse time. Felicity's pesky stubbornness had long been a thorn in Ronan's side since they were children and she had forced him to play dolls with her. He would celebrate her newfound confidence, if only she did not feel inclined to direct it at him.

"It's true and you know it. Promise me you'll come back and step into Father's role." She stepped towards him and set her hand on his arm. "Please Ronan, promise me."

His cravat seemed to tighten like a noose around his neck. Ronan nodded at Felicity, unable to squeeze the words of assent past the chokehold laying siege upon his throat. Felicity smiled at him, then went to the large vase of flowers beside the coffin and began to rearrange the blooms. He had already promised to never desert the title, but she did not need to know that.

"Excuse me a moment. I need to check on something." Without waiting for his sister's reply, Ronan made a hasty escape from the room.

Once ensconced in the library, he leaned against the door and attempted to slow his racing heart. Yet, with each breath, his chest tightened and the edges of his vision blurred. Ronan slid down the solid door, collapsing into a heap on the floor. He pulled his knees to his chest and rested his head upon them, willing himself to think of anything but the impending funeral and Felicity's accurate concerns.

A year. One thousand pounds for a year of his life. He only had to dedicate himself to the role his father so eagerly wanted him to fill before he could escape. It was an agreement he had made with his father. A year of his time, fully devoted to being the marquess, before he could take the money and run. Set up an estate manager to run the vast lands and fortune that would survive long after Ronan was gone. With the funds he made from his writings, he could disappear to Heathermore and never be required to partake in society again.

Thoughts of the future fled as each breath became harder to take. His entire body shook, nearly vibrating with energy, and his heart pounded in his chest in an attempt to keep up. The rushing in his ears grew louder, drowning out any sound but the chaos taking place in his own body. The quiet room and the internal torment that plagued him only emphasising how alone he was.

A knock on the door had him lifting his head. "Yes?"

The word was a croak.

"The mourners have begun to arrive, my lord," Jenkins said from the other side.

"I'll be out in a moment."

Ronan forced his lungs to take in air, imagining he stood on a ship bound for somewhere other than a stuffy parlour filled with his father's friends and an ungodly amount of society gossipmongers. Brisk air would dance against his cheeks, ruffling his hair, as the sea salt spray misted the breeze like falling snow. Ronan closed his eyes and imagined the sparkling blue expanse before him. Could smell the salty spray of the water.

His chest eased, the tightness collapsing to a dull ache where his heart resided. As he stood, his knees shook. Ronan leaned against the door, a sigh escaping his lips at the stability the wooden portal provided. He could do this. He would do this. For his father, for Felicity, he would push through the next few hours.

With shaking hands, he brushed at his trousers before adjusting his cravat and coat. 'One, two, three,' he counted, before opening the door. Shutting it behind him, Ronan forced himself to release the handle, but was jostled by a remarkable force. The weight bumped into his back, pushing him into the door, his nose slamming into the solid wood trim.

"Christ," he said, the words muffled against the trim.

"Blast, I am so sorry," said a female voice from behind him. Her small hands pushed against his back and her weight lifted off him. "Are you all right?"

Ronan rubbed his nose, dabbing to see if she had drawn blood. "I'm fine." Swinging around to confront his assailant, he blinked multiple times, certain he might have hit his head as well, given the vision standing before him.

The woman was petite, her head barely reaching his shoulders, but the brilliance of her gaze could cut a man to his knees. The smattering of freckles along her nose and cheeks highlighted the emerald depths of her eyes. Her full red lips parted in a gasp as she took him in from head to toe. She stepped closer, a hand raised as if to touch him, before realisation dawned and she stepped back, the hand falling to her side.

"I apologise for my reaction, madame. You caught me off guard," Ronan said.

"I'm the one who should apologise. I got a bit jumbled returning to the parlour and wasn't as aware as I should have been. Are you certain you're all right? Can I get you anything? Some ice perhaps, or shall I call for a doctor?"

Ronan frowned at the woman. The last thing he and Felicity needed was to draw more attention to their family. "No, a doctor isn't necessary. I'm afraid my pride is more bruised than my nose."

A crooked smile formed on her lips. "I know what you mean. It wasn't my intent to injure a man today."

"Do you normally plan your attacks on unsuspecting males?" He longed to see her smile in its entirety.

"I do. You, however, are my first spontaneous assault. If you have any advice on how I could do better the next time, I would appreciate it. I hope to have my technique perfected in the future."

Ronan smiled for the first time in days, possibly weeks. How on earth could this woman be sparking joy now when she had nearly bludgeoned him with a door mere moments before? He leaned against the door; his arms crossed over his chest. If not for the members of the aristocracy crowding his parlour, he would invite her into his library for tea and conversation, if only to keep the warm feeling in his chest alive.

That realisation worked like a bucket of cold water thrown over his head. His father's body lay in a coffin in the front room while Felicity tended to arriving guests, and here he was contemplating isolating himself from the world with a woman he did not know, all because she had made him smile.

"I should return to the wake." He stepped away from the door and dropped his arms.

Her smile dropped at the words, and she nodded, taking a step back. "As should I."

"May I escort you there?" he asked, wishing he could bring the stunning smile back to her lips.

"No, thank you. I shall follow shortly. Please allow me say once more how sorry I am for bumping into you."

"No apology necessary." Ronan bowed to the woman, curious as to how this lovely creature had come to be in his home. She returned the action with a curtsy and he smiled at her one last time before forcing himself down the corridor towards the foyer. It was for the best she had refused his offer to walk her into the room. Not only would it be questionable for her reputation, whoever she was, but it would have been disrespectful to his father's memory to arrive at the wake with a woman on his arm.

Inside the parlour, he found Felicity talking with Lord Strathmore while a few other members of the aristocracy gathered around the casket, their hushed murmurs filling the space.

Lord Ignatius Strathmore had been a permanent fixture in their lives since childhood. Tall and thin, he towered over Felicity and the others surrounding him, his skeletal frame fitting with the theme of the day. The man had been an unending shadow that had clung to his father, following him about Parliament and the town like an affectionate stray dog, but there had always been something about him that had been unsettling. His presence should have been soothing, a familiar presence that offered comfort, but it did little to calm Ronan. If anything, it was an annoyance. Another unnecessary specter hanging about, reminding him of his unaccomplished duties.

Ronan bowed to Strathmore, who shocked him by wrapping him in a hug, his frail arms like clinging vines, their touch suffocating. "I'm so sorry, my boy."

Ronan forced a kind smile to his lips. "Thank you, my lord."

"None of that, lad. We're family."

Ronan nodded, his hand reaching out for Felicity's and giving it a squeeze. He scanned the room for the mysterious hallway miss. When she walked through the doorway, his heart skipped and he squeezed Felicity's hand harder.

"Who have you spotted?" Felicity asked next to him, breaking the spell.

"I'm not sure. Do you have any idea who that woman is? The blonde in the grey dress."

Felicity's body froze next to him and he looked down at her, a frown pulling at his lips. "What is it, Lissy?"

"I don't know who she is, but I'm fairly certain the man whose arm she has taken is none other than Remington Knight." Ronan's stomach dropped at her reply.

✧   ✧   ✧

"YOU'RE DOING WONDERFUL, El," Knight whispered. Opening her mouth to reply, Eloise was forced to a stop. Her eyes rushed to Knight's face, frown lines bracketing his mouth as he stared across the room. Her superior's normally serene demeanor had disappeared entirely, and in its place, she saw longing. Following his gaze, she nearly gasped as she spotted the man from the hallway talking with Lord Strathmore. On his arm, a dazzling redhead stood, her gaze flummoxed as she took in Knight.

"Knight?" Eloise said, tapping his arm.

He seemed to shake himself free from his thoughts. "My apologies," he said.

For that brief moment, Knight had dropped his calculated temperament, and abject longing had taken over. She had never seen him do that before. He guided her to the group and bowed. Eloise curtsied, her gaze returning to the giant of a man who stood across from her.

Knight cleared his throat. "Please allow me to introduce the Duchess of Harcourt, the Earl of Strathmore, and, of course, the Marquess of Vaughn. This lovely creature is Eloise Delacroix." The man flinched as Knight said her name, and Eloise could not help the slight smile at her lips. Her reputation, it would seem, preceded her.

"Mrs. Delacroix, a pleasure," Strathmore said. "Lord Knight, it's been some time. How is your mother? I'm afraid I haven't seen her about town lately."

"She is well, my lord. She's currently in Bath taking the

waters, otherwise, she'd have been here as well. We were both heartbroken when we heard about the late marquess," Knight said.

Eloise kept her gaze on the pair across from her, watching as they took in the interaction between Knight and the earl. They wore a matching set of frowns as they shot lethal looks at Knight, which he ignored. When the marquess looked at her, Eloise smiled, but his lips merely tightened in return, as if he had tasted something foul. Something was clearly amiss with the three of them, the tension so palpable she was confident her hair stood on end. She was not certain if she should intercede or watch the goings-on like a spectator at the theatre.

The earl glanced at the young pair who stood in mulish silence, then back at Knight. "It's been a pleasure to see you again. We should meet for a drink soon." Nodding to Eloise, the group departed, the duchess and marquess disregarding them both.

"What the hell was that about?" Eloise whispered.

"Just some old acquaintances." She opened her mouth to respond, but he glared at her. "Leave it, Eloise. It doesn't concern you."

Their respects paid to the family—who seemed to have little interest in receiving them—Knight pulled Eloise towards the door. She followed to his waiting carriage, but her mind kept replaying the image of the captivating man who had snagged her attention. "What do you know of the new Marquess of Vaughn?" she asked, picking at the hem of her sleeve.

"He's a spoiled rotter who used to be my closest friend. Why so interested?" Knight asked, one blond eyebrow raised.

"He seems a unique sort."

"His father was on that list you found in Eastwick's study. Does that change your answer?"

A smile crept across her face. "It does, actually. Now, I know my next step."

CHAPTER THREE

S WEAT STUNG ELOISE'S eyes, but with the heavy mask she wore, she could do nothing to get rid of it. Her arm ached from her hold on the rapier, her fingers numb from gripping the hilt, but she took a calming breath and faced her opponent once more.

Raising her weapon, Eloise stared at the figure across from her. At his quiet *allez*, she attacked. He parried her thrust, forcing her backward on the carpeted floor of the ballroom. Redoubling, she came after him, nearly landing a shot to his shoulder. Niraj spun, his movements like lightning. With minimal effort, his arm shot out, the tip of his rapier landing against her heart.

Eloise tore off her mask. Throwing her rapier to the ground, she wiped her face with her forearm, her heart's thunderous pounding echoing in her ears. *Bollocks.*

"Again," Niraj said, wiping sweat from his dark brow before securing his mask over his thick, black hair.

"My, aren't we the sadist today?" Her arms shook from exertion and every muscle begged for reprieve, but her mentor merely resumed a ready position.

Mask back over her face, Eloise picked up her rapier and faced him. The ballroom of the Foreign Office's Marylebone townhouse had been transformed into a training facility, its days of dancing and parties long since passed. For the foreseeable future, the stylish townhouse acted as the current home of the notorious Eloise Delacroix. The main rooms were bedecked in luxury, ever appropriate in the latest of styles, while the rest of the home remained shrouded in dust cloths and cobwebs, the space unnecessary for the minimal staff that remained.

With a quiet word, Niraj attacked, forcing Eloise back toward the edge of the rug. Eloise parried his thrust, swinging her blade overhead and watched in amazement as Niraj lunged. His rapier drove towards her shoulder. Pivoting, she skittered along the edge of the carpet, her bare feet avoiding the wooden floor as if it were lava. Then she turned back and renewed her defense. Niraj's motions were effortless as he attacked, but his touch was soft as it landed on her abdomen, ending the match effectively.

"You consistently hesitate when there's an opening." He took off his mask once more and wiped at his brow with the sleeve of his linen shirt.

"I want to ensure my hits are precise," she said, her lungs burning as she forced the words from her lips.

"You're signing your death warrant. An enemy won't hesitate because you're a woman, El. Do you realise what they'll do to you if they're shown a moment of hesitation?"

Eloise frowned as she looked at her mentor. "You think I don't know what they would do to me if given the chance? You forget, I have seen hell in the belly of St. Giles," she said, looking at the carpet. "I've watched the vilest of people rape and steal, and all for the ability to survive another night."

"You're a long way from St. Giles, Eloise. This is entirely different."

Eloise took a drink from a cut crystal glass, the cool liquid soothing the sting in her throat. The piece would have fetched enough to feed her family for a week in St. Giles, but here in Marylebone, it was standard. Required. An essential piece to the ruse they played. And just like the staff that walked the halls of the home, each piece, each person, had been picked with precision for the case. "Yet, all of them are the same, taking what's not theirs, harming those who cannot protect themselves. The classes may be different, but the scum is identical."

"There are good people in this world, you know?"

"So you say." She waved her hand dismissively. "Enough with the mind games. Did Knight send you a copy of the list I found?"

"He did. All the names are members of the aristocracy, but there doesn't seem to be a pattern. Their statuses differ. Incomes vary, from debtors' prison to richer than the king. I hate to say it, but there isn't much to go on."

Eloise tapped her top lip as she recalled the names on the list. "Are any of them friends or acquaintances? Any children who've happened to run into some sort of trouble?"

"Nothing I can find. On the exterior, they all seem like unassuming men who want to do their part for king and country," Niraj said, a sarcastic look taking over his face.

Eloise paused in the removal of her jacket and smiled at him. "Well, that could be something."

"What?"

"If they're all part of the aristocracy...," she tapped

her finger against her lip once more, the action soothing as her mind calculated. "Do each of them actively participate in Parliament?"

"I hadn't checked. It seems a rather bold move to be such a prominent figure while committing treason, don't you think?"

"Yes, but it would make sense. An understanding of the proceedings, the ear of the king and his consorts. It's quite brilliant, actually. There's a massive amount of information ripe for the picking, for which the French would pay handsomely."

Hearing someone clear their throat, Eloise forced her eyes up. Her younger sister, Sophie, stood in the doorway, her midnight-black hair and sapphire eyes gleaming in the candlelight. "Sorry for the interruption, but there's a man who says he's the solicitor of Lord Eastwick requesting your presence."

"Blast!"

"Eastwick? Did you forget to tell me something?" Surprise laced Niraj's usual calm and even tone.

"Eastwick intends to have a contract made up as my new protector." She resisted the impulse to sigh. It would be a glorious day when the earl became nothing but a distant memory. "He can hardly afford Eloise Delacroix; however, I'm intrigued by his tenacity. I wonder what his wife will do if she finds out he has a mistress."

"The countess is rather territorial of her swine of a husband, isn't she?" Sophie asked, her eyebrow raised in confusion.

"Indeed. Any chance you can send him away, Soph?"

"Sorry, no. He's most insistent on seeing you. He mentioned the earl would be stopping by later," Sophie said.

"Bollocks. All right, have the gentleman escorted into the parlour. Niraj, if you could please be your usual overbearing self and interrupt my time with the man, it might make our guest leave a bit quicker."

"Shall I bring my sword and stare menacingly at him?" Niraj asked, swishing his rapier in the air.

Eloise stuck her tongue out at her superior before storing her equipment.

"You're right, it's a bit much," Niraj said as he placed his rapier back on the wall. "How long do you need?"

"Ten minutes should be enough time to state my decision."

"Do you need help changing?" Sophie asked.

Eloise grimaced at her clothing. "No, but I would enjoy the company while I dress for battle."

"That, I would be happy to provide."

Sophie followed her into the darkened hallways of the house, the need for candlelight unnecessary after the amount of time they had spent trudging the familiar corridors. "We could trade places. We're of the same height and build. You become Eloise Delacroix for a bit and I'll be Sophie, the inconspicuous maid," Eloise said as they traversed the worn carpet that lined the scratched unshapely floors. If anyone ever made it past the front of the house, they would wonder at the lack of care the home was receiving.

"Yes, the sudden change in hair colour and eyes would never give it away," Sophie said. "Besides, we know you're better at this than I."

"Your acting skills are superior. Remember when you

hid the money we'd pinched in the lining of your cap and lied to father about coming up empty?"

Inside her bedroom, Eloise removed her sweat-filled garments, tossing them into a pile on the floor, and washed herself with a damp cloth. Sophie sat at the bench against the window and stared out into the night.

"That wasn't entirely a lie, Ellie. I only hid the money so he wouldn't spend it on gin."

"True, but that night, we ate like kings." Eloise winked at her, then tied her stockings and slipped her feet into ornate slippers. A black silk banyan was her last piece of armor. Pulling out the pins that held her hair into place, Eloise brushed at the blonde locks until they shone before applying powder to her face and a hint of rouge to her cheeks. Picking through the tins of colour, she grabbed her deepest vermillion and applied it to her lips with expert precision. She glanced at her reflection, pleased by the flush of her cheeks and the gleam in her eyes. She re-pinned her hair in a haphazard style and adjusted her bosom. If all went accordingly, the solicitor and Eastwick would be out of her home within the hour.

But five minutes into the meeting with Eastwick's solicitor, Mr. Petrean, Eloise was exasperated and certain she had overestimated her tactics. Draped on the chaise lounge in her parlour, the solicitor sat across from her, his gaze focused on the slit of her banyan that played a constant game of peek-a-boo with her ankle. It was as if he was waiting for her entire leg to expose itself to him, and she was tempted to cross them both, if only to see if his eyes would grow any larger.

"As I was saying, Mrs. Delacroix, Lord Eastwick's

offer is most generous. He'll provide a house, and all the trinkets you desire. And of course, the earl will generously pay any outstanding debts you may have, as well as any you incur during your time together."

Eloise swallowed a snort. What a pompous man. If she were still in St. Giles, she would tell the solicitor where the earl could shove his generous offer. But alas, she was Mrs. Delacroix. Although her body was on display like a piece of art, she had to remain dignified. Pursing her lips, she eyed the young man. He could not be more than twenty, his face still full of spots, yet sporting nary a wrinkle. What she would not give to be that young, ignorant of the cruelty that lurked in the world. Deciding to go easy on the lad, Eloise smiled at him.

"Mr. Petrean, do you see the home I live in? The items furnishing my floors and walls?" She gestured to the ornately furnished parlour, its walls covered in a blue and white paper, then to the plush rug beneath their feet. Lastly, she pointed to the fine china sitting in front of her. "The tea you so eagerly sipped was imported from China, by my request, using my funds. Everything surrounding you was purchased with my own money. What need do I have for the earl?"

The young man swallowed audibly, his gaze darting around the room.

"I'm flattered by the earl's offer, truly, but I believe I must decline. Give him my best, of course," Eloise said, keeping her smile in place.

"M-Mrs. Delacroix," the solicitor said.

Standing, Eloise walked to the pull and tugged on it with a force built from irritation. The solicitor's unnecessary appointment was an absolute waste of her time.

"Madame, please. My employer will be devastated if I return to him with this as your answer. Is there not something he can offer for your, uh, services?"

"I'm afraid not." The tension in her shoulders released as Niraj entered the room. "My bodyguard will see you out."

Niraj escorted the muttering solicitor from the parlour. When the door closed behind them, Eloise paced the room, counting out her steps until her nerves settled.

"That seemed to go splendidly," said Niraj.

Eloise glared at him. "It was an absolute waste of time. If I'd anticipated that Eastwick would send his blasted solicitor, I would have disappeared for the afternoon." She frowned as she peeked out the window at the retreating hack. "I seem to always underestimate the magnetism of Mrs. Delacroix."

"You entranced that poor solicitor as well. I wouldn't be surprised if he returned with an offer of his own," Niraj said, his stunning blue eyes crinkled in mirth. His mop of black hair was piled on top of his head, and while his trim beard gave him a friendly look, it was a far cry from his true nature.

"Don't make me hit you." She smiled at him.

Niraj returned her smile and put up his fists. "I'd like to see you try."

"I wish you would have said something more than a growl or grunt," she said, gesturing to his tall, muscular frame.

"It's part of my disguise."

"Maybe so. Wouldn't everyone be surprised to know

the truth?"

"What? That your bodyguard is one of the most sought-after assassins in England, or that he works for a secret sector of the Foreign Office?"

"No. That your voice is truly lovely."

With a snort, Niraj walked to the door. "Let's get back to training before Eastwick arrives in a sobbing mess. I would prefer to get my exercise in before I must deal with another of your admirers."

"Old codger," she said affectionately. "Let me change and I'll meet you."

Niraj nodded before he took his leave. Eloise headed to her chamber, exchanging her banyan for trousers and a shirt, and wiped away the ornately applied makeup with a damp cloth. She stood before the mirror, twisting her hair into a tight chignon. After a cursory inspection, Eloise left the room, closing the door behind her with a quiet *snick*.

The home had been under the ownership of the Foreign Office for a century, a property kept in the heart of London to keep agents close to the city in case there was trouble. There were rumored to be hidden passages within the home, built for a time when operatives had to make a fast exit, but her and Sophie's late-night expeditions had turned up very little proof of their existence. Instead, it was merely a boring, half-used home, filled with retired agents acting as staff and a faux courtesan with a highly-trained assassin acting as her bodyguard.

Eloise walked through the halls, her strides echoing in the dim walkway, before she stopped at the second door on her right. A turn of the doorknob revealed the ballroom, or what should have been the ballroom. In its place stood a chamber nearly empty, except for an assortment of weapons and a stuffed leather bag. Eloise wrapped her hands in a strip of linen as she eyed it. The bag hung suspended from the ceiling by a chain, swaying from the slightest movement of air. She closed her eyes and took several deep breaths. Counting each inhale and exhale, she waited for her muscles to relax, imagining each fiber of her being smoothing with her breaths. Creating a picture of stillness in her mind, she opened her eyes, bringing her fists to her face.

"Jab, jab, cross," Niraj said from the corner of the room.

Executing the moves with ease, Eloise stalked around the bag.

"Jab, uppercut, cross."

She settled into a rhythm, attacking the bag with measured strokes. With each punch, the tension of the day drained away, leaving only strength and conviction. She would find proof that these men betrayed England. She would complete this assignment, proving once and for all women held the same power, if not more, than men did. They deserved to fight for their country.

Aggressively, she drowned out everything but the bag and Niraj's quiet voice.

✧   ✧   ✧

As HIS CARRIAGE rumbled down the sunny morning streets of London, Ronan groaned as the rocking jostled his stomach. His skin was grimy from the long journey from Heathermore, and the jolting of the carriage made his head throb after a long night of little sleep.

After the wake, Ronan had walked behind the darkened carriage that carried his father's body. Plumed black horses led the conveyance past St. George's where the bell tolled nine times to honour the fallen lord. He then joined the procession on the road south of London towards Sussex.

The burial had been fast, faster than the two-day journey to Heathermore. Ronan was certain he had lost decades of his life inside the carriage to Sussex. The knowledge that he could be on his horse, galloping at a brisker pace than the slow parade the carriage made, only further aggravated him, as did the amount of time he spent alone within the plush confines of the carriage, with nothing to keep him company but his own ramblings.

The memory of his father's voice kept time with the tromping of the horse's hooves, the repetitive chant, *one year, one year*, played throughout the journey. The commotion turned the conveyance into a movable jail cell of which he could not escape. A year of his life in exchange for the ability to disappear from the aristocracy all together. He knew his father hoped that within the year Ronan would change his mind, find a sense of duty within the daily requirements it took to be the marquess, but in truth, he had been willing to agree to anything if it meant there was a chance to lead the life he wanted. An estate manager could easily take over the mundane tasks required and when he died, the title would fall to a second cousin who greatly desired the opulence of London and all it entailed.

Once the burial in the family crypt was completed,

Ronan had met with the land steward at the family estate and checked on the tenants before having the carriage readied to return to London. Felicity had not been wrong to worry that he would submerge himself in the country, and the fear of failing her and the children was truthfully the only thing that had driven him back to town within the week. They were all he had left in this world since Remy had abandoned him, and he would do whatever it took to keep her happy.

Well, that, and the fact that whenever he sat down to complete his manuscript, the words failed him. It had been this way since his father's ultimatum and subsequent death, as if his creativity had been buried alongside the man. Without his words, the seclusion of Sussex had become a tightened cravat, choking the air from him.

Ronan patted his coat pocket in search of his flask. Coming up empty, he swore under his breath. Turner was doomed to lose his post as soon as he returned to Mayfair.

His mind kept replaying Felicity's pale face, frozen in shock when she saw Remy. The man should have never set foot in his home, and when the bastard had introduced the remarkable woman on his arm, it took everything within Ronan not to lay him flat. Felicity's tightened grasp and shallow breathing were the only thing holding him back from decimating his old friend, funeral be damned. Knocking on the carriage roof, Ronan redirected the driver. Between his father's wake and comforting Lissy, Ronan had been tempted to leap on the first boat to America. Instead, he would go to the Rogue's Den. Perhaps he would have a chance to pulverise Remy once and for all, then drink all the whiskey his coin had purchased.

A crushing silence had filled the rooms at Heathermore, and he was certain the near-empty townhouse was a similar state. Just the notion of the loneliness that awaited him left Ronan longing for the pandemonium he would find at the Rogue's Den. However, the wailing that met him at the doors sounded inhuman. If he was not seeing it with his own eyes, he would have sworn an animal was being slaughtered.

The Earl of Eastwick sat in a plush velvet chair before the roaring fire, sobbing. Tears streamed down the swollen cheeks of the man's face, creating wet spots upon his jacket. The empty bottle of whiskey next to him explained the unnatural display. Attempting to slide past him, Ronan was astounded when the earl lurched towards him, his arms stretched out as he stumbled.

"Vaughn," the earl slurred drunkenly.

"Hello, Eastwick. If you'll excuse me, I'm headed to those chairs," Ronan said, bracing himself against the man's onslaught.

"Wonderful, I'll join you." The earl hiccupped as he followed Ronan to an empty seat. "I envy you. So carefree, unaware of the heartbreak that awaits you once you've fallen in love."

Ronan called over a footman and requested two fingers of scotch, forgoing anything for the earl, who seemed to be already headfirst in his cups. "Are you speaking of your wife?"

"No, no. I'm speaking of a beautiful woman with eyes that sparkle like flawless emeralds. Such a magnificent woman, and I could've had her. Everyone would've known she was mine. I would've been praised. Envied," the earl said, his sobbing beginning anew.

"Eastwick, I'm afraid you leave me confused."

"She's a diamond, a star that shines bright in the night sky."

"Are you speaking of Mrs. Delacroix?"

"Don't say her name. It only makes my heart ache anew," Eastwick said, his foul breath wafting from his chair.

"Good God, man, did you drink the entire bottle?"

Eastwick emitted a burp and nodded. "I might have done."

"What could this woman have possibly done to cause you to be in this state?" Ronan nearly kicked himself for engaging with the man, but he would give anything to hear news of his hallway miss.

"She's refused me."

The thrill of joy that leaped into Ronan's pulse left him frowning. Why the hell did he care?

"She sent my solicitor scurrying out her door yesterday with nary a word as to why. It's unbearable." Eastwick swiveled in his seat but overcompensated and landed on the floor with a thud.

With a sigh, Ronan helped him to stand. "Let's call for your carriage. All will look better, although slightly more painful, tomorrow."

Ronan motioned to the footman standing at the door, and they each grabbed a side of the bumbling lord. Together they half-walked, half-dragged him to the doors of the club. As Ronan stood with a swaying Eastwick awaiting his carriage, the earl mumbled something unintelligible.

"What did you say?" Ronan asked.

"It's simply the damnedest thing. I cannot remember my night with her. With someone so marvelous, you'd think I'd remember. It's all I have left of her," Eastwick said as he rocked back and forth.

Ronan opened his mouth to question the earl further but stopped as Eastwick's carriage rumbled into the street. Wanting to be rid of the drunken fool, he guided the stumbling lord to his conveyance, and with the help of Eastwick's driver, hoisted him inside.

As the door swung closed, the earl said, "Perhaps I imagined it."

"I wonder what could have caused such a ludicrous outburst from Eastwick?" asked a jovial voice from the doorway.

Ronan scowled. Of course, the bastard would choose now to show up. He missed all the drama but was certain to reap the reward that was Eloise Delacroix. And damned if it did not rankle Ronan.

Requesting his carriage from the waiting footman, he whistled a shanty as he inspected his nails.

"So quick to leave when you only just got here?" Remy asked, leaning against the door and lighting a cigar. "You haven't even enjoyed your drink."

"I'm finding I dislike the company this establishment caters to. Perhaps I should call in my loan. You wouldn't happen to know who I need to speak with about that?"

"Ro—"

Ronan pointed at the giant oaf. "You had a lord bellowing inside over the loss of his ladylove and I was the one to handle it, Remy. I think my money might be wasted here."

"It was well in hand. Eastwick needed a good cry before he returned home to his wife. It's not every day you're turned down by Eloise Delacroix."

"Says the blighter who showed up at my father's wake with Eastwick's desired companion on his arm. It's as if you're trying to make me beat you to a pulp."

"She's not my companion. We're friends, Ronan. I wanted a friend by my side through what was understandably a hard time. Does that sound familiar?" Remy asked, taking an idle puff.

Ronan chuckled. "A hard time? For you? How is it possible you are still so utterly self-involved?"

Remy's cigar hung out of the side of his mouth. Ronan resisted the impulse to make the club owner eat it. Jealousy was not a welcome emotion, yet Ronan could not help but feel its claws sink into him at the memory of Remy and Eloise. Instead of starting a scuffle with the blond lummox, Ronan turned towards the street, hoping Remy would take the hint and retreat.

Instead, Remy, who had never appeared to be an unintelligent man, walked down the stairs of the club and stood next to him. Ronan's hands turned to fists at his sides as he stared at the street. "I wish you would put aside this feud and talk to me," Remy said, his voice close to a whisper as he scuffed his boot against the dirt lined street. "I spent so much time with your family as a child that it was as if they had become my own. I didn't know your father was sick."

"You don't know a lot of things, Remy. That's what

happens when one abandons their family."

Remy sighed. The smoke from his cigar tinged the air with a peaty scent. "I'm worried about you."

"Nothing to worry about." Ronan's carriage rounded the corner and the relief that washed over him was instant. "Now, if you'll excuse me, I'm late for a meeting."

"You never know when you'll need a friend," Remy said, as Ronan jumped into his carriage without waiting for it to stop.

The words were ominous, but he shook them off. Remy was many things, but a prophet he was not. The last person he would seek out as a friend would be Remington Knight.

CHAPTER FOUR

T HE NEXT MORNING, Ronan was entering the breakfast room when he paused in the doorway, unnerved by the silence. He leaned against the frame, his gaze taking in the empty room. His father would have been at the head of the table, documents scattered around him as he ate toast points and eggs. Grief filled him at the memory, but he was ravenous and unwilling to have yet another tray sent to his room.

Spontaneous was not a word that came to mind when Ronan ruminated on his father, the previous Marquess of Vaughn. Clinical, yes. Regimented, absolutely. Tedious, most definitely. He would meet with his man of business directly after breakfast before enjoying a light luncheon. Ronan was certain his father even scheduled his trips to the water closet, but he had never gotten the courage to ask him.

Taking a plate from the sideboard, Ronan filled it with the offerings. His head throbbed from lack of sleep, and when the footman blessedly provided his cup of tea before he had even set his plate down, he groaned in relief. He chose a seat several places down from the head of the table, where his father usually sat. His stomach growled in anticipation, but anxiety kept him from picking up his fork. He could only stare at his father's empty chair.

Each morning would begin in a similar fashion since his father had passed. Breakfasts once filled by his father's gentle probing were now memories inside the empty room. He would never live up to the standard his father had set, and the daily reminder of how unacceptable he was chipped away at what little confidence he had left. As the percussion of his eating filled the quiet room, Ronan swore the eggs in his mouth grew in proportion. Ronan gulped the tea in front of him, the steaming brew burning his tongue.

He had to get out of this house. Snatching his journal and tucking his pencil into his pocket, Ronan ordered the carriage.

His fingers drummed upon his thigh as the conveyance travelled the busy streets of London. The hustle and bustle soothed his rampaging thoughts. The clatter of carts and shouting of people drowned out the whispers of failure that threatened to consume him. As the carriage slowed, Ronan opened the door and jumped out. Adjusting his attire, he walked into Hatchards bookshop. Nodding to Miles, the lad who manned the counter, Ronan headed towards the section for travel and geography. He skimmed his finger along the titles, stopping when he found his prize.

Adventures of a Gentleman in Greece stood bound in green leather, the gold threading making it appear like a jewel in a sea of monotonous text. Slipping it from the shelf, Ronan thumbed through it, a smile forming on his lips. Utterly focused on the text in his hand, his foot caught on a stack of books. He swore his heart stopped as a female's voice cried out. Ronan caught himself before his face met the floor, arms extended at an awkward angle, effectively stopping himself from squashing the petite blonde who sat on a low stool, her skirts spread out around her. The stack of books he had tripped over lay scattered across the floor.

"I'm so sorry," he said, pushing himself up from the floor before offering a hand to the woman. Her plum-coloured bonnet had fallen forward over her face, and she brushed at it with vicious swats, attempting to straighten the purple monstrosity. As her head lifted to look at him, his gaze met brilliant green eyes framed by blonde lashes. Her brows rose in surprise before she took his hand and he pulled her to stand.

"The fault was mine, my lord. I appear rather intent on seeing you maimed," Mrs. Eloise Delacroix said, brushing at her blue day dress. Her bonnet remained askew, covering half of her face from his view. "Only a lummox stacks a monstrous tower of books in the middle of an aisle."

"You weren't injured, were you?" Bending down, Ronan corrected the stack of books that had been his downfall. Expecting the usual novels that lined the shelves of the women of his acquaintance, he was delighted to find travel guides. Italy, Greece, and a book on Roman architecture littered the floor. After stacking them, he stood and faced her. She once again straightened her bonnet, peeking up at him.

"I'm unharmed, my lord. And yourself? I hope my pile of books didn't harm you." Mrs. Delacroix worried at her bottom lip, and Ronan was hypnotised by the action.

"Quite fine," he mumbled. "Blast, I'm sorry. I'm being

an utter idiot. Can I take these to the front for you? Miles can set them behind the counter until you're ready to make your purchases."

She eyed him, before nodding. "That would be nice."

Ronan watched the woman walking alongside him. She should have exuded sex and indulgence, yet she looked as if she belonged in this dusty bookshop surrounded by paper and ink. Perhaps it was her comely appearance, or the fact that she seemed so down to earth, but whatever the reason was, he was beginning to understand why the town was fascinated by her.

Her lofty stack of books raised a million questions about who she was behind the façade. More than likely, she was different from the scandalous creature she was known to be. Clearing his throat at the silence, Ronan said, "You enjoy travel texts?"

"I do." The captivating woman kept her eyes hidden as they walked to the counter.

"About Europe, specifically?"

"I enjoy reading about everywhere and everything."

Ronan set the books down and looked at her. She stared back at him before her gaze moved away to inspect her stack, straightening each so they lined up perfectly. Her plum cap still sat askew, shielding her emerald eyes from his. "Do you enjoy traveling?"

"I've never left London. However, I do believe I would like it. It fascinates me."

Ronan recognised the longing in her voice as it matched his own. Tapping her stack of books, he waited for her to look at him. "These are good for information, but I know some that will make you swear you've been transported to other worlds."

She frowned as her gaze scanned his. "And I'm to trust that you're knowledgeable in this endeavor?"

He picked up the book which he had been absorbed in only moments before. Handing it to her, he watched her open the cover and peruse the first page. He was like a child, fidgeting as he waited for her to tell him her thoughts. Noticing his disquiet, she glanced at him.

"I'm impressed." She smiled, closing the cover and running her slim fingers along the green material. "By A Gentlemen Adventurer. Very intriguing, my lord." Handing it back to him, she asked, "Might the gentleman have anything else besides Greece?"

Ronan held out his arm to her and guided her to his favourite section of the shop. She perused the other tomes written by the same author, each title cloaked in a different colour of leather. Italy seduced with a dark red, the gold script curling along the cover. Spain enticed with its jewel blue, a delightful rendering of a bull and matador sketched in its corner. Her eyes widened with each volume he presented.

Most endearing of all, she sat with him at a small table in the back, each tome laid out in front of her as she inspected them. Ronan could only watch in silence as she attacked each book with delight.

After skimming through the Gentleman's works, he then introduced her to other authors he loved. She crinkled her nose at Laurence Sterne's *Sentimental Journey Through France*. "Whatever is wrong with it?"

"Nothing. I'm sure prosperous marquesses such as yourself enjoy texts from stuffy clergymen who like to boast about themselves."

"Goodness," Ronan said, taking the book from her and putting it back on the shelf. "Thankfully, we prosperous lords, at least the ones with a brain, have also read Wollstonecraft."

Ronan retrieved a copy of Mary Wollstonecraft's, *A Vindication of the Rights of Woman*, handing it to Mrs. Delacroix without a word. She smiled as she read the title before she met his eyes. "You've read this?"

"Every word."

"Hmm." Opening the cover, she read the first page. Ronan knew he had her when she smiled and looked at him as she closed the book. "This one I'll read." With the quirk of a brow, her mouth pinched. "Might I offer a suggestion for you?"

Ronan's brows raised in surprise. "I would love that."

She smiled, and the sight was breathtaking. "How many stories of romance have you read, my lord?"

Ronan's hand rose to his neck, and he rubbed at the skin there, hoping to ease his embarrassment. With a laugh, he said, "Not many. Is my preference that obvious?"

A soft laugh escaped her lips as she indicated he follow her. Down another long aisle, Mrs. Delacroix stopped, her gloved finger tracing the spine of an unassuming brown leather spine, the words *First Impressions* written in black. A laugh escaped Ronan's lips and Mrs. Delacroix turned to look at him, her brows raised at the sound. "If I had known that would be your reaction, I wouldn't have offered a suggestion, my lord."

Ronan shook his head, his hand reaching out to take

the book off the shelf. "I beg your pardon, Mrs. Dela-croix. It's simply that women's novels have never been my preference."

Her mouth pinched, the motion appearing to be that of a challenge. Opening the cover, Ronan read the first sentence, promising himself that if it did little to captivate him that he would return it to the shelf, the woman beside him be damned. Instead, his eyes finished the first line, only to follow to the second and on to the third. "Good-ness, this is magnificent." Looking at Mrs. Delacroix, he smiled. "Is the entire book like this?"

With a laugh, she nodded, standing on her tiptoes to peek at the book over his shoulder. "It is rather magnifi-cent, isn't it? It's one of my favourites."

"Hmm," Ronan said, surprise colouring the sound.

By the end of their foray, Ronan carried a stack that reached his chin that contained each of the works by the Gentleman, along with the novel by Wollstonecraft and the women's fiction suggested by the enchanting lady. He accompanied Mrs. Delacroix to the counter and waited as she paid for her purchases, peeking up at him from the rim of her bonnet. "I had a wonderful time this afternoon, with the books, I mean."

Ronan chuckled. "I'm happy I was available to help with the books, of course." She blushed and Ronan was quite certain it was the most beautiful thing he had ever seen. Her face was barren of the paints used to tempt and entice, the colour taking over her cheeks genuine. "In truth, I could spend all day here, reading different novels, exploring other sections. I tried to get them to hire me when I was a boy, but they had no use for a scrawny heir with a penchant for reading."

"A bookseller would be an extraordinary position. Think of all the worlds that lie inside a book. And each day, you get to share a new adventure with someone," she said, smiling at him.

"There aren't too many people I could imagine sharing an adventure with, but I think I might have just found one."

She paused at the words, her gaze searching his face, as if to be certain he told the truth. "It sounds like a lovely life, my lord."

Ronan carried the heavy stack of books to her waiting carriage, her bodyguard glaring at him as he placed them inside.

"Thank you for your help, my lord." She executed a deep curtsy before turning to enter her conveyance, but paused to look back at him. "If it wouldn't be too forward, may I invite you to tea someday so we can continue our discussion?"

Ronan stopped at her invitation, his heart and head at war in their answers. It would not do well for his reputation to associate with a woman such as Mrs. Delacroix. Yet, he could not seem to view her as anyone other than Eloise, a fascinating woman with a blossoming interest in travel. He smiled at her, his decision easily made. "I would like that."

"Wonderful," she said, returning his smile. "I'll send an invitation soon."

"I look forward to receiving it, Mrs. Delacroix."

Ronan handed her into the carriage. As her conveyance pulled away, Ronan stood baffled by the twist the day had taken. Eloise Delacroix had turned out to be an enchanting creature. One he desired to know better.

✧ ✧ ✧

"GOOD HEAVENS," SOPHIE said, her gaze taking in Eloise's purchases as the stack teetered in the moving conveyance. "Please tell me you did not buy all of those? Honestly, Eloise, the lengths you'll go for your cover. What the devil were you thinking?" She eyed the books with distaste.

"I'm going to read them, Soph. Well, some of them. I do enjoy a good literary escape on occasion."

"That isn't news," Sophie said, a smirk taking over her lips.

Eloise stroked the books sitting next to her on the bench. The informational guides could be returned to the shop tomorrow, but the books Lord Vaughn recommended had grabbed her notice. She sighed, wishing she had time in her day to laze about and read.

"The bookstore was a wonderful idea." Sophie said.

It had been an astronomical idea and Lord Vaughn had slipped into her trap so simply that she was almost sorry for the man. Almost, but not quite.

"Lord Vaughn is a unique creature. One of habit, but also one with interests outside of the aristocracy." She sent a knowing smile her sister's way. "I invited him to tea, and he accepted."

Sophie smirked at her. "Bravo, sister dear. Bravo."

CHAPTER FIVE

THE PAPER IN front of Eloise blurred as the hour grew later. She had stared at the same information for so long she could not be certain whether her spectacles were helping her vision or hindering it. Several names were written on the paper, along with every bit of information she could find. But still, the web seemed tangled. Aside from being members of Parliament, little connected the individuals on the list. Sipping the glass of lemonade in her hand, she sighed. She should call it a night, but sleep would not come easily.

At the ripe age of seven and twenty, she was exhausted. Life had by no means been easy for her as a child of St. Giles. Her early years were spent in constant survival, a fight for her life. Had Knight not intervened and pulled her from the refuse heap, she no doubt would have spent the remainder of her life picking pockets or selling her body on the street. If she did not find a lead to the Fall of Caesar, the secretary would force her to leave the Foreign Office, and she would no doubt return to the cesspool of St. Giles and the grimy one-bedroom apartment her family had occupied, sharing her shelter with every rat and pest nearby.

A quiet knock ended her melancholy. The door opened and Niraj entered the office. She took off her glasses, resting her eyes as she told him, "You should be in bed."

"I was just heading there. You got a missive from Vaughn this afternoon," Niraj said, handing her the folded page.

"The seal is broken."

"I was curious."

"Curiosity has always been your weakness." She threw the note on the desk without reading it. "Well, what does it say?"

"He accepted your invitation to tea tomorrow." He glanced at the clock on the wall. "Perhaps I should say, today."

With a sigh, Eloise rubbed the bridge of her nose. "I assume you plan to have someone in place at his home?"

"Already taken care of. His father's office has remained locked since his passing, so there is a large chance our contact will get caught combing through it. The butler, a man named Jenkins, is reportedly very astute." He frowned at her as she yawned. "You should rest, Eloise."

"Perhaps I should," she muttered, pushing herself to stand.

"Is it to be the laudanum again?"

"Sophie thinks I've drugged too many lords," Eloise said with a snort. "She might have a point. Mayhap I shall just be my charming self and see where it takes me?"

Niraj chuckled, his laugh filling the silent room. "Charm is not the word I'd use for you. I won't be far if he gets out of hand." At her scowl, he walked to the door. "Get some sleep. That's an order."

Eloise wanted to salute him, but was far too fatigued

for even a smidge of sarcasm. The door closed behind him with a click. She finished her drink before dousing the lights and heading to her room.

Several hours of fitful sleep later, Eloise sat in the hip bath, allowing the warm water to penetrate her aching muscles. The knuckles of her hands were pink, the only outward sign she had trained earlier in the morning. Laying her head back, she stared into the fire, letting her mind wander as she watched the flames dance.

"Which dress did you have in mind?" Sophie asked.

"The ivory one," Eloise said, scrubbing at her skin. The lemony scent of her soap filled the air, soothing her exhausted nerves.

"I adore that one, although it's a bit demure."

"What do you suggest instead, my chemise and a bit of rouge?" Eloise asked with a smile.

"It would certainly get you the information quicker, but you already wore your battle armor this week."

Eloise threw a washcloth at Sophie for her impertinence. Once she was done, she dried herself off with a towel and set it aside, crossing the room to sit at her vanity. "You should assist Niraj this evening on his reconnaissance." Sophie paused at her words. Eloise swiveled on the bench to face her. "Your knife skills are amazing, far better than mine."

"Do you think I'm ready?"

"I do. It should be a simple assignment."

"So, a simple job. That's what you're suggesting?" Sophie asked, her forehead crinkling in frustration.

"We all start on easy jobs," she said. "Take what you can get, for now. Bide your time, and when the moment is right, you'll prove to Knight and the Foreign Office what an asset you are." Sophie nodded tersely. Eloise threw a clean chemise over her head and continued. "But before you become the greatest spy the office has ever seen, you need to help me get into this blasted maze of a dress."

Sophie returned her smile with a conspiratorial grin. "Dear sister, I shall do my best."

Eloise eyed her reflection, noting the smile that tugged at her own lips. Things were finally starting to look up.

✧   ✧   ✧

HE WAS TRAPPED, his back against the wall as the villains descended upon him, flanking him from all sides. Blocking the chief's daughter, Sakima, with his body, he removed his pistol.

"Get back," he snarled.

The sound of a throat clearing brought Ronan's head up. "My lord, you requested that the carriage be brought around at a quarter to four," said Jenkins.

Ronan sighed and looked back at the page in front of him. He could remember when he had written it, the moment perfect. It had been so real he could smell the sweet spice of Sakima's soap. But now? Nothing. How could his creativity have fled him like this? Ronan scowled at his journal. "Right then."

He quickly checked his appearance in the mirror, adjusting his cravat and running his fingers through his hair before heading out the front door to his waiting carriage.

Ronan's fingers drummed on his leg as he sat inside, traveling to Mrs. Delacroix's home. This was a terrible idea. Was he foolish to accept her invitation to tea so early in his mourning? True, the rules for mourning were considerably less strict for men than they were for women. Hell, all he was required to wear was a band of black on his arm. Even so, what was he doing taking tea with Eloise Delacroix? Especially when she had arrived at his father's wake on the arm of the man he hated most in London.

Certain this tea would be a disaster, he nearly ordered the coachman to return home. He was already formulating the missive he would send to explain his absence, excusing himself due to a plight of ague, but he disregarded the idea.

She had hesitated before issuing the invitation, as if certain he would rebuke her offer. The twinge of discomfort he had experienced at witnessing her indecision only furthered him to say yes. And her joy as she sat in that dusty bookstore with him, surrounded by the texts he loved most, had been the highlight of his week.

As the carriage drew up before her home in Marylebone, Ronan forced himself to take a deep breath before opening the door and heading inside. Her bodyguard stood at the entrance wearing the same foreboding frown as he had at the bookstore. Ronan smiled at him before turning as Mrs. Delacroix walked down the stairs.

Clothed in an ivory gown, she appeared like a debutante, the sleeves cupped her shoulders, showcasing an intriguing line of muscle running down her arms. The intricate design along the front would draw an onlooker's eyes to her breasts, yet they were hidden from view by a pink fichu. Her blond hair was pinned to her head, but a few curls escaped their capture, the golden colour glistening in the afternoon sunlight.

And yet, it was her eyes that entranced him, and her smile which sent a jolt of pleasure through him. The sensation was familiar, similar to standing on the bow of a ship, off to another world. It was intoxicating, and he was suddenly very glad he had not turned back home.

"Mrs. Delacroix," he said, executing a brief bow.

"My lord," she said, dipping into a perfect curtsy. "Sophie, have the kitchen send up tea and sandwiches, please." He assumed she spoke to the maid, who stood at attention at her side. Once the request was made, Mrs. Delacroix turned and walked towards another room.

"Of course," the maid said to the quiet foyer.

Ronan followed her into the parlour.

"Please, sit." She motioned towards one of the over-stuffed cream sofas that bracketed the fireplace. As she moved to sit across from him, her skirt swishing along the floor, Ronan struggled to keep his gaze from following her. Clearing his throat, he took a seat on the one she had indicated.

"I must admit, I was delighted you accepted my invitation." She paused, her eyes assessing him.

"Why is that?"

"Men who receive any sort of invite from me are typically looking for one thing, and a conversation regarding travel texts is not it. Thoughts, emotions," she said, waving her hand in the air, "those are all beyond what they desire. Heaven forbid they ask my opinion on Corn Laws or my interests in other civilisations." She frowned. "Goodness, I seem to be quite free with my thoughts in your presence."

"I'm glad." Her eyes widened at his admission. "So, have you begun any of the books?"

"I started *Adventures of a Gentleman in Greece*, and I must say, it's rather remarkable. I know it's only a novel, but the way he writes about the colour of the water and the salty smell of the air makes you feel as if you were there alongside him. The gentleman is a wonderful writer."

Ronan's heart swelled with pride at her admiration of his work. "I'm pleased you like it."

"I love it. His descriptions are stunning. Do you...- Well, do you happen to know who the author is?"

Ronan's pulse stumbled at her question.

"I only ask because it seems he knows Greece as if he has been there. I thought he might be able to tell me more."

"I don't, but perhaps I may be of some assistance?"

"I would like that a lot." A quiet knock sounded at the door, interrupting them.

"Enter," she said.

The maid arrived with tea and a tray laden with sandwiches. Once the fare had been laid out, she left, and they were alone once more. "How do you take your tea?" Mrs. Delacroix asked.

"Two sugars and a splash of milk, please." Mrs. Delacroix poured two cups of the steaming brew, then set about adding milk and sugar to each. After handing him the dish, she sipped the liquid in her own. Ronan almost missed her nose wrinkling.

"Is something the matter?"

"No." Even though a smile graced her lips, two narrow lines had taken residence between her brow.

Ronan set his dish on his knee and raised a brow at Mrs. Delacroix. "Any particular reason you're lying, Mrs. Delacroix?"

She laughed before quashing the sound. "Honestly?"

"Absolutely."

"I hate tea. I much prefer coffee, if you must know." She smiled at him. "I know it's not very dignified, but I cannot stand the drink. Very un-British of me."

"Thus, the copious amounts of milk and sugar."

"Exactly."

"Why not just order coffee instead when you have visitors?" he asked.

She frowned at him. "You know, no one has ever asked me that before. I think I always serve tea because it's what is expected of polite society."

"Ring for the maid to bring coffee. I promise I won't tell Prinny you violated the sacred British oath of only drinking tea during teatime." She chuckled at his words, and Ronan's heart skipped at the sound.

"If you swear it will be our secret, then I don't see why not." Mrs. Delacroix called for the maid once more and when the coffee arrived, she sat across from him and took a deep inhale of the steam coming off the brew. "I love that smell. Now then, you mentioned being of assistance regarding my interest in Greece. How did you come by such knowledge?"

"It was one of the many stops on my grand tour. It was marvelous. No, that word is too flat. It was," he paused, searching for the best expression to describe the region he adored. "It was breathtaking. And the area is steeped in history. Stories of gods and goddesses. Monsters roaming the earth. And food! Olives, dried figs, loaves of bread so thick they could feed you for a lifetime. Freshly caught fish, and wine, unending amounts of wine."

"It sounds surreal, almost Utopian."

"It was magical. But it wasn't just Greece. Venice, Madrid. All of them were wondrous adventures waiting to be uncovered."

"I do believe you fell in love." She smiled, causing charming crinkles to form at the corner of her eyes.

"I did. With every last one of the regions."

"You mentioned India yesterday at the bookshop. Have you travelled there?"

"No." His stomach ached at the loss. "No, I think my days of travel are at an end."

"Whatever for? You're still young, my lord. I'm sure you have another decade before your aristocratic responsibilities force you to marry and procreate. I know it's what I would be doing, was I you."

"Is that what you would like to do? Find an adventure?"

"No, there is no adventure to be had in England." Mrs. Delacroix frowned.

Ronan swallowed; his throat dry. Her words drummed at the part of him that longed to throw the title aside and jump upon the closest ship. Gulping the tea in his hand, he frowned. The soothing liquid did little to provide the relief he sought, the loneliness in her voice holding an all-too-familiar ring.

Mrs. Delacroix set her cup down. "I enjoy novels for the adventure they can give you without leaving the comfort of your own home. I'm quite content with it remaining that way."

Ronan chuckled, the motion creating an odd twinge in his cheeks. He had not smiled this much in a long time and his facial muscles were protesting. He was sorely out of practice. "Come," he said, standing and reaching for her hand. "I promised to talk with you about the other books."

They wiled away the time perusing the texts she had bought the other day. Mrs. Delacroix sat on the floor next to him, curling her legs under her as they both read over the tomes he had brought. Had any woman besides Felicity ever seemed as tranquil around him? He could not recall. She enlightened him with stories her bodyguard told her of India and admitted her fascination with the vineyards of Italy. He tried to sketch an image of the greenery, even telling her about the time he participated in a grape stomping festival. She laughed at the notion of him covered in fruit scraps, and for a moment, he wished she had been there with him. Instead of second-hand stories, she would have her own to tell about squishy grapes and Italian air.

When the light left the room, he bid her farewell, leaving behind the sanctuary he had found with her and the crisp, clean, lemony scent of her skin. Ronan rubbed at his lips, conscious of the smile still sitting upon them. He could get used to this feeling.

CHAPTER SIX

AFTER SHUTTING THE door to her room, Eloise stood still, closing her eyes tight and taking in a deep breath to center her rioting emotions. Her time with Ronan had been nice, almost bafflingly so. In truth, she could have spent the rest of the day in that room with him, listening to stories of his travels and skimming over the books he had brought. He had listened when she spoke, his attention solely on her as a person and not as an object. It had been wonderful, and yet, all too dangerous. The ease she felt around him sent alarm bells ringing, her nerves reminding her to keep her guard up. How could merely talking to one man create such havoc within her?

Leaning her head against the wooden portal, she closed her eyes and counted her breaths, attempting to calm her body. It was ill-fated that the first man to grab her attention in months happened to be her target. Of course, she would be stuck with a beautiful, brooding lord whose father also happened to be connected to a devious organisation. Dear God, she needed a fight. Somewhere to direct whatever this energy was. Eloise yanked on the pull before ripping off her slippers and stockings as she paced her room. Shaking her hair free of the pins, she walked to the pull and tugged on it again. Her blood pumped through her veins energising her as she waited for Sophie to appear.

"Help get me out of this blasted contraption," she said, her voice snapping when Sophie entered the room.

"Hello to you as well, sister dear," Sophie said. "I take it the tea didn't go well?"

"It went fine. He's fascinated by Mrs. Delacroix."

"So, the hostility is from …?"

"Perhaps it's from pesky little sisters."

"Well, if that's how you feel, I'll remain quiet." Sophie sat on the bed and picked up a book from the pile that littered Eloise's nightstand.

"What are you doing?" Eloise asked with a sigh.

Sophie looked at her, eyes wide with feigned innocence. "Reading. I thought that was obvious."

Eloise sat on the bench of her vanity, her fingers drumming on the velvet fabric. Counting to four inwardly, she looked at Sophie. "I'm being a complete termagant, aren't I?" At Sophie's raised brow, Eloise groaned. "Sophie, I'm sorry."

"As well you should be." Setting the book aside, Sophie sighed. "Get up then. Let me unhook you."

"Aren't you going to interrogate me about the tea?"

"No, because I don't care. As long as you reel in Lord Vaughn, I couldn't give a toss about anything else."

"He's not a fish," Eloise said with a laugh. Then, she frowned. "He didn't mention wanting to see me again."

Sophie let out a snort. "You sound perplexed at the notion."

"It was so simple with the others. Be my charming self, remark upon how wonderful they are and they follow like a horse on a lead." She looked at the book Sophie had abandoned. "We may need to set up another encounter." Holding Sophie's hand, she stepped out of the skirts of her dress, the fabric falling to the floor.

"You seem flabbergasted that a man isn't throwing himself at you, and yet, you said it yourself. Vaughn is a different creature. He isn't interested in the ton, nor, would it seem, in having any sort of physical relationship with you." A curious expression crossed Sophie's face. "Do you think he prefers the company of men?"

"I haven't heard any information confirming that he does, but even befriending him is becoming a rather tricky endeavor."

"Because you have to do the chasing?"

Eloise groaned and collapsed onto the vanity bench. Her eyes burned from exhaustion and she rubbed at them indelicately, more than likely smearing the kohl and rouge she had applied earlier. "I sound ridiculous."

A hand touched her shoulder. "Ellie, when was the last time you slept?"

"I have a very long nap scheduled as soon as this assignment is over," she said, her face buried in her hands.

"How hilarious you are." Sophie took a deep breath as her hands brushed Eloise's hair. "You should rest, Ellie."

"I need to solve this assignment, Sophie. We have agents dying, betrayed by their own citizens. Meanwhile, the French are working to end our very way of life. And I have my entire career riding on this case, and yours as well. I cannot rest until I bring them down."

"Why must it be you?"

"Because I'm tired of having to work twice as hard to prove myself. I'm just as good as the male agents, if not better. It's time they saw us for who we truly are. We're just as strong and determined as the male half of our species. Women are, by far, more persistent than men, and I'm going to prove it."

Eloise had spent the early years of her life clawing her way out of the slum that was St. Giles, and now that she had control over the direction of her future, she was not going to let it get away from her. Neither Sophie, nor sleep, nor a marquess who caught her fancy was going to get in the way of making sure her path was set. If she had a reliable career, she would have a roof over her head and food in her belly. And if she was phenomenal at what she did, she would never be that scared little girl from St. Giles ever again.

Sophie cleared her throat, effectively pulling Eloise from her thoughts. "You can't make those changes if you work yourself to death."

"I'll do what I must to end this, to set an example for any other woman wanting to join the agency. They should not have to jump through hoops and falsify who they are, as I did."

"I wish you would let me help."

Ripping off her stays, Eloise looked up at Sophie. "You are helping. Keep digging for information about the people on the list, keep sharpening your skills. We will end this, and when we do, no one will ever doubt the value of a woman in this field again."

Sadness showed in Sophie's eyes before she turned away, and Eloise fisted her hands to keep from reaching for her. "Don't overwork yourself, Ellie," she said, shutting the door behind her.

Closing her eyes in frustration, Eloise rubbed at her brow. What an utter joy she was becoming. It was not lost on her how nasty she was behaving. Everything was shoved to the wayside as she strived towards her goal, doing whatever she could to carve out a place for herself in this male-dominated field. Even her relationship with Sophie had begun to tarnish under her incessant effort. A day would come when Sophie gave up on her altogether, and the notion squeezed at her throat like a fist. Blinking away the tears that threatened to fall, Eloise forced herself to breathe. It would do her very little to worry about something that may or may not happen.

Exchanging her chemise for a shirt and trousers, she headed to the ballroom. Eloise trained mercilessly, hardly noting when the candles guttered and the room darkened. Moonlight filtered through the enormous windows, guiding her blows. Letting her mind go, she tore through each instrument until sweat ran down her back. She kept at it, each strike a release of frustration. Each new scuff in the bag giving her immense satisfaction. For hours she attacked until her limbs shook from exhaustion.

Taking a small break for a drink, Eloise returned to the bag, stretching her arms and shaking out her fists. Candlelight filled the room and she glared at the offending object and the person who held it in his hands.

"How did it go this afternoon?" Niraj asked, setting down his candle and leaning against the wall.

"As expected," she said, praying he could not hear the irritation in her voice. Heaven forbid he learned she had actually begun to like the marquess.

"Find out anything interesting?" he asked, like the

nosy nuisance he was.

"It was a getting-to-know you type of tea. It didn't seem the time to interrogate him about his father's traitorous activities." The words were sarcastic, even to her own ears.

"Goodness me, someone is in a foul mood."

Eloise hugged the massive bag, the earthy smell providing a smidgen of comfort. "I keep having to remind myself of the reward."

"Are you sure this is something you still want?"

He stood beside her but kept his hands to himself. She would balk at any sort of physical support, and frankly, Niraj was not the sort to offer it. Instead, he waited for her answer, his presence the only solace he gave. "I intend to join the Foreign Office and to do so, I need the connection Vaughn can provide. By his side, I will have access to information about his father and, hopefully, the Fall of Caesar."

"Then you keep going. There will be an end, just like there is to everything."

Swallowing the lump of emotion that rose in her throat, Eloise stood and wiped the sweat from her brow. "What's our next step?"

"We begin again in the morning. It means something that he accepted your invitation to tea. There is obviously interest there."

"We need to plan another run-in," she said, unwrapping the linen from her hands.

"He's scheduled to attend a discussion on North America tomorrow afternoon. Is that something Eloise Delacroix might be interested in?"

"Considering we discussed it today, I think she'd be most interested." She smiled.

"An accidental encounter during a dissertation?" Niraj asked. "He'll not stand a chance. Shall your menacing bodyguard attend with you?"

"That might put a damper on things." A laugh burst from her when he frowned. "You're rather foreboding with your brooding stares and crossed arms. You certainly terrified me when I first met you."

"I did nothing of the sort. I'm as cuddly as a puppy."

Eloise snorted, the sound utterly indelicate and absolutely inappropriate. The six-foot four-man looked nothing like a loveable pup and every bit a hardened assassin. When she had walked into the training room five years ago, his menacing stare left her questioning if she would have been safer on the streets. Yet, it had taken little time for Niraj to become her closest ally within the Foreign Office, his instruction ruthless as he put her through gruelling exercise after gruelling exercise. But his persistence had paid off. Through the years, the giant of a man had become her fiercest supporter. He had been merciless, but most importantly, he had taught her the greatest lesson she would ever learn: not everything was as it appeared.

Five years of tutelage under Knight and Niraj. Five years of a roof over her head and food in her belly. Five years of promised safety and security for Sophie. Even with all the obstacles still in her way, she was truly grateful for the reprieve from St. Giles.

Patting Niraj on the arm, she headed towards the door. She would get some sleep tonight if it killed her.

"Eloise," Niraj said before she could open the door. Turning, she looked at him in the shadowy ballroom, only able to make out his silhouette. "I wouldn't have taken the risk on you if I thought you weren't able to excel as a spy."

Tears misted her eyes, blurring her vision. Blinking them back, she prayed he could not see the moisture. "You cannot know what that means to me," she said, her voice husky with emotion. "Goodnight, Niraj."

"Goodnight."

After disrobing and settling into bed, Eloise looked at the books she'd unceremoniously deposited on her side table. Tapping on her thigh, she sighed and reached for the *Gentleman's Guide to Italy*. She should be readying herself for another day as Eloise Delacroix, but the book called to her.

Settling back against her pillow, she began to read, the text wrapping her in a blanket of description. She was transported, deposited into a land of warmth and hospitality. A country full of rich history, delectable food, and charming people. Her heart ached to go on an adventure. To feel the soil of the fields beneath her bare feet, and taste ripe grapes bursting with sweetness. But it was not to be expected in this life. Shaking away her melancholy, she huddled deeper in her covers, entranced by the words. "He had found his heart in this valley. Eternal happiness was another day under the majestic sun and endless blue skies."

Eloise laid back, the book resting against her chest. Dear God, how utterly beautiful it was. Moisture pooled at the corner of her eyes, but instead of her usual disdain for the show of emotion, she was ecstatic, reassured that she was still able to feel anything after everything she had experienced. Dabbing at the tears, she caught sight of her hands, the pale scars and calluses that decorated them a testament to the hardships. They were like her soul, battered and beaten. Between her bastard of a father and St. Giles' rough streets, she had weathered the storm, each setback creating another scar. Each blow toughening her heart.

Somewhere in the house, a clock chimed three times. Eloise swallowed a curse. In a few hours, she would rise for the day and begin once more. Folding the corner of the page, she set the book aside and blew out her candle, exhaustion pulling at her. Perhaps Sophie was right and she needed more sleep.

Not that she would ever admit it to Sophie.

CHAPTER SEVEN

THE LECTURE HALL was filled to the rafters by adventure-seekers, the air abuzz with excitement. Were he not in the midst of it, Ronan would have laughed at the commotion. He would have written the scene with the pack of gentlemen as a group of hornets, each frantic to get to their queen. Instead, he tucked his arms at his sides, consciously aware of the men who stood on either side of him. Sweat trickled down his spine from the stifling heat, and he would commit murder for a cool drink in the muggy room. Why would they not open the bloody windows?

The clearing of a throat from the podium caused the noise to quiet down, though not much, as several men still argued fervently about Roman architecture. Their debate over which was more stunning, the Coliseum or the Pantheon, left Ronan groaning. Bloody fools. Did they not understand both works were remarkable given the period?

Renowned explorer Alexander Mackenzie stood at the podium, his lean frame disappearing behind the wooden stand. Mackenzie's dissertation on his travels through the northern part of the Americas would be invaluable, yet with the noise of the room, Ronan was certain he would miss most of the discussion. He was tempted to scream at the crowd to shut up, but staunch society would not look upon his actions with the same humour he did.

A soft, "excuse me," was almost lost in the din, but he swore he would have recognised that voice anywhere. Peeking around the tall gentleman to his left, Ronan was surprised to spy Eloise Delacroix working her way around a group of men, each one looking more aghast than the next.

True to form, Mrs. Delacroix ignored them all. Instead, she inclined her head in thanks as each man moved out of her way, a soft smile playing about her lips. This woman was well aware of the havoc she wreaked on the male sex. Taking a position by the wall, she removed a small notebook from the mauve bag looped around her wrist. She fished out a pencil and began flipping the pages until she came upon a blank one. Holding the instrument against her lips, she listened intently to the man at the podium.

Her pencil flew across the page as Mackenzie waxed on about the trials he faced during his route to the Pacific Ocean. Her eyes grew large as Mackenzie described the antlers of a large animal called a moose, and Ronan's breath caught in his chest. Her fascination was utterly captivating. Like a magnet, he moved towards her, pulled in by her intrigue.

"I didn't expect to see you here, Mrs. Delacroix," he said as he took the sliver of space next to her.

Mrs. Delacroix looked at him and smiled. "I heard about the discussion and had to come. After our conversation the other day, I couldn't seem to get the Americas out of my head."

Ronan smiled at her, delighted. Leaning against the

wall, he crossed his arms as Mrs. Delacroix's attention returned to the speaker.

Her hair was covered by a straw bonnet, the flowers on top bobbing as she wrote, her pencil flying over the page, her script neat, but lacking the usual feminine swirls and loops. She wrote down the name of birds, the size of the trees, the dialect the native tribes spoke. It was as if she planned to investigate the land herself. On the opposite page, she drew a replica of the moose sketch Mackenzie had shown the crowd, her focus on detail astonishing.

Lowering his head to her ear, he asked, "Do you plan to add North America to your list?"

Her eyes shot to his. "Did the Gentleman write about North America as well?"

"He hasn't." But he would. It was the reason Ronan had come today. Once his novel on India was completed, he would base the next one in the Americas. This lecture was the closest he would come to traveling there. If not for the enchanting woman next to him, he was certain he would have been just as intrigued by Mackenzie's descriptions.

Ronan attempted to listen, but his eyes kept drifting to the blonde beside him. If Mrs. Delacroix was exhilarated by his presence, she never showed it. Her pencil moved against the paper as she tried to keep up with the man's ramblings. An hour and a half passed quickly and Mrs. Delacroix seemed to have filled up the entire notebook. His legs were shaking from the length of time he had been standing, but he shook it off. Mrs. Delacroix tucked her implements into her drawstring bag as the room began to clear.

"Are you hungry?" he asked her, surprised at himself as the words spilled from his lips.

"I am, but I don't want to intrude. I'm sure you have other plans after the dissertation." Her brow furrowed as she watched the individuals around them shuffled towards the door.

"I have no other plans except to delight in your company. I enjoy spending time with you, Mrs. Delacroix." Her brow rose at his admission.

Offering her his arm, Ronan escorted her from the building, aware of the eyes following him, including those of Lord Strathmore's. The raised brow he sent Ronan as he took in the woman on his arm sent a jolt of guilt coursing through him.

His father would have banned him from attending the lecture, and it was a good thing he was dead or he might be spinning in his grave at the thought of his son keeping the company of a courtesan, but Ronan could not help it. Even after the hours spent at her side, he longed for more time with her. The relief her presence provided had become his only escape, and he was greedy for the feeling.

Several men seemed stunned as they passed her, whispering to one another before sending her disgruntled looks. "I might be damaging your reputation and I'm not certain that is something I can bear." Her eyes never left the group of men.

"There is nothing to bear. I'm out with a friend."

Her gorgeous green eyes went wide as she looked up at him. "Are we friends?"

Ronan touched her hand, his fingers wrapping around hers. Even with her gloves on, he could feel the connection vibrating between them. "I would like to hope we are. Are you all right being friends with a surly aristocrat who has an obsession for travel?" he asked, delight dancing across his skin at her smile.

"As long as you're all right being friends with a courtesan who also has a budding fascination for travel." Her fingers tightened around his arm and she eyed him before nodding her head. "Come, my lord. I know the best establishment in town for a proper feast." She inclined her head towards the exit before releasing his arm and leading the way.

Ronan followed as she walked towards the doors, but instead of sliding by the men who had whispered about her, she stopped and smiled. Dipping into a deep curtsy, she said, "It was a pleasure, gentlemen."

Ronan swallowed a snort at the number of dropped jaws Mrs. Delacroix left in her wake. She winked at him, then turned and strode from the auditorium. He followed on her heels, practically skipping out the door.

"You were bloody fantastic."

Mrs. Delacroix turned to look at him. Her green eyes sparkled in the afternoon sunlight. Ronan adored the smile that danced on her lips. "In truth," she said, leaning towards him, "it felt fantastic."

Ronan laughed, the joy saturating his body as he held out his arm to her. How had he been impervious to the true woman she was? She was a wild sunflower blossoming in a garden of dull roses.

"Where to?" he asked.

Mrs. Delacroix peeked up at him. "Is my home all right? I know for a fact my cook made strawberry tarts with cream this morning." The words tumbled from her lips in a rush.

"It sounds wonderful." Hailing a hack, she gave the driver her direction. As Ronan helped her inside, the clasp of her hand sent a thrill racing through him. The streets of London flew by as the hack made its way to Marylebone.

Inside, they were greeted by Mrs. Delacroix's bodyguard, who glared at Ronan as he took his hat and coat. His remarkable blue eyes and knowing smirk made Ronan's brain niggle with memory, but as he attempted to focus on what it was, the recollection floated away on a wisp. Mrs. Delacroix requested refreshments and led the way to the parlour.

Ronan took the couch he sat upon the last time they had met, and Mrs. Delacroix sat across from him once again. Had it only been two days since he was last in her company?

"I never did ask you when we last met, my lord," she said, looking at him. "Do you have anyone who shares your love of travel?"

Ronan's throat tightened at the question. In this passion, he had been very much alone, although it had begun with a small spark from his father. He cleared his throat. "My father gifted me a copy of *Gulliver's Travels* one Christmas before I left for Eton. I'm sure he intended to give me something to occupy my time and keep me out of trouble. Instead, it was the catalyst for something that I became rather passionate about."

"*Gulliver's Travels*?" she asked curiously.

"Christ, tell me you've read it? Mrs. Delacroix, we shall have to cease being friends if you haven't."

Mrs. Delacroix shook her head.

"This must be remedied." He shook his head at her. "I shall have Hatchards send a copy over immediately."

She smiled at him. "I'm sorry, my lord, but I've already so many books to read..."

He sat forward, his hands between his legs. "Put those aside at once. This man, Gulliver, he travels to different lands and meets the most incredible beings. Pirates, an entire island occupied by the smallest of humans, and a land filled with giants. He fights enormous wasps and is taken hostage by a monkey."

"It sounds like something a child would read, not an adult. What would the ton think of me?" Her laughter was melodic.

Ronan winked at her. "You and I both know you don't give a toss what the ton thinks of you. If I send it over, will you read it?"

She sent him a crooked smile. "Of course, I will. You're the wise bookkeeper, are you not?"

"I am," he said, swallowing. "My father gave me that book and that was it for me. I was sold on the life of an explorer and no one could understand why, nor convince me otherwise."

"Do you do anything for fun? Outside of dissertations about moose and the Americas, I mean."

"Are you certain it's moose? I've always been rather convinced it should be meese." He smiled at her.

She frowned at him. "Are you avoiding the question?"

A knock interrupted his response, and Ronan was thankful for the reprieve. Even though she was just making conversation, it was as if he were dodging an inquisition. A tray of sandwiches and strawberry tarts, accompanied by lemonade, was delivered by the staff. After the food was distributed, Mrs. Delacroix retook her position on the couch.

She avoided the sandwiches altogether, instead reaching for a strawberry tart. As she nibbled on it, Ronan ate the food she placed upon his plate, but his eyes kept falling to her face. While the sandwich was enjoyable, roast beef with some sort of spread that was creamy and yet held a delightful tanginess, it was nothing in comparison to Mrs. Delacroix.

Her eyes were closed in rapture at the delicious treat, and her pink tongue snuck out to lick up an errant drop of cream. It was such an innocent gesture, and yet his heart picked up its pace at the sight. Want pulled at him; for the treat or the woman, he did not know. The emotions he had found in her presence were like nothing he had ever known before.

Swallowing the last of his sandwich, Ronan set the plate aside and leaned back to watch Mrs. Delacroix. When her gaze met his, she smiled. "Do you enjoy watching people eat?"

"What?" he choked.

She shrugged. "Some people have a predilection for it."

"Can't say that I do."

"Are you ever going to answer my question, or shall we stare at each other in silence and eat until we are terribly uncomfortable?"

Ronan examined the sandwiches on the plate before him.

"Dear heavens, my lord, I was jesting," she said with a

laugh. Setting her plate aside, she waited until he met her gaze. "If you don't want to talk about anything other than travel, we can do that. I can become your companion in conversation on all things that reside outside of England and we shall only discuss those items and nothing more. Just say the word."

"No, that's not what I want at all. I'm sorry, your questions caught me off guard."

"There's no need to answer them. Tell me to bugger off and we can move on."

Her honesty was refreshing. "Telling you to bugger off is the last thing I want to do." He sighed and rubbed at the tension between his eyebrows. "In truth, there is nothing else but travel. No hobbies, no charitable endeavours. No friends, really." His stomach ached at the confession. He had never admitted to anyone, let alone himself, that there was truly no one to lean on besides his family. After the Duke of Harcourt's untimely death and Remy had all but abandoned Felicity and the children, their friendship had met its end. He had never been truly capable of allowing anyone in after that.

Mrs. Delacroix stood and walked around the low table that sat between the two couches. When she sat next to him, she took his hands in hers. "That sounds like a rather lonely existence."

Ronan laughed softly, the sound more like a burst of air than a chuckle. "It is. I struggled to fit in with the other boys at Eton and Cambridge, but they never quite understood me. It didn't matter that I boxed as well as they did or rode a horse just as fast as they could; they still saw me as different, odd. I liked to read and had little interest in practical jokes or one-upmanship. With Remy by my side, it was easier to brush off their disdain, but now," he shook his head. "Now those old insecurities have cropped back up and I feel even more out of place."

Her small hands squeezed his, calluses marring the skin. Her reassuring squeeze reminding him that she was not going anywhere.

"These men are now all active in Parliament, and if they aren't, their fathers ensure that they're involved in London society. They attend balls and court women. They race carriages and hold duels, and I'm just this man with an obsession for travel and a title he never wanted," he said.

"A title you never wanted?" she asked, the softness in her voice matching each gentle stroke of her fingers. It was odd, the comfort he found as her bare skin touched his.

Ronan shook his head before squeezing her hand in return. "Nothing. That got rather melodramatic fairly quickly, wouldn't you say? Any more of that nonsense and I'm likely to drive you away."

"I'm not going anywhere." She squeezed his hand one last time. "What did you think of the dissertation?"

Her question was a well-needed reprieve. "I found it fascinating. North America is full of such wondrous things waiting to be discovered. To be honest, I was surprised to find you there. What prompted you to come?"

"Our discussion the other day about the Americas raised my fascination. When I learned Mackenzie would be speaking, I knew I needed to go."

"You were taking notes," he said. "Are you planning to become an explorer and traverse the vast reaches of

North America?"

Mrs. Delacroix laughed. "Doubtful. But the conversation felt like I was transported there, if only for a bit."

"I know what you mean. Eternal happiness can be found in learning of other places in this world." Glancing at the clock, Ronan stood and brushed at his trousers. "I cannot believe I'm saying this, but I must be going. I asked my sister to join me for dinner this evening and I cannot be late."

"I understand." She stood as well, shaking out her skirts. Ronan took Mrs. Delacroix's hand, bowing over it. His lips grazed the top her hand, and he swore he felt her shudder. Meeting her gaze, he searched her face for an inkling, an iota, that perhaps she felt the same attraction as he did, that perhaps this friendship of theirs was taking a slight detour, but he found nothing. Only her friendly smile and green eyes crinkling at the corners.

Clearing his throat, he said, "Thank you for a lovely afternoon, Mrs. Delacroix," and took his leave.

Ronan hailed a hack outside Mrs. Delacroix's home and made the brief journey back to Grosvenor Square. When the door opened, a serious Jenkins met him in the foyer.

"Your sister has arrived early, my lord. Cook has dinner prepared if you would like to eat earlier than usual," Jenkins said.

"That would be perfect."

Walking into the parlour, Ronan headed for the decanters and poured a large measure of scotch. "How are you, Lissy?" he asked the petite redhead sitting on the butter-yellow settee.

"I'm well, Ro. You, however, look a bit rough," Felicity said.

Although she was three years older than him, Ronan was still protective of her. Felicity was by no means fragile or meek, but over the past years, the damage her husband wrought had taken its toll. The woman who once stood strong, and spoke with enthusiasm, had withdrawn into a shell. If her husband were not already dead, Ronan would have ensured that the duke rued the day he married Felicity Tomar.

"I'm better than I look." The ringing of the dinner bell was a sharp crack of a judge's gavel, sentencing him to an evening at his father's table without the man's massive presence.

As he escorted Felicity into dinner, his mind wandered back to his afternoon with Mrs. Delacroix. In those few hours, it was as if he could handle anything thrown at him, he was the commander of his destiny. Those feelings remained as he pushed in Felicity's chair and took his place beside her at the head of the table. The clockwork motions of the footmen as they delivered each course was enunciated by the silence filling the room.

"How was the Mackenzie dissertation?" Felicity asked, picking up her fork. "Was it the one about North America?"

"It was. Rather an interesting discussion. I—" heat crept into his cheeks. "Well, I was there with someone."

"Oh, who?" Felicity asked.

"Eloise Delacroix."

"Oh," Felicity said, looking at her hands. "I thought she was Remy's mistress."

"Felicity!"

She frowned back at him. "I'm not unaware of what unattached, and even attached men, for that matter, do for companionship."

He paused, then said with a sigh, "I'm not certain if she has a protector at the moment." Ronan twirled his fork.

Felicity nodded, her mouth pinched. "I've been meaning to talk with you," she said, changing the subject. "I plan to take the children back to Yorkshire tomorrow."

Ronan paused as he lifted his glass of wine to his lips. "What?"

"A matter has arisen at the estate that needs my attention and it really cannot wait another moment," she said, taking another bite of her pheasant.

"Surely there is someone who can see to it while you're here?"

Felicity shook her head, her gaze focused on the plate before her.

"This is about Remy, isn't it?"

She closed her eyes. "Ronan, please understand..."

"That blighter. He should be the one dealing with estate matters, the one seeing to Georgie's schooling and locating a nurse for Bea. He should be welcoming you into his home and ensuring you are safe and taken care of, and yet, he is nowhere to be found."

"This isn't Remy's fault. He lost his brother and is grappling with the grief of it, same as I am." Ronan made a rude noise and Felicity frowned at him. "Ro, I can't remain in Harcourt's home. There are too many memories there. I jump at the slightest sound. I can barely sleep for fear that he will walk through the door between our bedrooms."

"Then move back in here," Ronan said, setting his glass down on the table and leaning forward. "There's plenty of room in this large house and I'd love having you and the children near."

"I can't stay in London." She pressed her lips together, their outline turning white at the pressure. "It's too much. With father's passing and the ton in season, it would be simpler if I remain in Yorkshire, especially since I'm in mourning."

Ronan looked at Felicity, noting the fine lines that had begun to outline her eyes. Dark circles shrouded her brown eyes and her cheeks had taken on a sunken look. Whether they had formed during their father's funeral or the signs of exhaustion had always been present on her face, he was unsure. Ronan would be a bloody rotter, and a terrible brother, if he begged her to stay, even as the thought of remaining here by himself was terrifying.

Smiling at her, he took her hand in his and gave it a gentle squeeze. "I understand. Promise me you'll write to let me know you made it safely. And please do not hesitate to contact me if you or the children need anything."

"Thank you for understanding."

When dinner ended, they removed themselves to the drawing room. Felicity sat by the fire with a book in her lap while Ronan poured a measure of brandy and lit a cigar. When Felicity set the book aside and got to her feet, Ronan's throat tightened. "I best get going," she said. "Their nanny will need all the help she can get collecting the children's belongings. Will you be all right? You know you're more than welcome to join us in Yorkshire."

Ronan shook his head and forced himself to smile. "I shall be fine. Get on with you and see to your children."

After placing a kiss to her forehead, Ronan watched Felicity leave. Terror set in as she left the room and he was once more alone. The enormous expanse loomed before him, and even with the multitude of servants that filled the place, he was isolated.

After refilling his brandy, Ronan walked the hallways of his father's home. In each room, he pictured his father. His massive presence still presided over the dining room and each time Ronan sat at the head of the table, he swore the man's ghost stood behind him, calling him a fraud. His father's rooms remained closed, as was his office. Ronan could not bring himself to move his things into the very spaces his father had occupied daily.

Removing himself to his apartments, Ronan sat at his desk and took up his manuscript. Tapping his pencil against the wooden surface, he read the previous paragraph he had written. Usually, all it took was a single sentence and the words came back to him, flowing like the tide. Yet, in the week since his father's burial, they had dried up, and try as he might, he could not find the passion for writing that he once had.

His father was dead, Felicity and the children were leaving London, and his career would soon be washed down the Thames. The only bright side Ronan could find was that if bad news happened in threes, nothing else could go wrong.

CHAPTER EIGHT

T HE SOUND OF a slamming door jolted Eloise from the plush seat in her office and sent her sprinting to the kitchen. Finding both Niraj and Sophie at the table, she jerked to a stop. Sophie's shirt was torn and across her cheek she sported cuts that brought a shock of red to her pale skin.

"What the hell happened?" she asked.

"Just a minor scuffle," Sophie said, dabbing at her cheek with a cloth. The blood that covered the linen sent Eloise's heart pumping at a frantic rate.

"A scuffle, my arse. Now tell me, what happened?" Narrowing her gaze at Niraj, she watched as he stirred a spoonful of sugar into his tea and took a dainty sip. The urge to punch him grew. "So help me..." Eloise said on an exhale.

"We met with some trouble on the way back from the publisher's office. A couple of roughs thought they could take on Sophie," Niraj said with a chuckle. "Boy, were they wrong."

"How many is a couple?" Eloise asked, her eyes taking in Sophie's dishevelled state.

"Three." Niraj took another sip of his tea. The clown was acting as if he were discussing the weather instead of a brawl involving her baby sister.

Yanking out a chair, Eloise gripped the back of it until her knuckles turned white. "Are you planning on sitting down or were you thinking of hitting Niraj with that?" Sophie asked, her words muffled by the cloth pressed against her face.

Plopping into the seat, Eloise's eyes volleyed back and forth between her mentor and Sophie. "You allowed three thugs to attack my sister? And what precisely were you doing, adjusting your cravat?"

"I had it well in hand, Ellie," Sophie said.

"What utter nonsense. Your face is covered in blood and your shirt is torn!"

"Eloise..." Niraj said.

"No." Eloise slammed her fists on the table. "This was supposed to be a reconnaissance trip, nothing more. She could have been killed!"

The chair scraped as Sophie pushed to her feet, her hands slamming down on the table. "Stop treating me like I'm some insipid miss! I've had the very same training as you, and I'm just as capable of handling myself in any situation." Sophie stormed from the kitchen, and Eloise flinched as the door slammed behind her.

Sighing, Eloise placed her head in her hands.

"You shouldn't be so hard on her," Niraj said, his voice soft.

Eloise lifted her head and looked him in the eyes. "How can I not be?"

"You don't give her enough credit. She's been training just as hard, if not harder, than you ever did. She did everything by the book. It was just circumstance that those men arrived when they did." He paused and looked down at his tea. "She begged me not to say anything, but one of them had a gun. Your sister is lucky she's as fast as she is. The shot almost hit her."

Closing her eyes, Eloise struggled to remain in control, forcing the lump of fear down her throat. She could have lost Sophie. Looking back at Niraj, Eloise cringed when he glanced at her cheek. She brushed away the tear afraid the man would see the crack in her armor.

"Were you able to find anything?" she asked.

Niraj pulled a piece of paper from his jacket and slid the crumpled slip across the table to her. Eloise tore at the document, her mind barely able to discern what she was reading. "I don't understand. Ronan is the author of the Gentleman books?" she asked.

"He is. No luck on your end, I take it?"

"None. He's only just started to let me in. I doubt he'd tell me something this astronomical."

"Yes, but we're not using him for information. We're using him as your way into the home," Niraj said. "It's as if you expect Vaughn to sit across from you and tell you all his secrets."

"I know."

"Eloise, you need to remember your true purpose with Vaughn. You need him only for the connection he provides. Whatever emotions you have begun to feel for the man need to be ignored. You only have a few more weeks to prove yourself. Do you really want to put your career on the line for some obscure aristocrat?"

"Niraj..."

"I'm not saying this as your superior, but as your friend. Do not let your heart get in the way of this mission.

You will come to regret it."

Her heart raced in her chest. "I need to apologise to Sophie," she said, pushing away from the table and making her way to the door.

"Eloise," Niraj said, stopping her. "Your sister did wonderfully tonight. You've trained her well."

"I only taught her what you taught me, you loon."

"Then try not to be so hard on her. You made your share of mistakes as well."

With a nod, Eloise walked out of the kitchen and to her room. Grabbing her things, she made her way to the training room, knowing Sophie would be there. As she stepped through the door, she could hear the punches Sophie was throwing.

Clearing her throat, Eloise approached her. Sophie's punches never ceased as she continued to strike the bag. "Niraj said you were astounding tonight."

Sophie's strikes never slowed. Her only response was a grunt.

Eloise sighed. "Why is it I'm constantly having to apologise to you?"

"If you weren't behaving like a shrew, you wouldn't need to apologise so often," Sophie said, landing a punch that sent the bag swinging in chaotic motion. Eloise felt as if the strike was to her heart.

"You're right." Walking to her, Eloise took Sophie's hand. "I have been a shrew. This dratted case is making me insane, but I have no right to take it out on you. You're an amazing sister and a stunning agent. I apologise for all of it, Sophie."

Eloise drew her into a hug, uncertain how her sister

would take the motion. The tension eased out of her as Sophie wrapped her arms around her. "I couldn't imagine losing you, Soph."

"You'll have an awfully long time before you have to do without me." Sophie pulled back and grabbed the strip of linen from Eloise's hand. "I have a sudden urge to pummel you silly."

Smirking at her, Eloise said, "Darling girl, I would love to see you try."

A knock on the door drew their attention, the emotional moment now past. Niraj entered the ballroom and Eloise smiled at him. "Were you planning on training?"

"Not tonight. You have a visitor, El."

"Whoever could it be at this hour?" she asked, looking at Sophie with a frown.

"Lord Vaughn is asking to see you. I put him in the front parlour. You probably should change before you go and see him," Niraj said, gesturing to her buff breeches and white shirt.

Eloise's heart tripped at Ronan's name. Dismayed, she turned to Sophie. "Can we reschedule your trouncing?"

"I'm going to hold you to it. Have fun with your target," Sophie said with a laugh, turning back to the bag.

After a rushed change of clothing, Eloise hurried to the parlour, slowing her steps before she reached the door. With a deep breath, she opened it. Ronan sat on the sofa, his legs bouncing as he looked at his hands. His brown hair shot out in a million directions as if he had raked his fingers through it one too many times, and she ached to know what caused such distress.

"Lord Vaughn? Is everything all right? It's rather late."

Her words sent him to his feet, and Eloise shook her head. "Sit," she said, taking the seat beside him on the couch.

"Yes. Yes, everything's fine," he said, his leg continuing its rhythmic movement. "Christ, I'm only just noticing the time. What a blighter I am. You must have been readying for bed. I'm sorry, I shouldn't have come."

"I was still awake and reading in the library. You didn't disturb me at all. Can I have the servants bring you something to drink? Have you eaten?"

"No, I... No." He shot up from the couch and began pacing back and forth. The energy that poured off him was chaotic, his strides frantic, as if there were not enough room to exorcise whatever demon had brought him here.

Her heart hammered in her throat as she observed him, and the notion shocked her. More thoroughly appalling was that a part of her wanted to fight off whatever caused him this much agony.

Eloise approached him, placing her hand on his arm to stop his motions. Cupping his scruffy cheek, she raised his eyes to look at her. "Ronan, are you all right?" she asked, his name rolling off her tongue with ease.

"No," he said, his voice a whisper. "God, no, I'm not all right." He leaned his cheek into her hand and closed his eyes. Eloise yearned to hug him.

Instead, she grabbed his hand and brought him back to the couch, forcing him to sit before tugging on the bellpull. After ordering coffee from a servant she had summoned, she joined him on the sofa, taking his hand in hers. She stayed silent, her hands rubbing warmth back into his own as she waited for him to talk.

"Felicity and the children are leaving tomorrow for

Yorkshire."

Eloise squeezed his hand.

"The house. I can't stay there. It's so quiet, and I just..." He released her hand and buried his face in his own. His groan was muffled. "I sound ludicrous."

"You don't." She pulled his hands from his face. "You sound like someone who is grieving. It's completely understandable that Felicity leaving has caused you to feel alone."

"No, it's irrational. Any other nobleman would be able to handle these circumstances with honour, and yet I come running to you." Ronan raked his hands through his hair. "No. That's not what I meant."

"What did you mean?" she asked, sitting back.

Ronan opened his mouth to respond, but stopped at the knock on the door. Taking the tray from the maid, Eloise set it down on the low table and resumed her seat.

Ronan looked at the items on the tray before reaching for a spoon and adjusting it so it aligned with the others. "Outside of Felicity and the kids, I don't have anyone else but you. Your friendship this past week has meant more than you could know. I'm just..."

"Just what?"

"Angry. Angry that I'm having to do this on my own and that I can't run away as Felicity can. Furious that my father passed years before his time and that I have to take on responsibilities I wasn't ready for. And I'm lonely. God, I'm so fucking lonely." He leaned back against the couch and stared at the ceiling. "I'm sure my confessions weren't what you had in mind when you agreed to a friendship with me."

Ronan's deep, heart shattering confession left Eloise breathless. Regret grasped hold of her with its powerful fist, and for a moment, she felt shame.

This man, this genuine, kind man, was in need of a friend during this tumultuous time in his life, and she was using it to her advantage. Using him. His loneliness was so familiar it was as if she were looking in a mirror. While one part of her heart yearned to help him through the storm, the other argued that her actions were for the greater good, emotions be damned.

Eloise forced a laugh, then leaned against the couch, matching his posture to stare at the fresco on the ceiling. "I'm not sure I had anything in mind when I decided we were friends. Perhaps, like you, I hoped you would be someone I wouldn't feel alone with."

Ronan reached out for her hand and held it as they both continued to stare at the ceiling. She squeezed his hand and his answering squeeze sent warmth to the region where her heart resided. The guilt that accompanied the motion ate away at the moment, and Eloise yearned to run away from his honest words and empathetic gestures.

"I'm going to make myself a cup of coffee. Do you want one?" she asked, sitting upright and reaching for a saucer. Anything to keep her hands busy so she would not be tempted to return to the warmth she had found when they were entwined with his.

"No." Ronan continued to look at the ceiling, his eyes drifting from open to close. He sighed, rubbing at his face with his hands before sitting up and looking at her. His blue eyes were half-closed and his brown locks stood at attention, bursting out in every direction of his head like the flames in the fireplace. "Are you certain I'm not interrupting your plans for the evening? I'm sure the last thing you want to do is entertain a melancholy aristocrat."

"I have nowhere to be and nothing I would rather do than spend time with you, melancholy demeanour and all." Eating one of the remaining tarts from earlier, she handed him the other. He took an enormous bite, sighing as the pastry filled his mouth. "Plus, you have an exceptional taste in baked goods."

Ronan smiled at her, his hand reaching out to her lips. Eloise's breath caught in her chest as his fingers danced across her skin, their silken texture sending jolts of lightning skipping along her nerves. When he pulled his hand away, his thumb carried a small dollop of whipped cream. Ronan placed the digit into his mouth and released a sound of delight that forced Eloise to look away. Her desire was certain to have transformed into a blush on her cheeks and she certainly did not need to spoil the moment with unsolicited physical reactions, no matter how tempting the individual was.

"I'd move in with you for your cook's tarts alone."

"You're such a flatterer. How did you know a woman always wants to be told she is valued for her chef's baking abilities?" Eloise swatted his shoulder.

"I mean, the company is pretty decent as well." He winked at her. She could not help but laugh, but her mirth stopped when his smile fell. "I wish I could stay here and never return home to that empty marble palace."

"Then stay," she said, surprising herself. Her stomach pitched. The request was sincere, scarily so, but it revealed far too much of her. In truth, she enjoyed his company far more than she should.

Ronan reached for her hand, his fingers lacing with hers. "Truly?"

At her nod, he smiled, his eyes scanning her face. "Do you have any plans for this evening?"

"Nothing whatsoever. What did you have in mind?"

"Does an evening of reading and perhaps a raid of the kitchen sound adventurous enough for the illustrious Eloise Delacroix?" he asked, raising a brow at her.

"Depends on what we find in the kitchen."

Ronan took one of the pillows that sat on the couch and hit her with it. Eloise laughed and retaliated with her own pillow. Her heart filled with delight when Ronan chuckled in return. Bollocks and blast, she was in deep.

CHAPTER NINE

L YING IN BED, Eloise stared at the book in her hands, yet it did not capture her attention. Her mind continued to replay the night before and she could not stop the warm feeling those images created.

Ronan had fallen asleep in the parlour surrounded by books and a plate filled with the remnants of cheese and bread she had appropriated from the kitchen. Instead of retreating to her room as an intelligent woman would have, she had lain beside him, watching the dying embers cast their elusive dance across his face. Guilt had gnawed at her as the hours passed, keeping sleep just out of reach. When he had left in the morning, it took everything within her not to tell Niraj she could not continue. That notion alone was unsettling.

With a groan, Eloise opened the book, unfolding the page she had dogeared. She stared at it for what had to have been an hour, knowing she had not taken in any of what she read. Collapsing on the pillow, she looked at the pale blue canopy over her head. Would things ever get simpler?

In want of a change of scenery, and knowing there would be no rest while her mind chewed away at the what-ifs, Eloise pushed the covers off her. Grabbing her robe, she left her room, tiptoeing down to the kitchen.

Perhaps a glass of milk and some chocolate cake would turn her mood.

She found the room occupied. Sophie sat at the scarred table, her gaze lost in the flames dancing in the fireplace. Not wanting to disturb her, Eloise tried to retreat, but the creak of the door sent Sophie's head spinning.

"Oh, I didn't know anyone was up," Sophie said.

"I couldn't sleep. I didn't mean to interrupt."

"You weren't. I was just daydreaming. And you, I wager, were angling to get some of that cake Cook made."

Eloise smiled. "Guilty. I couldn't sleep, so I thought a treat might cheer me up."

"Why so thoughtful at this late hour?"

Taking the plate Sophie offered her, Eloise poured herself a glass of milk and sliced herself some of the cake that sat on the table. "Last night with Ronan has me wondering if I'm doing the right thing."

"Eloise, if you were doing this for personal gain it would be different, but this is for the protection of our nation. You're only doing what is required to keep England safe."

"And the small matter of my career riding on it means nothing?" Shaking her head, she popped a forkful into her mouth and chewed. "No. There is a bit of selfishness in it. And for what?"

"Whatever do you mean?"

"I can't help but wonder if we're wrong about all of it?"

"You and I both know that things aren't always as they seem. His father's name was on that list and there's a reason for it."

"You're right. I know you're right. I just feel…"

"Guilty?"

"Yes." She groaned and rested her head on the table, the thump echoing in the room. "All he wants is to live up to the standard that his father set and here I am, dragging him into this complete farce of a friendship. Our entire time together has been based on lies."

"Ellie, what is this really about?"

Eloise traced her finger along a jagged scar on the table. "I like him. He's intelligent and funny. He's genuine, and in any other circumstance, I could see us being friends."

"But you're deceiving him into thinking this is real. Yes, I can see how that would muddy things."

"Once again, thank you for your glaring optimism." Eloise stuck her tongue out at Sophie, making her laugh, before the brat stole a bite of the cake from Eloise's plate, popping it into her mouth. Footsteps in the hallway alerted them to Niraj's presence before he made his appearance.

"Come to join the late-night sweets theft?" she asked.

"I'm afraid not. Chip sent a message from the Den. We have a problem," Niraj said.

"What sort?"

"One of our informants has gone missing."

The cake she had been so eagerly bringing to her mouth paused as she asked, "Which one?"

"Nigel Loge."

"Bollocks."

"What?" Sophie asked.

"I had him watching some of the members from the list

when they were at the Rogue's Den." Eloise dropped her fork to the plate.

"We can assume one of its members may be behind this," said Niraj.

"Let me grab my things."

"Dressed like that?" he asked, looking at her nightshirt and robe.

"Blast. Give me a minute to change." From the kitchen, she sprinted towards her bedroom.

"I shall have the coach ready out front," Sophie said, her voice following her down the hallway.

Eloise raced to her room and donned her trousers and shirt, finishing off the ensemble with boots and a large overcoat. After sheathing her knives, she grabbed an old hat and stuffed her hair into it. Outside the house, Eloise scrambled into the carriage, shutting the door herself.

"What does Loge look like?" Niraj asked.

"Tall, brown hair. He has a mole on his cheek that is shaped like France."

Niraj laughed.

"What? I notice things." She crossed her arms across her chest. "We'll go through the servants' entrance. See if you can find out anything else from Chip or the serving lads."

As they pulled up behind The Rogue's Den, Eloise hurried to the entrance and performed a series of knocks. The door opened a crack, revealing a bald man standing, in the open doorway.

"Wut?" he said.

"Hello Chip," she said.

"Ellie girl? Come on in, then," he said, opening the

door wider. Inside, the kitchens bustled with activity. Serving lads scurried around, gathering items for the club, while others prepared food. Chip walked back towards the stove, his height and girth making him appear gigantic in the small space.

"Chip, Niraj has a couple of questions about Loge. Is it all right if I do a quick run inside?"

"Sure thing. Don't let them nobs catch ya," he chuckled, waving a spoon at her.

Giving the cook a quick wink, she made her way into the club. Moving quickly, she questioned several of the footmen about Loge. None of them had any idea where he was or when he had left the previous evening. Eloise walked back to the kitchen, her fists clenched tightly at her side. She found Niraj sitting at a wooden table while Chip stirred a big stew pot.

"Anything?" she asked Niraj.

"I'll tell ya wut I told 'im. Nigel left last night in a rush. 'E usually stops by the kitchens for a bite 'fore headin' home. Ran outta here like a ghost was on 'is tail," Chip said.

"Thank you for your help, Chip." She buffed the old man's cheek with a kiss.

"Any time, luv."

Exiting the kitchens, they waited as the door closed, and then Eloise examined the alleyway. "He left in a rush. He must have heard something. Or found something."

"He didn't show for work today, which means he was most likely stopped. The question is where," said Niraj.

"How far can you get after leaving the kitchens?" she asked. Their carriage remained parked at the side, and the other end of the alley exited onto a side street. "If someone knew he had overheard them, they would've waited for him to leave."

Looking at their carriage, Eloise chewed on her bottom lip as she analysed the situation. Turning in the opposite direction, she walked down the alleyway, Niraj following behind.

"That street is not very busy. They could have boxed him in," Niraj said, pausing, his head pivoting back and forth, scanning the grime covered side street before them.

"Damnation." Eloise took off at a run down the alley, Niraj keeping pace beside her. Rubbish littered the sides of the street while brown-coloured muck slithered down the center of the narrow space, splashing at her feet as they hit each puddle, keeping pace with her heart. She skidded to a stop when she spotted the body.

A tall man in torn livery lay behind a crate, his mole the only thing recognisable on his mangled face. A puddle of blood surrounded him, the metallic scent filling the air with death.

Eloise's stomach rolled. Glancing at Niraj, she grimaced. "Bollocks."

"I think we have a larger issue to deal with at the moment. We are being followed." Niraj whispered.

Keeping her eyes trained on Niraj, her body tensed at the slight movement she spied out of the corner of her eye. "Double back and come from behind."

"You have your knives?"

"Always."

Niraj walked down the side street while Eloise turned back to the body, pretending to examine it. Bending down for a closer look, she slid her knives out of her boot. The intruder was closer now, his pace quickening towards her. Before she could react, Niraj came up from behind and bashed him over the head with the butt of his gun.

"You were faster than I thought you'd be." Eloise tucked her knives back into her boots.

"He was moving quickly. I wanted to be sure I made it in time," Niraj said, his breaths short. Lighting a Lucifer, Niraj held it close to the prowler's face, and they both released a curse.

Ronan Tomar lay on the ground, unconscious.

CHAPTER TEN

R ONAN AWOKE WITH a groan. His head throbbed and the scent of mildew made his nose itch. As he moved to rub it, he was met with resistance. His hands were tightly tied behind the chair he sat in. A low-burning lamp sat on a small table in the corner near a door. With a flex of his shoulders, he tested the tautness of the rope. It bit into his wrists, tightening as he strained against them.

Christ, what had happened? Ronan closed his eyes, attempting to remember what he had done last. He had been at his club, nursing a drink, avoiding going home or returning to Mrs. Delacroix's for another night. A boy dressed in black was flitting around, talking to each of the footmen. He would not have paid attention at all, except the boy looked oddly familiar. Ronan had followed him, but where to? An alleyway. The boy turned, the moonlight illuminating his face.

"Eloise! Eloise, where are you?"

Footsteps in the hallway filled the quiet room, and Ronan screamed her name once more. She could be injured. Whoever had knocked him out would have gone after her as well. "Let me out of here! Eloise, where are you?"

The door opened with a rough scrape, and Ronan squinted at the dark figure who filled the space. "What am

I doing here? Where's Eloise?"

"She's fine. No harm has come to her," a man's smooth voice said.

"You didn't answer my first question. What am I doing here?"

"What do you remember?"

"I was following a friend of mine into the alley behind my club. She was dressed as a boy, standing over a dead body. Then I was knocked over the head. Did you want a further recollection? Perhaps what I had for breakfast?"

The figure chuckled softly as it stepped further into the room. "No, that's quite all right, Lord Vaughn. I wanted to ensure we took you for the right reasons, and it seems we did." The shadow stepped into the light, revealing a tall man dressed in black. A black cloth covered the lower half of his face, leaving only his eyes viewable.

"Who are you?" Ronan asked.

"I'm not someone to be trifled with," he said.

"Where is Eloise?"

"She's safe."

"What is it you want? Money? I'll give it to you. Just show me she is all right."

"You care for her? How intriguing."

He sounded surprised. The skin on Ronan's neck tingled in a warning. "What do you mean?" he asked.

"You'll see," the other man chuckled. "Eloise, his lordship wishes to see you're well."

Ronan began to sweat at the man's familiarity. She could not be involved in whatever this was. When a second figure filled the doorway, his stomach dropped as the petite form stepped into the lit doorway. Her svelte frame was missing its familiar drapery of satin and silk. Instead, she was cloaked in tight buff trousers and a dark linen shirt.

"Eloise? What the hell is going on?"

"It's my turn to ask the questions, my lord. Why did you follow me?"

"You walked into my club dressed as a boy. What else was I to do?"

"What did you see?"

"You and your bodyguard were standing over a body. What were you doing with a dead body?"

"Never mind." She waved her hand. "Was there anything else?"

"Your bodyguard walked off. I went to approach you and I assume tall, dark, and hostile knocked me over the head," he said, nodding to the man. "I don't know what this is about, but I'm not interested in playing. You know who I am, Eloise. You know the power I wield. Let me go, and I'll make sure you are not held responsible for the kidnapping of a nobleman."

She cracked a smile. "Perhaps we tell him the truth," she suggested to her accomplice.

"We're not going to do anything of the sort," said the man, his voice rising an octave.

"Humour me for a moment. We tell him and watch how he responds. If it's bad, we ship him north until this whole thing is over."

"You-know-who is going to be bloody furious."

"I'm bloody furious," Ronan said. "Not that either of you seems to care." Mrs. Delacroix paused her pacing and glared at him. "Glad to see you remembered I'm still sitting here," he said.

She closed her eyes, her mouth moving as if she were counting. "Lord Vaughn, what do you know of the French?"

"Revolutionists? War? Waterloo? That bit, you mean?"

"Napoleon has a lot of supporters who would pay well for information about our government. About the king."

Ronan sighed loudly and pulled at the ropes once more. "Napoleon is in exile in St. Helena, so the likelihood of them gaining anything from it is slim."

"He's there for now, but his supporters would love to see England overthrown," she said, watching him. "Have you heard of The Fall of Caesar?"

"And now you're asking me about Shakespeare? Eloise, what is this?"

"You're currently inside the Foreign Office. We work for a branch that investigates governmental influence from outside sources."

"You expect me to believe the most wanted courtesan in London, nay England, is a spy for the Foreign Office? A woman who has had more lovers than the Prince Regent himself? Madame, I hate to be the bearer of ill news, but you are no more a spy than I am the Duke of Wellington."

Mrs. Delacroix glared at him, but he could not hide his incredulity. What could possibly prompt the Foreign Office to hire one of the most well-known figures of the ton? It was not that she was a woman, no, women could do anything men could and he would be the first to throw his support behind gender equality. No, it was the notion that someone as highly recognisable and sought-after as she would sacrifice herself and her livelihood for the greater good of the nation.

"You're no Wellington." Her gaze raked over him, and she smirked.

"You responded as if you know him." He laughed at the idea.

"I do. I know how he takes his tea, which pistols are his favourite, and that he and Kitty separated quite some time ago. Not that they're letting on to the ton. Knowing the gossips, I'm sure they'll figure it out at any moment," she said with a laugh. "My lord, whether you believe it or not, this is where you are, and I demand you cooperate. If you don't, this will become quite uncomfortable for you."

The man in black opened a cabinet and began to remove ghastly tools. He seemed almost filled with delight as he set each one on the table. "You've got to be joking!" Ronan shouted as the man in black removed an impressive knife with a long, thick blade.

"You think I'm kidding? I've been on this case for months trying to prevent what could potentially be the fall of England, if not Europe. I've watched friends disappear, never to be heard from again. I don't have time for a troublesome nobleman," she said.

"Then let me go, and we can discuss this."

"Answer my questions and I'll let you go," she retorted. "What do you know about the Fall of Caesar?"

"Nothing, I've never heard of it. Why?"

"Don't concern yourself with it. What about your father's finances?"

"What?" he asked, stunned at her question.

"His finances. What condition is the estate in?"

"Our estate is fine. I've never encountered an issue," he said, pausing before asking, "What does my father have to do with this?"

"We think he was involved."

"You would accuse my father of treason?"

"We have not accused anyone."

"You've lost your bloody mind if you think I'm going to help you implicate my father," he said, shaking his chair.

She frowned at him and he swore it was with pity. "If he is tied to this, I won't need your help."

"My father was a good man. He was honourable to king and country. He would never betray it."

"Then you shouldn't have any concern answering my questions, Ronan."

"Don't call me that," he said through gritted teeth.

"My apologies, Lord Vaughn," she said. "If your father is innocent, then there should be little concern with what you tell me." She looked at the man in black. "You were right. Take him north and stash him there until we get this sorted out."

"You truly think they won't notice a peer has gone missing?" Ronan asked.

"They haven't seemed to mind before. And if I remember correctly, your sister invited you to visit her in Yorkshire. Wouldn't take much at all to spread around the ton that's where you went."

Fury filled his body as the pieces of the puzzle before him clicked together. "You used me."

Her head swung back to look at him, her eyes cutting his heart to pieces with the emptiness he found there. With a sigh, she looked back to the man in black, her mouth parted to speak, and Ronan shook the chair he sat in. "No! Don't look at him, look at me. You did, didn't you, Eloise?"

"Yes." The word was said without emotion, cold and empty, just like her eyes.

"Why?"

"I needed the connection, and you supplied it quite willingly," she said with a smile. "If you hope to remain in my good graces, you'll continue to provide me with what I want."

He looked at her. This woman who had entranced him with her gentle demeanour now stared him down with intensity. The curls that had framed her face only a night ago were pulled back into a tight queue. She looked formidable, unsympathetic, and altogether more appealing than she had ever had. Even as frustration skulked inside him, his heart yearned for her.

"I know who you are. What you are," he said.

"And?"

"I could make this entire assignment much harder on you."

She laughed, the sound chilling. "I highly doubt you can wield that power, Lord Vaughn."

"It would be hard to continue an assignment when all of London knows you are a spy."

"I'm not the only one with secrets, am I? How would the ton react if they learned of your father's treachery? How would his legacy be tarnished when it is found out that he betrayed his country? And then, there is your publishing contract. It would be a shame if they abandoned your books for some unknown reason. You'd be penniless, and your poor sister and her children banished from society."

Any warmth he had held for her dissipated, the hurt covering each fond memory he had with a tint of blue. Each laugh, each moment of comfort, now held a tinge of dishonesty, a blanket of lies, and, in truth, a modicum of sorrow. She had used him. Shamelessly. Brutally. Took advantage of every opening into his world, and manipulated it for her own good. It was agony and anger, a morbid soup that stirred in his stomach as he looked at her.

Forcing a cool lilt to his voice, Ronan tried to hide his hurt. "Ah yes, but then what would happen to the connection you so desperately need? Why, you would be back at square one. All your hard work, the effort you have put into this case. Gone."

The deceiver dared to shake her head at him.

"My lord, I'm not the one with the most to lose. You are but one connection in a sea of thousands. However, it seems you've forgotten what your father's treachery would do to his legacy in Parliament. And then, of course, there is your sister."

"What about my sister?" Ronan said, clenching his teeth.

"Hasn't she been through enough scandal? The horrendous death of her husband, a useless brother-in-law who leaves her to run the estates. And of course, there's the abuse she suffered at the hand of the duke. It wouldn't just be your career that would make its way to the ton's ears, my lord. It would be every single skeleton your family holds in their closet."

"You're shameless." He shook his head, the ropes that bound his hands biting into his skin.

Her eyes narrowed, and she took a step towards him. "I am, and you'll do well to follow my directive to save your family's legacy. You will supply my entry into society. You'll do my bidding, or I will ruin everything you love. I'll give you some time to think it over."

"You will regret blackmailing me, Eloise," he said, anger surging through his veins. He wanted to wreck her. Wanted to ensure she ended up as devastated as he was. It made sense, after all. Misery loves company.

CHAPTER ELEVEN

ANGER AND REGRET poured through Eloise. The entire evening had become a muddle of complications, and the last thing she had anticipated was Ronan.

Another obstacle. Another opportunity lost. Another connection severed. The urge to punch something was strong, even as she began to count. Centering became harder as her mind swirled, a mixture of chaos and sadness.

An informant was dead. She had no leads, and her target now sat bound to a chair, aware of who she was and what she was doing. She wanted to shriek at the sky. To apologise to him profusely. To beg him to understand. Instead, she opened her eyes and forced herself to grin at the marquess. "The only regret I will have at the end of this is that I was forced to spend so much time with you," she said, before sauntering from the room.

Niraj followed, shutting the door behind him as she leaned against the wall. Pain throbbed between her eyebrows and she jabbed her thumbs into them, trying to rub the ache away. She glanced at Niraj. "We might be able to make this go away."

"How?" asked Niraj, ripping the scarf from his face. "His highness is currently bound to a chair, and knows you're a willing participant."

"You could at least try to be creative."

"Oh yes, let's try to make this even more of a farce than it is. You're lucky I doubled back or this could've ended up worse."

"I doubt much worse, considering we have a lord tied to a chair and we're currently blackmailing him."

"Now is not the time for humour, Eloise."

"You're right," she said. "We should continue with the original plan."

"You cannot be serious."

"What else am I to do?" she asked. "I need him. He is my only key to bringing down this organisation and keeping my job."

"This isn't something to be taken lightly, Eloise. He could ruin the entire operation. He could expose your connection to the Foreign Office."

Shrugging her shoulders and looked at the door they had just closed.

Niraj frowned. "It's another thing for you to contend with, El."

"It is, but I can handle it."

"Perhaps it's too much. There has to be another way that doesn't include working with a hostile participant."

"Niraj, I've been working on this approach for a week. We can't risk losing him and the access he provides, nor do we have the time."

"We're taking this to Knight and allowing him to decide," he said, striding down the hallway.

Turning the corner, they ran into Knight's assistant, Dorman. "Ah, I was just coming to ask how the interrogation was going," he said, pushing his glasses up his nose.

"Not well," Niraj said as he strode past him into Knight's office. Smiling at Dorman, Eloise followed and shut the door behind her.

"Well?" Knight asked.

"The bastard knows nothing. And worst of all, Eloise wants to blackmail him into continuing to provide her with the entry she needs."

"Truly?" Knight's blond eyebrows rose in surprise. "I doubt Ronan took well to the demands. He's a good-humoured man, but not one to be trifled with."

Knight stood and poured a tumbler of scotch, offering one to Eloise and Niraj. Eloise shook her head, grimacing. She still had not recovered from the stench of Eastwick. "Nothing for me, thank you."

"Right," he responded with a chuckle. "Don't suppose you'll be able to get over your adversity any time soon?"

"Be pinned down by a man who weighs fifteen stone and reeks of scotch, then we shall discuss my aversions," she said, taking a seat in the plush leather chair across from his desk.

"Fifteen? I was sure he was closer to eleven." Knight leaned back in his chair, the monstrosity specially made to fit his enormous frame. His blond hair was brushed out of his face either by a talented valet or his own repetitive motion. Brown eyes creased as he smiled, giving him a besotted look, but Eloise saw the calculation behind his grin.

"It's the corset. It creates the illusion he's trimmer than he appears."

"Can we get back to business?" Niraj said with a growl.

"Have a little fun, Niraj." Knight frowned at him. "If you can't laugh with us, at least have a drink. It might remove the stick you have wedged up your arse."

Eloise muffled a snort. Niraj scowled at her, then stood to pour a drink for himself.

"If I have a stick up my arse, it's because of this bloody situation."

"I think our solution is simple. We send Ronan away and Eloise goes after someone else on that list," Knight said, sipping his drink.

"No." Eloise sat up in her chair and met Knight's surprised gaze. "I think we should continue to use Vaughn, regardless of the threat he poses."

"Your cover is already blown, Eloise. Do you think this is the best idea?" Knight's brow was furrowed and Eloise could feel her stomach tighten in panic.

"I've already invested so much time in him, I can't take the chance of starting over. Not now. My month is almost up."

"You haven't seen the way he looks at her. He's besotted. Well, he was." Niraj chuckled. "Before he found out who she was, I'm sure he would have done anything she asked. Now? Most definitely not."

"I can't start over, Niraj." Eloise crossed her arms to hide how tightly she was clenching her hands.

"No, I can't allow it." Niraj shook his head and looked at Knight. "This will not end well. He was becoming invested in their relationship and we both know what happens when those ties are severed. We need to send Vaughn away and start again."

"If she is willing to continue, I don't think we have

much say," Knight said, his words measured as he evaluated her. "And as much as you hate to admit it, Niraj, you're allowing your own decisions to drive your position. You made your choice in Marseille. You chose to follow Evangeline into hell knowing what she was, and who she was, but that doesn't mean the same will happen now."

"But I paid dearly for it."

Knight scoffed. "Always the victim, Niraj. If you could only see …"

"Can mother and father stop fighting for a moment so I can speak?" Eloise interjected.

Niraj and Knight straightened, glaring daggers at each other. When they both quieted, she spoke. "I'm going to continue down the planned path. If you two hens will stop pecking at each other, we could come to an agreement."

"I'm all aquiver to hear your infallible plan." Niraj leaned back against his chair and raised a single dark brow.

"We blackmail him to work with us."

The bastards dared to laugh.

"Hear me out. We have enough information to keep him in line and have him continue to follow our demands. We'll make it so the ton thinks he has taken me as a mistress, which will allow me to visit his home to search it, and give me an invitation to certain events where other members of the group might be in attendance."

"Fine." Knight stood and straightened his jacket, shooting Niraj a glare when the man attempted to argue. "But you need to find something valuable soon, or I am calling it off."

"Deal. Let's hope he doesn't discover your part in this," Eloise said, glancing at Knight. "If he learns you're involved, he will have your head."

"Don't worry about me. He'll do everything he can to make sure you fail. Are you sure you wish to continue?"

"I will not start over. I've already put in too much time with Vaughn. It will be his mistake if he underestimates me."

"My fear is that it's you who is underestimating him."

"I can handle this." Without waiting for a reply, she left. Storming down the corridor to the interrogation room, Eloise seethed.

She was tired of being miscalculated. Tired of having others determine her path. This was her life, and she would do everything required to ensure that she never returned to the streets of St. Giles. Never go back to a life of crime, picking pockets to put food on the table and coal in the stove. No, she would ensure Ronan followed her directive and gave her the information she needed. There was no other option.

Opening the door, she came to a crashing halt at the sight that greeted her. Ronan had managed to topple his chair, and now lay upon his back, his legs in the air. His arms were still tied behind his back, making him look like a turtle. A giggle built in her chest. When he wiggled his legs in an attempt to right himself, it burst from her in an unattractive snort.

Ronan frowned at her. "Are you going to help me or not?"

She met his scowl with a smile. "I'm sorry to laugh," she said as she helped to fix the upended chair.

"I'm glad you've found joy at my expense."

She paused, her lips curling into a smile at the irritation in his voice. "Were you attempting an escape?"

"Yes, but these blasted knots are tighter than the devil." He rolled his wrists, showing her the knots she had expertly tied hours ago. "Any chance I can convince you to loosen them?"

"I'll do you one better. I'll untie you after we discuss our arrangement."

"What a gentle way of saying kidnapping."

Eloise looked at Ronan. His disheveled dark locks fell in front of his face and his clothes were wrinkled and smudged with dirt. But even in the state he was in, he was still the most handsome man she knew. Even as her mind told her to focus on the assignment, her heart ached at the lost connection between them.

"I'll accept any proposal you have, but I have a few conditions."

Eloise shook her head. "I don't think you are in any position to negotiate." She smiled at him. "You forget, my lord, I can have you dispatched. Yes, I have need of you, but you're not the only fish I have on the hook." The lie rolled easily off her tongue. "So, you will agree to my demands, or I'll send you north to wait until this task is over. And while you wile away in the country, your sister and her children will be left to deal with the repercussions of your decision."

Ronan scowled at her response. "What must I do?"

"As of now, you have taken Eloise Delacroix as your mistress. You'll attend every engagement I wish you to. You won't question my methods of obtaining information, nor will you tell anyone who I am or I promise you I will make your father's treachery known." His brow furrowed, and Eloise swore she could see the cogs moving in his head as he ran through her demands.

When his gaze met hers, she knew she had him. "We have a deal."

With a nod, she walked around his chair and untied the ropes that bound him. He stood, rubbing the abraded skin at his wrists. Eloise looked at his hands, the fingers calloused from where he held his pencil.

"I'm afraid I'm rather handy with knots."

"Of course you are," he mumbled, his gaze raking over her body. "Why lemons?"

"How hard did Niraj hit you?" she asked, tempted to run her fingers through his hair to check for a bump.

"The scent. Why do you smell of lemons?"

Eloise looked at Ronan, those familiar blue eyes pulling her in. "The first time I ever smelled something clean was when I smelled a lemon. The rot fell away, and I swore, for a moment, the world sparkled."

"Really?"

"No. A maid put them in the first proper bath I ever took and I continued the habit."

"I like the first story better."

"I did too," she said, her voice quiet. "How about a drink to seal the deal?" Pouring them each a measure of sherry, she brought the glass to him. "To us."

"To us."

Eloise looked at him, her body heating as his tongue followed an errant drip on his lower lip. He frowned at her. "What is it?"

"You were rather upset when you learned I was involved."

"Of course I was. Believe it or not, I did think we were friends," he said, his eyes losing focus as he dropped his glass. "What the hell?"

Eloise wrapped her arm around his waist, helping him to sit on the floor. When his eyes met hers, she gave him a quick smile. "You're all right." As his eyes slid closed, Eloise lowered him to the ground and brushed back a strand of hair that had fallen over his brow.

The door opened with a loud bang. Niraj strode in. "Christ, Eloise, you said no more dosing!"

CHAPTER TWELVE

T HE SUN WAS blinding as it shone through the window. Most aristocrats were still abed, but Eloise had been up for hours.

After a brisk ride through Hyde Park, she had returned and spent several hours in the training room attempting to ease the wild swarm of thoughts inside her head. Lifting the cup of coffee to her lips, Eloise gulped the liquid with enthusiasm. Those nobles and their insipid addiction to tea. They did not know what they were missing.

The exhaustion that enveloped her could only be the result of the night before. Eloise had collapsed in bed after returning a heavily sedated Vaughn to his Grosvenor home, and even as her mind argued to search the home while he was incapacitated, her heart would not allow it. Instead, with eyes heavy and bones weak with fatigue, she had returned to her home, but sleep had eluded her.

Ronan's new role filled her mind, needling her for solutions. When the sun finally peeked into her room, she accepted that sleep would never come.

Looking back down at the list she held in her hand, Eloise fought the urge to lay her head down on the dining table. The paper she had smuggled from Eastwick's home was filled with names, each with a number written beside it. Some had checkmarks next to them, but it revealed nothing else. They would not get much from it, but with Ronan's cooperation, perhaps she could find some insight.

Staring at the silver pot in front of her, Eloise debated another cup of coffee. Fatigue pulled at her, but another serving would make her jittery. She could not afford to lose focus. Not now.

The door to the breakfast room opened and Niraj stepped inside. "You're up early."

Eloise lifted the list of names. "I'm going over the list again, trying to figure out which events to attend."

"I see. And what are your plans for today?" Niraj went to the sideboard and filled a plate with kippers, eggs, and a stack of toast.

"I have a special trip planned to learn more about the Vaughn estate. What about you?"

Niraj sat in a chair and sighed. "Since you've dragged Vaughn into this, I'm left waiting on tenterhooks as he makes his next move."

"I'm sure he'll barge in here demanding I release him from the arrangement, but heaven knows when that will be. Perhaps you should take the day off to repair your frayed nerves?"

"Don't treat me like some maidenly aunt," he said, ripping off a piece of toast with his teeth.

"Then stop acting like one. Accept his involvement and move along. Mayhap I shall let you punch him a couple of times to make you feel better."

"Promise?" he asked with a smile.

"You're terrible."

A banging at the front door sent Niraj into curses. "Who the bugger could that be at this time?" he asked, shoving back from the table. "Can't a man have a decent breakfast before saving all of England?"

Eloise smiled as he strode from the room.

Setting aside the list, she allowed her mind free rein, hoping to uncover a detail she had missed. Instead, her body reminded her of Ronan's hands, calloused from his pencil, gently cradling her own.

This fascination with Ronan was a weakness. Brushing it off, she re-examined the list. Anything to divert her thoughts.

Niraj pushed through the door and threw a letter down to the table. "Your protector will be by this morning. He would like to know what is required of him in his new duties." Sitting down at the table, he picked up his fork. "And now my breakfast is cold. The things I do to help you, Eloise."

"Answering the door? We do have someone for that." Picking up his plate, she refilled it with warm food from the buffet.

"That ancient beast? He'd have taken ages to answer it."

"My friend, you would complain about the sky because it was too blue. When was the last time you had a woman?"

His jaw dropped. "What an inappropriate question."

"All I'm saying is your emotional state might change if you were to relieve some energy."

"Solve this case and my emotional state will fix itself. Until then, I shall take out my energy in the training room."

"I highly doubt physical exercise and meditation are

going to solve your problem."

"Are you speaking about me or yourself?"

"I'm not sure what you mean," she said, studying her coffee cup.

"Vaughn was ready to break his restraints to ensure your safety. It seems things were progressing quite splendidly. At least that was before he inserted himself into our investigation."

"He is a target, nothing more." She inwardly winced at how easily the lie rolled off her tongue. "Your powers of observation are mistaken if you believe there is anything more."

"Your protestation says it all, El." He watched her across the table, one brow raised. "Just be careful. I know how easy it is to become ensnared in a target. For it to take control of a mission."

Eloise swallowed her annoyance. "I will," she said, pushing back from the table. "Alert me when Vaughn arrives."

She left the breakfast room and paused in the hallway, her hand over her chest. Niraj certainly must be wrong in his worrying. She most assuredly had not developed feelings for Ronan. It was only guilt at using him that ate at her, nothing more.

In her office, she closed the door behind her and leaned against it. If one of the greatest agents of the Foreign Office could have been led astray during a case, it did not bode well for her if she allowed any feelings to develop.

At her desk, she sat and stared at the wooden surface before her. Then, forcing out a breath, she removed a file tucked away in a drawer. It contained the financial status of every individual on the list. Family matters, governmental involvement, and whatever information they could get from the Den filled the file. It was thick, stuffed to the brim.

And yet, it was useless.

While the information was enough to bring down some of the highest in the kingdom, the knowledge within was as useful as bits of sand in a sea of boulders.

Picking up her pen, Eloise removed a clean sheet of paper, dipped the sharpened end into the ink, and began to write. She wrote down every connection, question, and possibility she could fathom with this case. She wrote until she had created a stack of papers at her elbow containing all of her reflections and theories. A knock on the door interrupted her, forcing her to look up.

"Yes."

"Lord Vaughn is here," Niraj said.

Eloise frowned at her ink-stained fingers before nodding at him. As she stood, she clenched her fists in a valiant attempt to prevent herself from wiping them on her skirts. "You may send him in. Ask Sophie to send up refreshments." Eloise stuffed the papers back into the file.

Taking a handkerchief from the pocket of her skirt, she rubbed at the ink. She ensured that everything was in place around her before she stood behind a chair at the hearth. Her fingers gripped the back of the chair, and she forced herself to count her breaths willing her heart to slow.

The door to her office opened, and a somber Vaughn entered the room. Eloise's heart ached, and she desperately wished she could go to him and offer solace even though she was the one who had harmed him the most. "Are you having me followed?" he asked.

"Followed? By whom?"

"Some rough-looking lad who is much too young to be someone's tail. Whatever is the Foreign Office doing, hiring a child?"

"My lord, I haven't had you followed and even if I did, I wouldn't have hired a child. It could just be a coincidence."

Ronan shook his head, his lips pinched.

"Well then, is the lad outside now?" Eloise asked, peeking out onto the street.

"No, I lost him, but I wouldn't be surprised if the urchin popped up soon. You truly didn't hire anyone?"

"I did not. There is, however, another matter. We have an appointment to keep," she said, as the door opened and Sophie entered with refreshments. "Wonderful! Would you care for something to eat before we depart?" Seating herself in one of the chairs, she waited while Sophie placed tea and scones on the small table.

"What appointment?" Ronan asked, waving away the plate of sandwiches Eloise offered.

Setting the plate on the low table in front of her, she poured him a cup of tea, forgoing the loathsome drink herself. After placing two sugar cubes in his, she rotated the handle towards him, then added a splash of milk. "We're going to your solicitors to have our contract drawn up. As I said, my lord, you're to play the part of the dutiful protector."

Ronan stared at his teacup for a moment before taking a sip. "You know where my solicitor is?"

"I know quite a lot about you." At his perplexed look,

she shrugged her shoulders. "You were a mark."

His frown made her throat clench. The shift in their relationship was a hard one, but necessary. As long as she continued to keep him in a state of disappointment, the longing for what might have been would diminish.

"When is our appointment?"

"In a half-hour. Do help yourself to the food, my lord. We wouldn't want you to be famished when we get there. I know your temperament when you've not eaten." His brow furrowed.

Picking up a sandwich with smoked salmon, she nibbled on it while watching him. The lines between his eyebrows had become deep indents, as had the areas bracketing his mouth. She could nearly feel the frustration rolling off of him.

Eloise polished off several more sandwiches before setting aside her plate and standing. Shaking out her skirts, she glanced at Ronan, noting he had not touched any of the food. "Afraid I was planning to dose you again, my lord? You have little reason to worry. I merely did so to ensure you were unable to identify your location later on."

"I don't believe you," he said. "Either way, I seem to have lost my appetite. Must be due to all the surprises I've had." He stood as well, brushing at his buff jacket.

"Shall we?"

Ronan left the room without a word. It would seem she had struck a nerve, and while she missed his soft touches and simple conversation, perhaps it was best he thought her the villain. Taking her spencer and straw bonnet from Clarence, the elderly man who acted as their butler, Eloise left the house. She strode towards her carriage but stopped short when Ronan touched her elbow. Looking at him, she raised a brow.

"We are taking my curricle."

"That will not do. I need Niraj to accompany us."

"You're a spy, Mrs. Delacroix. I doubt you require a bodyguard." Ronan guided her to his curricle. Two gorgeous bays waited while he helped her into the seat. Taking the reins, he set the horses in motion, merging onto the busy lane.

"I know how it bothers you to be reminded of my position, but to keep up appearances, I do need Niraj."

"The ton will assume I'm your protection. And honestly, I can keep you safe just as well as he can. What skills could he possibly have that I do not?"

Eloise's spine shot straight at his comment, and she sent a glare at Ronan. "Niraj has many talents, my lord. He can take a man down with a single strike, disarm an assailant before they even know it happened. Knock out a lord who sticks his nose into business not his own."

Ronan appeared slack-faced. "You will catch flies, my lord. Best to keep your mouth closed, especially considering your misguided and repulsive prejudices. Don't be fooled by appearances. People see what they want to see in this world, and those far smarter will use it to their advantage."

"Niraj was the man in black from last night," he said, disbelief in his voice. "How is it possible? The man had an accent more refined than my own."

Smiling, Eloise turned to watch the crisp London morning.

"Who else?" Ronan asked.

"I beg your pardon?"

"Who else in your household is working for the Foreign Office? I'm sure there are more individuals. Does the gardener hide bodies in the flower beds? The maids have secret ways of cleaning up blood splatter?"

"What an imaginative mind you have." She smiled. "Not everything is as it appears."

"So it would seem."

✧ ✧ ✧

RONAN CONTINUED TO glance at Eloise as he steered the horses towards Chancery Lane. The crowded street held the morning rush of servants and tradesmen, but few of the ton were out at this hour. Eloise kept her gaze trained on the chaos of the street. Whether it was because she was avoiding him, or her training had taken over, Ronan did not know. She charmed him even as she enraged him, and his anger had by no means tapered.

Guiding the horses to a stop, Ronan jumped down, then held out his hand for Eloise to descend. Handing the reins to the stable lad, he escorted her into the building that held the offices of Miller and Sons. The parlour was sedate, holding several chairs, along with a small writing desk. The young clerk who sat at it froze when his eyes met Eloise's, his jaw dropping at the figure she cut. Scowling, Ronan cleared his throat at the man, who muttered a quick apology.

"Inform Mr. Miller that Lord Vaughn is here for his appointment," he said. The clerk nodded, then rushed from the room to inform Eugene Miller of their arrival. He turned to Eloise with a frown.

"No need to be so hard on the lad, my lord," she said.

"His behavior was rude. He should treat you with respect."

"He was admiring the wares. I'm a courtesan, remember? Do I not look the part?" she asked, holding her hands out to her sides.

Ronan raked his gaze over her. She had removed her bonnet and spencer. Her day dress was a pale-yellow spotted muslin with loose-fitting capped sleeves. While not what he would call provocative, the dress showcased her figure delightfully. He had seen something similar on Lady Jersey once, yet on Eloise, the effects were ravishing.

He cleared his throat. "You look fine."

She raised her eyebrow at him. "You dislike my dress?"

He said nothing, allowing the silence to be his answer.

"I beg your pardon, my lord," she said, her brow furrowed. "I'll return home after our appointment and don a shroud, shall I?"

Before Ronan could respond, Mr. Miller came into the parlour. "Mrs. Delacroix, what an honour," he said, kissing her gloved hand. Ronan was speechless. Miller never escorted him, let alone any other peer, to his office. That job was for the lowly clerks, and yet here the man was, paying homage to Eloise.

"Mr. Miller, how lovely to meet you," Eloise said, a husky tone slipping into her speech. Ronan turned to face the wall to hide the smile that pulled at his lips. Even hurt as he was from her lies, he could not help but find the humour in her acting, especially now that he knew the truth.

"Lord Vaughn," Miller said, executing a brief bow before returning his attention to the woman at his side. Ronan gaped at the solicitor. Did all men act this addle-pated when she was about? "Shall we convene to my office?"

Miller offered his arm to Eloise, and Ronan followed behind them down a darkened hallway and shut the door of Miller's office behind him. Eloise sat primly in one of the chairs in front of the man's desk, looking adoringly at his solicitor. With a frown, Ronan paced the modest office, glancing over the books lining Miller's shelves, each volume as boring as the next.

"Would you care for some tea, madam?" Miller asked.

"I would adore some." Eloise smiled at the solicitor and Ronan swallowed the protest that rose at the notion of her drinking the very thing she loathed.

After Miller rang a servant for refreshments, he returned to his seat and smiled at Eloise. "I must say, Mrs. Delacroix, I was very surprised to receive your request this morning. Typically, these types of arrangements are between your solicitor and the gentleman who wishes to…" he cleared his throat, "acquire your services."

Eloise simpered at the solicitor, drawing Ronan's brow even further into a frown. "Sir, I'm quite able to attend to my own settlements."

Attempting to stop his eyes from rolling, Ronan strode to Eloise and sat in the leather chair beside hers, hoping he looked like a man in love. He patted Eloise's hand as he looked at Miller. "I'm afraid I've become quite fascinated with Mrs. Delacroix and wanted to finalize our agreement before she chose another. She has a way of making a man feel unhinged," he said, glancing at Eloise, hoping she understood his meaning. The glare she sent him proved she did, and she withdrew her hand from his own.

"I want to ensure the settlement is the best for us both. I adore Lord Vaughn, but I also have a great number of requirements to ensure I'm taken care of. I want to be sure the marquisette is fit to meet them."

"I have no idea what you mean, madame," Miller said.

Eloise frowned at the man. "Mr. Miller, we both know the estate had been in debt for quite some time. I must guarantee there are still funds after the numerous debts accumulated by the previous marquess."

"I can assure you, madame, that the estate is quite prosperous." Miller adjusted the stack of papers before him.

Eloise glanced at the solicitor with a look of confusion. "What a very sudden change of events. How did the previous marquess come into such a large sum of money so quickly?"

"I apologise, madame, but I'm not at liberty to share that information. I do, however, want to reassure you the estate is thriving," Miller said. His brow had accumulated quite a bit of sweat since they had entered the office and Ronan worried for the man's health.

A soft knock at the door alerted them to the maid who brought in the tea. The maid laid the dishes out and excused herself from the room. Miller poured tea for them all, and Ronan looked at the brew, his stomach churning at what was to come. "Why was I not informed of the state the finances were in?"

"Perhaps we should save that discussion for another time, my lord," Miller said. "These are confidential matters pertaining to the marquisate."

"Whatever you have to say can be said in front of Mrs. Delacroix."

Clearing his throat, the solicitor looked at Ronan. "The debts were rather deep on the estate, both here and at Heathermore. Your father wanted to keep the ton's knowledge to a minimum so there would not be any gossip. I believe this is why you weren't informed of its disorder."

Ronan sighed. It seemed that he was paying the price for the lack of interest in the affairs of the title, and his father's transgressions were now coming to light.

When he opened his eyes, he observed Miller. The man was sickly thin, the translucence of his skin giving him the appearance of death. With the direction this appointment was going, Ronan was certain hell was near.

"Mr. Miller, how did my father absolve the debts?" Ronan asked.

Miller's pallor deepened, if possible. "My lord, as I've said, I'm not at liberty to discuss these matters presently, but I can set up an appointment and meet with you...."

"It would seem, Miller, you aren't at liberty to discuss much with me today." Ronan glanced at his fingernails and forced an air of casualness into his voice. "It's quite odd, considering I'm the marquess. I'm not sure how I feel about the way this firm is handling my accounts."

Miller's mouth gaped and the sweat on his brow increased until beads ran down his cheeks. "My lord, I'm quite sorry..."

"As am I, Miller. As am I," Ronan said, rising from his seat. "Come, my dear, I believe it might be time I hire another firm to manage my estates."

"He didn't tell me where the money came from," Miller said, his voice a squeak as he hastily wiped at his brow. "He arrived one day with a rather sizable sum and said his luck had changed. That's all I know."

"Thank you, Mr. Miller," Eloise said, smiling at the man. "You've been very helpful. I'm afraid we have another appointment, but we'll be sure to return and have the contract drawn up soon."

As she put on her spencer and tied her bonnet, Ronan swore the floor shifted beneath him. She had arranged the meeting to investigate his father's finances, setting the line of questions in motion, knowing he would demand answers.

Glaring at Miller, he escorted Eloise out of his office towards the front parlour. "It starts already?"

"We will discuss this outside," Eloise said with a whisper, smiling at the clerk.

"Mrs. Delacroix…"

"Please, use some common sense and keep your mouth closed. A lover's quarrel is not the best idea in the office of your solicitor." Eloise stood patiently waiting for him to open the door, and Ronan felt like growling.

Fury and confusion bubbled beneath the surface and he held it back as he opened the door. Every fiber of his being tingled with unleashed energy and so many questions that he wanted to scream, but heaven forbid the clerk think he was fuming. Once the door closed behind him, he turned on Eloise.

"Why are you doing this?" he asked, not caring about their location or audience, even as his upbringing chided at him to not cause a scene.

Eloise smiled at Ronan. "Pretenses, my lord."

Ronan took her hand and walked her towards the alleyway. When they stopped, she pulled her hand from his. "What are you doing?" she asked, her eyes looking anywhere but at him.

"You deliberately set up this appointment to find out information about my father."

"Of course I did! His name was on the list I found. I need to know everything I can about him, including his finances."

"I'm a means to an end for you." Even he heard the resignation in his words, but he could not drum up enough energy to care.

"Yes, and you played your part quite well. You gave me the opportunity I needed. Like every other aristocrat, your knowledge of your family's estate was lacking. I needed to be sure I could cross your father off as a suspect. From what I've learned today, that will not happen. Who walks in with a large amount of banknotes and no other information? He had to have been paid by the Fall of Caesar."

Ronan drew back as if she had struck him. "My father was not a traitor. He could have won the money at The Rogue's Den for all we know. It could have been a gentleman's bet between another member of the aristocracy."

"Is there a lord you're aware of that is hiding a large vault in his home? Perhaps in his ballroom?" she asked, sarcasm lacing her voice.

Ronan opened his mouth to reply, but Eloise's hand

clamped over his mouth. "Don't say anything," she said with a whisper, backing him towards the wall. Ronan struggled against her. For such a slight thing, her grip remained firm as she shoved him hard, her eyes never leaving the entrance to the alleyway as she held him.

"Damn you, stop wriggling, and don't make a peep." She looked to the other end of the alley and cursed. "They've boxed us in." She removed her hand from his mouth and reached into the pockets of her dress. "Can you fight?"

The question sent Ronan looking towards the street. Four men walked towards them, two from each end, effectively closing off any means of escape. "What?"

"Never mind," she said, removing her outerwear and hiking up her skirts. Ronan averted his eyes as she deftly tied them off. "I hope you can fight. The last thing I need to deal with is your death. Especially after how much trouble you've put me through."

Eloise tucked her hands into the folds of her skirts and smiled at the four ruffians that had jammed them in from opposite ends of the alleyway. "Good sirs, how are you this lovely morning?"

"We're doin' quite all right, luv," one man said. His balding head was covered in brown spots and the gap where his two front teeth should have been slurred his words. "It's not you we're after, but the bloke with you, but maybe you'll be a bit of fun once he's dead."

As he approached Eloise, she stepped back. When his grimy hand reached for her shoulder, she ducked beneath it and delivered a punch to his nose.

The man shouted as blood poured from his nose. And then all hell broke loose.

CHAPTER THIRTEEN

THE RUFFIAN FELL to his knees in the dirty alleyway, his hands clutching his bloodied nose. Ronan gaped at Eloise as she removed her knife from the pocket of her dress and faced the other men, a smile on her lips. Dear God, was she enjoying this?

"Final warning," she said to the three still standing. At once they rushed at her, and he could not remain motionless any longer. Ronan grabbed the reedy man to his right and spun him around, throwing a quick punch to his ruddy face. The brute took the hit, then turned back to Ronan and smiled. He spat out the blood dripping from his lips. Ronan raised his fists, waiting for the man to throw a punch at him. When the bloke dove at him instead, tackling him to the ground, Ronan shouted. Grappling for purchase, Ronan shoved at him, finding him immovable.

"No use in fightin', me lord. Yer dead either way," said the man, his breath reeking of stale fish and sewage.

Ronan struggled as his assailant removed a knife from his pocket. He pushed at the man's arm, but the blighter hardly moved, his laugh maniacal as Ronan struggled.

"This will be fun. I'll kill you, I'll fuck the lady, and then get paid a king's sum," he grinned. "Best day of me life." As the dagger drew back into the air, Ronan froze, watching it swing like a pendulum back towards him.

A quick movement flashed out of the corner of his eye, and then the weight was gone. Pushing himself up, he stared in awe.

The other two men who had attacked Eloise lay on the ground groaning, while she had his attacker immobilised. Her bonnet was wrapped around his throat and held tight in her hands as she rode him down to the ground, pinning his arms with her knees while she tightened the ribbon. The thin man clawed at his throat, but she held firm, her gaze never leaving the other brutes. As the man's eyes rolled into the back of his head, his body fell slack, and Eloise released the strings. The man's head fell to the street with a sickening thud.

Before she could collect herself, the larger of the two men was on his feet and running towards her. He grabbed her by the hair with his meaty paws, holding her immobile. Her cry of pain had Ronan pushing up from the ground, staggering towards them like a drunkard. He made it only a few steps before she placed her hand on top of the hand gripping her hair. Eloise threw a sharp punch into the man's upper arm and he screamed. When he released her hair, she thrust the palm of her hand up, striking him in the nose. The villain collapsed to the ground.

In the stillness of the dingy alleyway, Ronan walked towards Eloise. "Is he unconscious?" he asked, looking at the criminal.

She shrugged her shoulders, grimacing. "Hopefully. I didn't feel his nose crunch when I hit him."

Ronan swallowed the bile that rose to his throat and

looked away. "The thin one mentioned a king's ransom for my death."

After wiping her knives on her handkerchief, Eloise discarded the soiled cloth and pocketed her daggers. "Any idea who could be behind this?"

"None," he said, eyeing the men that littered the ground before him.

She looked around the alleyway, then bent to untie her skirts. Slipping on her shoes, she retrieved her belongings from the damp and sullied street. "You're not safe here."

As she walked towards the street, a noise grabbed Ronan's attention. The balding man rose from the ground and rushed at Eloise, a knife raised in his fist. Ronan did not think twice as he stepped between the two of them.

The knife sliced into his chest, sending fire dancing through him. A scream tore from his lips. The bald man pulled out the knife and raised it to strike again, but Eloise shoved him to the side. Ronan fell to the ground, crying out in agony. Pulling himself up, he dragged himself to the wall, leaning against it. His chest burned while blood seeped from the wound, soaking his shirt.

Eloise evaded the bald man, his knife glinting in the light. As the man struck the knife towards her, she grabbed his wrist, and using his body force, pulled his arm down. Eloise swung the knife back around towards the villain, hugging him from behind, and plunged the knife into his chest.

One of the men rose from the ground beside him, staggering to help his fallen comrade. Ronan kicked out his foot, hitting him in the kneecap. The man released a guttural yell as he floundered to the ground holding his leg, confirming Ronan's blow had done some damage. Ronan leaned against the grimy wall at his back and closed his eyes. The screams dimmed as the pain engulfed him. How had a simple friendship with this woman turned into such a bloody nightmare?

✧　✧　✧

ELOISE LET GO of the knife, backing away from the balding man. Blood covered her hands and sweat dripped down her brow. Wiping her hands on her skirts, she looked around for Ronan. He sat against the wall, blood dripping through the fingers he held against the wound. She cursed, kneeling by his side. Blood pooled on his shirt, waistcoat and jacket. Reaching under her dress, Eloise ripped a layer of her petticoat, then shoved it into the gash. Ronan let out a guttural moan.

"I know, I'm sorry. I have to stop the bleeding," she said.

"You were magnificent. Where did you learn to fight like that?"

"It's a very long story. Do you think you can stand?"

"Yes," he said, groaning as he sat up.

Eloise braced him against her shoulder, and with agonising slowness, brought Ronan to his feet. His breath came in quick pants as they walked towards the curricle. Ronan dragged himself up into the seat while Eloise assisted from the outside.

"Stay here," she said before running back into the alley. The lone survivor rocked on the ground, holding his leg. "Who sent you?" she asked, bending down before the ruffian.

"Don't know 'is name. Rich bloke wif a classy accent'," he mumbled between whimpers.

"How do you find him?"

"Don't know," he said. Using her hand, she jabbed at his kneecap and he screamed. "I don't know! He finds you!"

"If I find out you lied to me, I'll find you."

"He'll kill me first."

"Take your friends and get out of here."

Eloise hurried back to the conveyance and found Ronan slumped to the side. Clambering into the vehicle, she sat next to him, reapplying pressure to his wound. Ronan hissed in pain. With one hand, Eloise took up the reins and started the horses back towards her home in Marylebone.

"Talk to me," he said, his voice gruff.

"About what?"

"Anything will do. Just take my mind off the pain. Tell me where you learned to fight."

"I grew up in St. Giles. My mother worked for a seamstress making dresses for the fancy ladies of London. Her laughter was contagious and it filled our small rooms. It's her joyfulness I remember most. She died when Sophie was five and after, well, our father was never the same. He started thieving, working with a local gang to break into homes. When we became old enough, he taught us everything he knew."

"That couldn't have been good," he said, his eyes halfclosed.

"Stay awake or I won't finish the story."

Ronan's eyes snapped open, and Eloise grimaced, urging the horses to a faster pace before continuing. "Picking was all we could do to keep food on the table and a roof over our heads. It didn't matter if it was right or not, it was what we had to do to survive. One morning, I was trying to round up enough money for a scrap of bread, and I got caught. The aristocrat noticed I lifted his pocket watch and grabbed me before I could dodge away. Instead of turning me in, he asked for it back and told me I could make better use of my skill. I agreed, willing to say anything for him to let me go. Thankfully, he didn't turn me in. When he released me and departed, I continued in my pursuit of coin. Little did I know I was being watched. The blighter followed me and caught me in my lie. I was taken to the Foreign Office. I was sure they were going to throw me on a ship or send me to Newgate, but instead, they offered me a job."

"They offered a job to a minor slip of a girl? Just like that?"

Chuckling, she glanced at him. "They didn't know I was a girl. Boys had better chances of being left alone on the streets. A girl can be raped, sold, or killed. I'd bound my breasts and stuffed my hair into one of my pa's old caps. I always wore trousers and a shirt with a large jacket to hide my upper body."

"So, they thought they'd given the job to a young boy."

"And instead they got me."

"They had to have found you out somehow."

"They did," she said as she slowed the curricle in the mews behind her home. "We're here. Do you think you can manage, or shall I get Niraj?"

At Ronan's scowl, Eloise jumped out of the conveyance and scurried around to the other side, bracing herself to catch him if he fell. His slow descent to the ground had studying his injury again. Blood still oozed from the gash.

Sliding underneath his arm once again, Eloise walked him inside. His soft chuckle in her ear made her glance at him. "What?"

"You're so small, and yet you act as if you can hold up an elephant." He smiled, his eyes slightly unfocused.

"I think the kitchen is as far as we're going," she said, helping him to sit in a chair.

Eloise ordered a maid to get Sophie before returning to Ronan's side. She reapplied pressure to his chest, his grimace the only sign of his pain.

"Keep talking," he said between his teeth.

"The aristocrat had me train with Niraj. It was the longest two months of my life. We worked on sparring and boxing. He was merciless. During one of our matches, his blade nicked me on the collar. While stopping the bleeding, Niraj had come to understand what everyone else had failed to notice. He kept it a secret while we trained, pushing me harder, intent on making me the best. I met with the aristocrat for my first assignment, still disguised as a boy. When I succeeded, I told him the truth. He was less than thrilled that I'd lied but realised the usefulness a female could have within the office."

"Not everything is as it appears."

"Exactly."

"Like a bodyguard who speaks as if he were the highest in the realm and a world-famous courtesan who is a spy for the British government."

She nodded. "Something like that."

A brisk knock sounded before the door opened and Sophie rushed in. "He was nicked. The bleeding has slowed, but it needs to be cleaned thoroughly and he'll require stitches." Eloise pushed on the wound again, causing Ronan to hiss in pain.

Sophie nodded her head and hurriedly began collecting supplies. Eloise knelt to help Ronan remove his jacket and waistcoat. "It might be easier to cut your shirt off rather than attempt to remove it over your head."

"You're the expert, it would seem, so do as you must."

Eloise took her knife and tore a small rift in the fabric, then yanked the pieces apart. "Impressive, Mrs. Delacroix."

"Dempsey." The word escaped her lips before she could think, and where once she might have wished to call it back, instead, she only felt a sense of relief at its utterance. A tipping of the scale back into balance, a sacrifice made to the man who had sacrificed himself for her.

"Beg pardon?"

"My name, it's Eloise Dempsey."

"A pleasure to finally meet you," he said, a smile tugging at his lips.

A slight movement out of the corner of her eyes notified her Sophie was ready. She moved aside before helping Sophie with the task. Eloise uncapped a bottle of whiskey and laid several towels behind Ronan.

"My lord, this will be quite painful," Sophie said.

"Do what you must," he said.

"How on earth did this happen?" Sophie asked in a

whisper.

"I don't know," Eloise said with a sigh. "He mentioned earlier that he thought he was being followed and, like an idiot, I brushed it off."

Ronan groaned as Sophie doused the cut with the liquor, nearly emptying the bottle on the fresh wound. The gash oozed anew, blood pouring from it once more. Ronan bit down on his lip, attempting to muffle the pain as Sophie mopped up the alcohol before grabbing a bar of soap and dipping it in the bowl of warm water by her side. She scrubbed the area with the soapy cloth until the skin turned pink, and all the while, Ronan never made a single sound.

When Sophie placed her first stitch in his chest, pulling the thread tight, he let out a bark of pain so loud it made Eloise jump. "What do you need?" She cupped his cheek, turning his gaze to meet hers.

"Keep talking to me?" he asked.

"I have no other stories to tell."

"Rather unfortunate. It seems we'll need a different distraction." Snaking his fingers into her hair, Ronan drew her down to meet him. He gently brushed his lips over hers, causing her to gasp. It was all the invitation he needed and he invaded her mouth with his tongue. Pleasure stole up Eloise's spine as she reached for him. His tongue stroked her own, capturing her breath with each caress. Angling her head, she allowed him to plunge deeper, causing a deep ache to settle inside of her. The clearing of a throat brought the yearning to an end and Eloise yanked her head back, staring at Ronan. When she met Sophie's knowing gaze, her cheeks warmed.

"I need to douse it once more with liquor," Sophie said with a smile. "Do you want to distract him again?"

"I think Lord Vaughn can handle it without a distraction."

"I don't know," he said. "I thought it worked well."

Frustration swirled as she glared at him. "Why did you kiss me?"

"Goodness, look at you. You become quite stunning when you're angry."

"If you think I'm stunning now, I'm about to become bloody gorgeous," she said through her teeth.

"I do hate to interrupt you both again, but I'm finished. My lord, you'll need to rest and ensure the laceration remains clean to minimise infection. If you start to feel ill, or it begins to redden, send for me," Sophie said.

Eloise gritted her teeth, certain it was a bad idea to beat the tar out of an already injured man. "I'll take you home."

With Sophie's help, she walked him out the door and hefted him into the curricle. All three of them sweating by the end of it. Getting into the seat, Eloise reached for the reins.

"You're bleeding," Ronan said to her, touching her cheek where a knife must have grazed her.

Snapping the reins, she set the horses in motion for Grosvenor's Square. "It's fine. I'll have Sophie patch it up when I return home."

"Do you think the man you stabbed is dead?" he asked. Eloise swallowed, then gave a brief nod. "How do you handle it, taking someone's life?"

"You don't. Every time it deadens a piece inside of

you, and you can never get it back," she said, steering the horses around a stopped cart. "When it's a battle between you or them, the choice is taken out of your hands. I always prefer to have them brought through the judicial system. Sometimes it doesn't work out that way."

"I couldn't imagine killing someone."

"It's not something I would recommend to anyone."

Ronan cleared his throat. "I haven't thanked you for saving my life."

Eloise waved her hand. "It was nothing."

"I wouldn't have blamed you if you'd allowed that man to kill me."

"It's part of my job, my lord. Keeping the informant safe," she said, brushing him off.

"Right. Just the job."

Eloise stopped the horses in front of Ronan's home. After exiting the conveyance, Eloise hurried to Ronan's side and held out her hand. His face contorted with frustration. "I'm helping you. I promise your manhood is not in any way endangered." His growl caused a smile to dance on her lips. "Have it your way, my lord. Just don't ask me to pick you up after you fall on your arse." She turned, her dirty skirts swirling at the motion.

His growl made her pause and turn back. "Yes?" she asked.

"Can you help me down?"

"Why, of course, I can," she said with a smile, holding her hand out to him. In her opinion, she would make the most remarkable footman. He eyed her hand with disgust before holding onto it and gingerly alighting from the curricle.

"Thank you." The sound was guttural, as if forced from the very depths of him.

"It was my pleasure, my lord."

As she walked along with him, she fought the urge to slide an arm under his shoulder and support him once more. His pace was slow, each step seemed to pull a little more energy from him. Thankfully, his dutiful butler chose that moment to open the front door. With a frown at Eloise, Jenkins sent two footmen out to get Ronan.

As the men wrapped their arms around his waist, he growled, and Eloise wanted to snap at them to be gentle. Instead, she swallowed the words back and followed behind them, attempting to squeeze past Jenkins. Before she could follow Ronan to his room, the butler reached out and grabbed her arm.

"What happened?"

"We were set upon by a group of thieves outside of the solicitor's office. Lord Vaughn valiantly fought them off but suffered a knife wound. I summoned my doctor, who cleaned and stitched him, but he needs to rest. Lord Vaughn insisted upon doing so at home," Eloise said, shaking the man's hand from her arm. Pushing past him, Eloise followed the footmen.

"Mrs. Delacroix, this is unacceptable. You cannot go up there," Jenkins said as he trailed behind her.

"Leave her be," Ronan said with a groan as he navigated the stairs with aching slowness.

The butler turned away with a scowl, and Eloise swallowed the urge to stick her tongue out at the man.

Inside Ronan's room, his valet helped to peel his jacket off. Unable to stay still, she went to Ronan's side and bent to remove his boots.

"You don't need to do that," he said, his words soft with exhaustion.

"Humour me."

The fatigue seemed to have taken over him, his entire body losing the want to fight against her command. His valet approached the bedside, and Eloise moved so the man could remove the remainder of Ronan's filthy clothes. The moment was entirely improper, and perhaps, if she had truly been his mistress, she could do more to help. "I should go." His gaze met hers, but he said nothing. His lack of response was the answer she needed.

As she left the room, Eloise was aghast at how greatly she wished he would call her back. And how willingly her heart wished to remain.

CHAPTER FOURTEEN

"**B**LOODY FUCKING HELL!" Ronan roared as his wound was filled with fire. His bastard of a valet, Turner, would be getting the sack as soon as he put Ronan to rights. The fiend rinsed the wound with whiskey, purportedly on the directions of Eloise's doctor, who just so happened to not be a doctor at all.

The physician had sent a directive on how to care for his injury, along with a salve to keep infection at bay. The pot reeked of cow dung and looked similar to vomit. He was certain Turner enjoyed every moment of watching his master laid low by a stab wound.

When Turner refilled the cup to cleanse the wound once more, Ronan growled at him. "If you come near me again, I'll skewer you."

Turner rolled his eyes but set the cup aside in favour of the bowl of steaming water and a bar of soap. "My lord, Mrs. Delacroix's physician clearly stated that we must cleanse the wound thrice with spirits."

"Mrs. Delacroix's physician was just being flippant. I'm certain the third time is unnecessary. Clean it and apply the salve, and then leave me in peace. I've had enough of your fluttering about."

"I'd forgotten how utterly disagreeable you become when ill," his valet said.

"You risk your job if you continue with your imperti-nence."

"Whatever shall I do if I'm not valet to the most im-possible lord in London? Why, I'm certain I would celebrate for a week."

"That can be arranged." Ronan smiled at the man, but his valet only shook his head.

"One can only hope," Turner said, wiping away the suds that had accumulated over Ronan's stitches.

As he opened the pot of salve, Turner's nose turned up and he gagged, causing Ronan to laugh, before groaning in agony. "Just get on with it. The faster you apply it, the less you'll have to smell it." Ronan covered his mouth and nose with his hand, desperate to minimise the foul stench.

"The reek will seep into my fingers, following me around all day. I'll be the laughingstock of the household. Mrs. Brown will kick me out and have me eat luncheon in the stables with the rest of the animals."

"Bloody hell," Ronan said, snatching the pot from his valet. "I'll do it. Take your fragile self out of here before I smear this putrid paste on your pristine waistcoat."

Turner hurried out the door before Ronan could change his mind. Taking a sizable scoop of the potent concoction, Ronan spread it across his wound, sucking in a breath at the pain. Placing the lid on the pot, he set it down on the side table, grabbed up his pillow, and placed it over his mouth. Screaming into the cotton-covered down, Ronan gripped the pillow with desperation.

"Did I come at a bad time?" said a voice next to him.

Ronan ripped the pillow from his face to shout at the intruder, but swallowed the sound as Eloise raised a brow at him. Her blonde hair was pulled up on top of her head and her stunning figure was cloaked in a grey spencer. In her hands hung a bonnet, the ribbons twirled absently around her fingers.

She looked utterly phenomenal, and here he lay, utterly useless.

A worthless noble smelling of cow dung with a stab wound in his shoulder. Not that it mattered, anyway. She was still a liar, even though he was still drawn to her presence.

After the kiss they had shared the night before, he was certain he could drown himself in her taste as well, but that was beside the point. He had only kissed her because he had been weak, desperate for a distraction from the fiery pain of his wound. It had nothing to do with her charm, nor her smile, nor the way her presence had stoked a warmth in him that he had never felt in his lifetime.

Certainly not.

A liar she still was, devastating kiss or not.

"What are you doing here?"

"I came to check on you. I see you got Sophie's note and healing salve. You smell delightful." Eloise pinched her nose, her eyes crinkled in barely-contained mirth.

"Lean closer and I can make you smell as wonderful as I do."

Eloise sat on the edge of the bed, her eyes raking over him before meeting his face. "You're looking well. How are you feeling?"

"Like I was stabbed." It was utterly vexing that she dared to visit while he was feeling so miserable, rubbing salt into an already festering wound.

"You're grumpier than usual. Have you eaten?" Eloise picked a piece of lint from her dress, unphased by his temper.

"Yes, mother. I had a delightful breakfast of mash and some tepid water, per your doctor's instructions."

Eloise chuckled. "Sophie was only kidding."

"You don't say?" He frowned at her.

"Well, partially. The diet was only necessary if you developed a fever, which I can see you have not. Let's get you something heartier." Standing, she tugged on the pull to summon a footman. When the man arrived, she requested bacon, kippers, toast with butter and jam, and a carafe of tea.

"Are you feeding an army?"

"No, it would seem I'm feeding a feral bear," she said with a small smile in his direction.

Being confined to the bed while such a stunning creature was in his room seemed to be a fate worse than death. The urge to trail behind her as she inspected the books on his desk and the trinkets from his travels was unnerving. She picked up a shell he found on the coast of Oia, rubbing her finger along the ridges of the smooth pink interior. "This is beautiful," she said, her voice soft in the still room.

"I found it during my trip to Santorini. It was sitting on the beach exactly like that. As if it were waiting for me."

"What was it like there? Your books are phenomenal, but when I read them, they only emphasise how much I've missed by never leaving London."

"Sorry, I save my stories for those I consider friends."

Setting down the shell, she presented him with her back. "You're still upset."

"Was it supposed to miraculously disappear overnight because you saved my life and I kissed you?" he asked before thinking. The stiffness of her back made him wish he could recall the words. "Eloise..."

She turned to him, her gaze hard. The soft demeanour she had arrived with had vanished in a plume of smoke, as swiftly as it had come. "Right. Glad to see you're keeping your wits about you. It wouldn't do for you to begin to have a fondness for me due to the events of last night. Which is actually why I'm here."

"Oh."

"You'd mentioned someone was following you. I think they alerted those men to our location. And the fact that they attacked us in broad daylight makes me worried about your safety."

"So, what? You're planning to employ a bodyguard for me?"

She smiled at him and Ronan's stomach dropped. "I've a better idea. I'll be moving in."

"What?" Ronan sat up in the bed, the motion jostling his shoulder and causing him to hiss in pain.

"I'm moving in. Well, my staff and I are."

Ronan's jaw dropped at her audacity.

She smiled at him before sitting on a chair that was positioned beside the bed. "Now don't make that face. Not all of my staff, of course, just Niraj and Sophie."

"Of course," he said, his mind still trying to wrap itself around her pronouncement.

"Oh, and we'll need you to open your father's office as

well so we can search it."

Ronan wanted to vomit at her words. His father's office had remained locked since his passing. He could not bring himself to enter the place without feeling beads of sweat accumulate on his brow, his stomach attempting to cast up whatever he had eaten that day.

Certainly, there were documents inside, financial records, and correspondence that the marquess had kept that Ronan would eventually need to look over. But it did not matter. As long as he kept that room locked and stayed away from it, he could maintain a modicum of sanity.

"You've lost your bloody fucking mind." The words tumbled from his lips.

"Ronan..."

"No. Absolutely not. You will not move your circus into my home, and you will certainly not be allowed access to my father's office. You'll have to pry the key from my dead fingers before I allow you to go anywhere near it."

"That can be arranged," she said with a tight smile, the gesture almost menacing.

A maid bustled into the room with a tray laden with the food she had requested, and Ronan's stomach made a horrible noise as he inhaled the delightful scents that emanated from it. Eloise smiled at the woman and took the tray, thanking her with soft words. The maid blushed at her kindness, then hurried from the room as quickly as she had come in.

"Ronan, you were attacked on the streets of London. I can't take the risk of losing you, and the ton won't question a man moving his mistress into his home. We've

been seen out enough times that there is already speculation about our relationship and we made a trip to your
solicitor yesterday. The supposition is already there for us
to use, and it will ensure that I can keep you safe." She set
the tray on the bed, then resumed her seat.

"I don't want your level of Bedlam brought into my
home. I'm already involved more than I want to be. With
you here, there will be no respite."

"You don't have much of a choice in the matter." He
scoffed but she merely shrugged. "I don't like playing that
card, but you and I both know what will happen if you
don't follow orders."

"So then do it already!" he shouted. "I've learned my
family estates were in arrears and my father found an
exorbitant amount of money to replenish the coffers. I've
been stabbed in the shoulder and have honestly seen
enough of you to last me a lifetime. You keep threatening
to expose my father's treachery, so do it already."

She stared at him. "You don't mean that. Ronan, you
would lose your title, your estates, everything. The crown
would take it all from you."

Ronan swallowed the lump that formed in his throat.
The notion that the title and its trappings could be taken
from him made his stomach clench. Yes, they were
trimmings of the life he never wanted, but they were his.
Generations of men before him had forged his legacy,
dedicating themselves to the title and all it required. It all
would be lost if word got out of his father's supposed
treachery. But only if what Eloise claimed was true, and he
still had his doubts. "We both know that won't happen
because my father isn't a traitor."

Eloise sighed and leaned back in her chair. Her hand came to her forehead and she massaged the spot between her eyebrows. "All right, how about I make you a deal?"

"A deal?" Ronan raised a brow at her.

"You work with me."

Ronan chuckled. "That's not going to happen."

She sat up and held her hand up to quiet him. "No, hear me out. You work with me, but with the intention of proving he didn't do it. Perhaps you're right and this whole thing is one colossal mistake."

"You're humouring me, Eloise." Ronan frowned at her.

"And what if I am? Prove my theory wrong, Ronan." She leaned forward, her lips pinched, waiting for his reply.

Ronan stared at the woman that sat across from him, her wine-red dress playing peek-a-boo under her grey spencer. Her bonnet sat in her lap and she fiddled with the ties.

It could be an act. She was adept at playing whatever role was required of her. Yet, a part of Ronan, the part that wished the Eloise he had met before existed, could not help but hope the woman before him was one and the same. The one who seemed to care for him, if only a bit.

"All right." Her jaw dropped, and Ronan took a moment to enjoy her shock.

"I'll be honest," she said, brushing at her skirts, "I didn't think you'd agree."

"I enjoy keeping people on their toes," he said with a grin. "Move your blasted staff in here and when I'm out of this bed, we'll discuss opening my father's office."

"Ronan…"

He held up his hand. "You've just gained a monumental win for the Foreign Office, Eloise. I'd leave the rest well enough alone for now."

She pressed her lips together once more and nodded her head. "Right then. I best get going as there is much to prepare." She stood and shook out her skirts before heading for the door. "Ronan?" Her back was to him, her hand on the door, ready to depart.

"Thank you," she said softly, and then she left.

CHAPTER FIFTEEN

THREE MORNINGS LATER, Ronan emerged from his rooms clean, fed, and less sore than he had been in the days before. While his injury still throbbed, he could not help but admit that he was indebted to Sophie's doctoring and her disgusting poultice. He showed nary a sign of fever and the wound looked like it would heal quite nicely.

Eloise and her group of Foreign Office comrades had taken over his home while he had lain in bed recuperating. Within the span of a day, the masked avenger formerly known as her bodyguard, along with her sister, had appropriated the quiet expanse of his home and filled it with their pandemonium. While the noise within the expansive townhouse had not risen, their presence was invariably felt.

According to Turner, they had seized the library and turned it into a home base of sorts, filling it with file folders and holding nightly meetings. Ronan swore he felt the family coffers lighten at the amount of coin he would be paying to ensure the servant's silence. Jenkins was already full of nonstop complaints below stairs about the new additions, even with his increased salary.

Ronan hated that Eloise's crew had taken over the one safe place that remained, but the knowledge that he was not alone created an envelope of security he could not disapprove.

Walking down the stairs, he found Eloise waiting for him in the foyer. Her blonde hair was pulled into a simple chignon at the back of her head, but that was not the extraordinary part. Eloise stood in a fitted pair of black trousers, a white linen shirt, and a pair of boots that fit her legs like a second skin. A navy-blue jacket finished the ensemble while brown kidskin gloves graced her hands, one rhythmically tapping the other with her riding crop. When her eyes met his, she smiled.

"There you are! How are you feeling?"

Ronan attempted to move his mouth, but his gaze could not leave her. He drank in the sight of her. She had rendered him speechless.

"Ronan? Are you all right?" she asked, coming towards him. She removed a glove and touched her hand to his forehead, her palm warm against his skin. "Should I get Sophie?"

"Fine. I'm fine. What in the blazes are you wearing?"

"Clothes?" she asked. "Come along, we're going riding." Grabbing his hand, she dragged him out the front door. They had barely reached the mews when he pulled her to a stop.

"Wait. You're not going riding wearing that." His gaze glided up and down her form. "What if someone sees you? You need to change. Where is your riding habit?"

Her sigh forced him to look back at her lips. Even pursed in displeasure and missing their usual rouge, they were delectable. Instead of responding to him, Eloise turned and strode towards the stables. She called back,

"Are you coming or not?"

Ronan took off after her, his shoulder protesting.

"Good morning," she said to his stable master.

"Morning, Mrs. Delacroix. My lord," the man said, doffing his cap.

"Mr. Grimsby," Eloise said, "His lordship will need a mare who enjoys easy strolls and cares not for speed." She looked back at Ronan with a smile.

Ronan bristled at her suggestion. "I'll have you know, madame, I'm capable of handling animals with a bit of spirit."

"I'm sure you are, my lord, but at present, you couldn't handle a pony. Your injury leaves you in a fragile state. Perhaps you should ride with me, so I can keep an eye on you." Her smile seemed filled with mischief.

Ronan cleared his throat and looked to Grimsby. "Have Hercules saddled and give Mrs. Delacroix Romeo." Grimsby nodded and began towards the stalls.

Outside the stables Ronan waited, reminding himself that the woman who stood beside him was not truly his friend, and the sting of that reality caused an ache in his heart. Even though he had agreed to her scheme, he was not certain they could ever regain what they had lost.

"I've read Shakespeare, my lord. If you've stuck me with a moody beast, I'll make you regret it," Eloise said.

At that moment, Grimsby and a stable boy led out two horses. One was a magnificent black. His coat glistened in the sunlight, his mane hiding hints of blue that appeared when he moved his head. "My God, he's gorgeous," she said.

"Which is why I named him Romeo. He cuts such a

fine figure that I'm sure all of our mares are dying to be near him." Ronan walked up to the tan beast Grimsby led out. "This is Hercules, obviously named for his size."

"He does seem larger than life," Eloise said, reaching her hand out for Hercules to sniff. His lips tickled her gloved palm, and she laughed.

"Don't let his size fool you. He's an oversized baby who adores apples and scratches behind his ears."

"A man after my own heart," she said, smiling at the brute of a horse.

Ronan stepped his foot into the stirrup and pulled himself into the saddle, swallowing the groan that tried to escape his lips. His body ached from lack of use and his wound smarted each time he overextended his arm, the motion pulling at the stitches. He squeezed his eyes closed against the sting before looking to see Eloise mount her horse. Her thighs gripped the horse's sides, directing him. She sat firmly, sure of herself and her control over the beast.

She smiled brightly at him. "Are you ready?"

Ronan shook his head to rid himself of the dangerous thoughts, before guiding Hercules down the drive towards Hyde Park. With the early hour, the street was nearly empty, as would be the park. It was not yet the fashionable hour and most of London society was still in their beds.

Ronan attempted to keep their ride sedate, leading their horses along Oxford Street at a measured pace. As they cleared the Cumberland gate, Eloise looked at him, an impish smile covering her face. Her eyes twinkled as she looked back towards the immense grounds. "How is your wound, my lord?"

"Healing. Why do you ask?"

Mischief filled her eyes as she said, "I'll race you to the Serpentine," she said, pointing some distance away. "Ready?"

"Eloise, I don't think that's the best idea—" he began, but she was already off. Romeo's sudden burst of speed had her screaming with joy as the stallion took off across the grass. Ronan's heart jumped into his throat. Urging Hercules to follow, he gave the horse free rein, praying he caught up with her before she injured herself with her foolish actions. As Hercules came abreast of Romeo, Ronan looked over, stunned to find Eloise leaning over the stallion's head, urging him faster. Her eyes were bright and her smile was the largest he had ever seen.

She was magnificent, an Amazon leading her steed into battle. Her hair had come free of the pins holding it in place and it whipped in the wind, twining with Romeo's dark mane.

She was a goddess.

She was stunning.

And Ronan had never been more perplexed.

As they crested the hill towards the river, Eloise slowed Romeo, whispering soothing words to him as she stroked his neck, her entire face alight with joy. "Well done, you amazing love," she said. "You were like the wind." The stallion's ears perked up at her words. When the horse finally pulled to a stop, Eloise slid from the saddle and turned to Ronan.

"Where the devil did you learn to ride like that?" he asked.

"I ride here every morning." She shrugged before leaning forward to stroke the beast she rode. Romeo leaned
into her caress and Ronan knew the stallion was already in
love with her. "He was brilliant. Do you race him?"

"Never."

"Are you fond of racing?"

"No. My father thought noblemen who involved themselves in horse races were uncouth."

She smirked at his comment. "It can be a bit barbaric,
especially if the trainers are abusive. With the right team,
Romeo would be wonderful." She leaned into the horse,
hugging his neck, and Romeo snuffled her hair, causing
her to laugh. Her ease with the animal surprised him. For
someone so controlled, she was unbelievingly gentle with
the brute.

As Ronan got down from Hercules, he could not keep
back the groan that left his lips. Eloise gasped at the sound
and hurried to him. Removing her gloves, she pushed aside
his jacket and unbuttoned his waistcoat and shirt. Pulling
it aside, she bit her bottom lip.

"Stubborn man," she said, looking at his reddened
wound. "You said it wasn't bothering you."

"It's only a bit sore and pulls when I move awkwardly," he said, in no rush to remove her bare hands from his
chest.

"It doesn't look infected, but if you continue to abuse
it, I'll send Sophie after you. She'll have your head."

"I'll rest tonight." His breath stumbled as her fingertips danced lightly around the wound.

Fixing his clothing, Eloise looked up at him. His throat
tightened and his heart thundered in his ears as he

searched her gaze. His fingers itched to cup her cheek, to slide into her hair and bring her lips to his. To repeat the kiss he had so simply brushed off days before.

"How are you?" she asked.

He swallowed the lump in his throat, his breath hitching as she put his shirt back to rights. "You've seen my injury. It's fine."

"Ronan," she said, her voice soft as she rested her hands on his chest. He suspected she could feel the thundering of his heartbeat. "Are you all right?"

"I suppose I'm how anyone would feel upon finding their father potentially lived a hidden life. I don't know how to reconcile the notion. We might not have agreed on my path in life, but I held him in esteem. I wanted to be like him; generous, caring, resourceful. He was a large presence in Parliament, a leader for our tenants. As much as I tried, I knew I would never measure up." He laughed, shaking his head. "I sound insane."

"You sound like someone grieving. It's understandable. The man you knew was not an aberration, it was merely one facet of a complex person. How much of an individual can we truly know?"

"It's odd hearing you say that after what you've put me through."

"What does that mean?" She frowned.

"You pretended to be someone else for a week before I found out who you truly were. For all I know, you lied about every aspect of yourself. Meanwhile, I bared my soul to you like an arse." He crossed his arms and stared at her.

She held her arms out for his perusal. "What you see is

what you get."

"We both know that's not true. A week ago, I thought you were a courtesan with a travel fascination and a desire for friendship. That turned out to be utterly inaccurate. There is more to you, Eloise Dempsey, and I think you owe it to me to be who you truly are. We can start with simple things if it's easier for you."

"Simple things?"

"Sure. What's your favourite colour?"

"Yellow."

"Mine is green," he said with a smile. "See, that wasn't so hard."

"You think by asking my favourite colour it shall give insight into who I am and mend our broken bond?"

"Perhaps."

She laughed, leaning against a tree and looking at him. The wind grabbed at her hair, twirling it around her. She looked like a siren, tempting him from his ship for a chance to be with her. "What, pray tell, does my favourite colour deduce?"

Ronan walked towards her, smiling. "Well, yellow is the colour of the sun, which makes me think you adore sunshine and warmth. It's also the colour of lemons, which is the scent you wear."

"You've caught me, good sir," she said, doffing a pretend cap and bowing to him. "Your deductions are so accurate. You should set up a guessing booth at a fair. You'd be quite profitable."

"Stop that." He crossed his arms as he stood before her.

"Stop what?"

"Using sarcasm and quips to divert the conversation away from what makes you uncomfortable." Eloise's jaw dropped at his statement and Ronan reached his hand out and closed her mouth. He gave into the impulse and let his fingers cup her cheek. In response, she scowled at him.

"We both know it's true, Eloise." She bit her bottom lip, and he rubbed his thumb across it, saving the delicate skin from her torment. "You know everything about me. I know it was for the assignment, but now we are both committed to this mission and I think it's only fair that I know you as well as you know me. After all, we're supposed to be working together now. It's time I know the real you."

"What makes you think I was ever dishonest about who I was?" Her voice was a near whisper, and when her eyes met his, it was a punch to the throat. "I do enjoy books about travel and everything else under the sun, but have very little time to read them. I love learning new things and setting tongues wagging with my outlandish behaviour because those stuffy old biddies truly think something as trivial as a neckline deems you worthy. I adore strawberry tarts and cannot stand tea. I never lied to you about any of that."

"No," he said, taking a step back from her. Her admissions sent the anguish he had tampered down surging through his veins once more. She was still guarded, doing whatever she could possibly do to stop from fully opening up to him. "No, but you did lie to me."

"For a good reason," she said, walking towards him. "Ronan, I know I lied to you, but it wasn't my intention to harm you."

"Yet, here we are," he said, motioning to the surrounding space.

"Why can't we go back to the way it was before? We were friends, Ronan."

"Eloise, you're holding me hostage in my own home and blackmailing me into helping you implicate my father." Ronan rubbed his hands across his face. "I just want to be done with all of this."

"Then open your father's office." She walked to him and set a hand on his arm. "I've been patient, allowing you to do it in your own time, but I'm not certain I can deter Niraj much longer. Let me look inside and see if there is anything that we missed. Maybe there is something in there that absolves him of any wrongdoing, but we'll never know if the doors remain shut."

Ronan moved his arm away, making her hand drop. His skin burned from her touch, whether from longing or dislike, he did not know. "I'll think about it."

"That's all that I ask," she said, moving around him. "We should head back." Climbing onto her horse, she said, "Race you," then took off back across the park. Ronan mounted Hercules, following behind her at a more sedate pace.

His stomach churned at the idea of opening the doors to his father's office and allowing Eloise and Niraj inside. It was a desecration of sacred space and a violation of his father's trust. Yet, what if Eloise was right and there was something in there that absolved his father of the crimes they accused him of? Then again, what if they opened the door to Pandora's box?

CHAPTER SIXTEEN

R ONAN LOOKED AT the journal in his lap, a frown furrowing his brow. A tepid cup of tea sat next to him, untouched, much like the journal.

His creativity had fled with each passing day, the stress of what had become his daily life ate away at whatever small spark of inspiration he might have had. His manuscript was late and his publisher had sent letters each day demanding to know when his book would be delivered. Yet, he could barely pick up a quill. Not to write the story, and certainly not to write them a response.

A knock on the door brought his head up as Niraj peeked in. "Eloise requires your presence in the ballroom."

With a nod at the man, Ronan rose and followed him, preparing himself for an interrogation on whether or not he would open his father's office. As the door to his ballroom opened, he came upon Eloise, wrapping her right hand in a strip of linen. Ronan stood, mouth agape, as he took in the changes to the home's ballroom. Plush rugs covered the floor, their varying shades a kaleidoscope in the cream-coloured room. One corner played host to an accouterment of weaponry, some of which he could not even identify.

"Good, you're here. Go change," she said.

Clearing his throat, Ronan glanced down at his clothes, then back at Eloise. "Is there something wrong with what I currently have on?"

"For what I have in mind, there is. Niraj has loaned you some garments," she said, waving her hand at the large man next to him.

Ronan raised his brow in confusion but followed Niraj to a changing screen, on which was draped a pair of pants and a tunic made of light cotton. He groaned at her demands, but soon his clothes landed on top of the screen.

"Leave off your boots and stockings. You won't need them," Eloise said.

"What is my life becoming?" he asked under his breath.

The garments hung loosely on Ronan's frame, allowing for movement as he walked out from behind the screen. The lightness of the cloth gave him a greater awareness of his body, and when he looked up, he caught Eloise staring at him.

Ronan cleared his throat. "Will this do?" he asked, spreading his arms wide.

"It'll have to. Niraj, I think we're set here. You're welcome to leave."

"Are you sure you don't wish me to remain?" Niraj asked.

"No, I'm quite all right, thank you."

"I wasn't asking for your sake, but for his." Niraj motioned to Ronan with a quick jerk of the thumb.

Eloise nodded towards the door, glaring at Niraj, who smirked at him before making his exit. When it closed, she turned back to Ronan. "How's your wound today?"

He rolled his eyes at the question. When she glared at him, he said, "Tender, but healing up quite nicely."

Eloise nodded as she finished wrapping her right hand. She motioned him over and administered the same attention to his own hands. With each brush of her skin against his, his body tightened and his awareness of her grew.

"Not that I'm lacking enthusiasm for our next foray into danger, but why am I dressed like this? A trip into town as errand boys, perhaps? I'm not sure this will disguise who we are."

"The other day, I realised a rather large mistake I had made. I assumed you knew how to fight and defend yourself. It seems I was mistaken."

"I beg your pardon?"

"You nearly died because you believed there are rules of etiquette to be followed. The only rule in a fight like the one you witnessed is to do whatever it takes to ensure you survive. This is not a bout with your fencing master, nor a round in the ring at Gentleman Jackson's. The only rule is the first one to die, loses. We need to remedy this."

"You're being silly. I know how to fight."

"You nearly died," she said, her voice tense. Her chest heaved as she took in large breaths, her shoulders so tight they made his own ache. "If I hadn't gotten to you fast enough, if I hadn't been able to shove his arm away, you would have been killed."

"And you would care if something were to happen to me?"

Her shoulders pulled back as she scowled at him. "Believe it or not, I would. And a dead nobleman tends to delay a lot of things. I need you to be able to keep yourself safe."

"So, your solution is what? For me to fight you?"

"Yes. Do you have an aversion to fighting a woman?"

"Yes, dammit. I don't want to hurt you."

Smirking at him, she walked to the carpets covering the ballroom floor, her small, bare feet disappeared in the plush rug. "You'll have to try awfully hard. Let's get to it, my lord." She nodded to the space in front of her.

Ronan stepped in front of Eloise and raised his fists to his face. As she walked around him, she inspected his stance, adjusting his arms and legs. Ronan's body tingled at each brush of her hand, and he swallowed hard. She stood next to him, her gaze focused and her brow furrowed. Sighing loudly, she looked at him. "I'm going to call out a command, and I want you to demonstrate it." He nodded at her.

"Jab," she said, and he executed a quick punch.

"Hook." He thrust his fist around.

"Uppercut." Ronan brought his fist up.

Eloise sighed, drawing his attention. Her eyes were closed and two lines had formed between her brows. Embarrassment flooded him, certain he was making an utter fool of himself.

"What?" he asked.

"When you trained, did you participate in a bout or did you hit a bag?"

"I don't train, Eloise. I boxed for exercise, not to make sure I knew how to engage someone in a fight."

Her eyes widened in mock-innocence. "Beg pardon, my lord, I forgot the aristocracy does not need to fight, what with your lofty principles and all. Meanwhile, the filth of London is forced to defend themselves in any way they can. When you exercised," she spat, "did you have bouts, or did you practise with a bag?"

"I've been in several bouts." He ground his teeth together.

"Did you land any punches?"

"A few," he said, tension filling his shoulders. Her questions made him uncomfortably aware of their differences. Being a nobleman came with power in regards to money and connections, but that was the only power he wielded. The fight in the alleyway had proved that.

"Can you show me any combinations?"

Ronan executed a few motions, self-conscious as her eyes followed him. He was on display; his aptitude being judged by a mere slip of a female who could bring him down with a few punches. In the battle for power, she continued to gain the upper hand.

She sighed again as she stepped in front of him. "I'm going to throw some punches. I want you to block them."

As she took the position, Ronan became fascinated by the muscles outlined through her linen shirt. When she threw her first punch, he barely had time to block it.

"Focus, my lord," she said. "Let's try again." She executed several more manoeuvres, all of them missing his face. When she pulled back, she frowned. "What are they teaching you at Gentleman Jackson's? It looks like we'll have to start from the beginning."

Ronan groaned. It was going to be a long afternoon.

CHAPTER SEVENTEEN

THE NEXT HOUR was spent in merciless torture as Eloise put him through his paces. She critiqued and adjusted each hit. She threw endless punches at him until sweat poured down his face and his arms shook with exhaustion. As Ronan dodged and parried, Eloise was hypnotised by his strength and grace. His body moved and flowed with each strike and block, a force to be reckoned with. With the right training, he could become an even better fighter than herself.

Disgusted by the train of thought, she executed a rapid series of moves in response. Before thinking, she aimed her hook shot directly at Ronan's jaw. She pulled as best as she could, but it hit him squarely in the jaw, knocking him to his arse. Ronan stared at the ceiling of the ballroom in a daze, his groan the only sound.

Eloise stood over him, frustration filling her. "This is useless and entirely my own fault." She wiped at her brow and whispered under her breath, "Why didn't I just dose you to begin with?"

"What did you say?" Ronan asked, rolling over and coming to his feet.

"Nothing. We're finished for today, my lord. Have a maid find something for your jaw. It's beginning to swell."

"I cannot remember any of it," Ronan said, his voice

low.

"What?" Eloise asked, turning back to him. "How hard did I hit you?"

"Eastwick wasn't drunk the night he claimed he was with you, was he? He doesn't remember it." Eloise froze at his words and Ronan pursued her across the room, taking advantage of her stunned thoughts. When he came before her, she stared at the rug at her feet, unwilling to meet his gaze. "Was he drunk, Eloise?"

Eloise swallowed. "No."

"What did you do?"

She shrugged her shoulders. "I drugged him. I needed to search his home and it was the simplest way."

"Jesus. Is that what you did to me in the Foreign Office?"

"Yes, but there is no need to discuss it," she said, turning away from him.

Ronan grabbed her hand before she could reach the handle of the door and turned her around. "Before that, before I found out who you were, did you intend to drug me?"

Eloise's eyes remained fixed upon the collar of Ronan's shirt, terrified her gaze would tell him the truth. He slid his fingers under her chin, forcing her to look at him. Meeting his eyes, she shook her head.

"Why not?" he asked, the words coming out in a croak.

"Because if there was a chance you felt the way I feel for you, I needed to see where it led."

It seemed to be the truth he needed. He crushed his mouth to hers, growling as she opened to him, allowing his tongue to slide inside. Eloise wrapped her arms around his neck as he lifted her and pressed her against the door. She delved her fingers into the silky locks of his hair, holding onto him and wrapping her legs around his hips. She shivered as he pressed his hardened shaft against her core.

Ronan ran his lips along her jaw and down her neck. His tongue wreaked havoc while his warm breath caused goosebumps to form on her skin. "Why? Why didn't you tell me?" he asked, kissing along her collarbone.

Arching her neck, she gave his skilled mouth more room.

Ronan tore his lips from hers and Eloise mourned the loss of his mouth. "You should have told me," he said.

Stroking his bearded cheek, she shook her head. "It wouldn't have changed anything." Smiling, she kissed his lips softly. "I lied to you, Ronan. And I used you. What I did was reprehensible."

He took her mouth with his, his tongue stroking her lower lip, begging for her to open to him. When she did, he dove in, his tongue sliding over hers. The friction of the kiss was astounding as his body mimicked what she ached for.

He drew back and rubbed his nose against hers, before resting his forehead on her chest. "Christ," he said, his breathing heavy.

Eloise chuckled as she ran her fingers through his hair, cupping his cheek and forcing him to meet her gaze. His eyes searched hers and she let him look his fill, afraid that if she broke contact, the moment would be lost. He groaned and captured her mouth once more, devouring her with his kiss. Her nails raked against his scalp, and Ronan growled. When his lips danced across her skin, skimming her jaw, then nibbling at her throat, she sighed. Her head fell back against the wooden door with a resounding thunk.

A brisk knock startled them. Ronan tore his mouth from her, his breath ragged.

"Eloise?" Sophie said from behind the unlocked door. "Niraj said you asked him to notify you when it was time for dinner?"

Eloise cleared her throat. "Yes," she said, her gaze never leaving his.

"It's time for dinner," Sophie said. "That is, if you and Lord Vaughn have finished with your training."

Eloise could feel the heat blossom on her cheeks. "We'll meet you in a moment," she said, as she lowered her hands to his shoulders. He lowered her to the ground, her feet making nary a sound as they touched the floor. He smelled like lemons and his own heady scent of paper and ink, and Eloise wanted to weep at the loss of him.

"I'm not sure that should have happened," she said, her eyes leaping around the room, avoiding his gaze.

"We're drawn to each other, Eloise. It was bound to happen." He cupped her cheek, bringing her gaze to his.

"It shouldn't happen again."

"Why not?" His brow was furrowed, and it took everything within her not to raise her hand and smooth away the creases.

"It's my job to keep you safe, my lord. I cannot do that if my focus is elsewhere," she said, meeting his eyes. "It would be best if we avoided another situation like this in the future." As she walked around him, Ronan stopped her with his hand. Her fists clenched as she forced herself to remain still instead of returning to his arms like she wished to.

"Is that what you want?"

"No," she said, closing her eyes. "But it's what I have to do." He let go of her hand and she left the ballroom.

✦ ✦ ✦

WHEN THE DOOR closed, Ronan rubbed his hands over his face, groaning at the sensation that still stung his lips. His scalp tingled from where she had raked her fingers through his hair and his body could still feel the press of her against him.

The line they had drawn between them was becoming muddled by this maddening need to be near her. To have her. To make her his own. Just the thought of her smiling at him sent his heart racing in his chest and left his hands shaking. How was it possible that after everything she had done, the lies and deception, he still longed for her?

Being near her, wanting her, was sheer torture. Ronan dropped to the floor, his head falling into his hands. If she wanted nothing more from him, he would respect her wishes, but it did not make him want her any less. If anything, it left him wanting to prove her wrong.

CHAPTER EIGHTEEN

ELOISE RUSHED OUT of the ballroom and headed straight for her room, for safety. She shut the door, her legs shaking from the onslaught of need. Sliding down the door, she rested her hands on her knees.

Her lips still throbbed from Ronan's kisses, and her heart raced. She knew she could go back to the ballroom and continue what they had started. Knew he would not question her change of heart, only give her the attention she desired. Yet, to give in to the attraction between them was nothing but perilous. What the devil was she doing fraternising with the man she blackmailed? All the while, the clock was ticking down to her eventual dismissal from the Foreign Office.

It would be different if she could have a brief dalliance with him as she used him for information, but her blasted heart had begun to like him as a person. To start an affair while she lived in his home? Goodness, she must be insane. It was as if she had lost all focus.

Eloise stood on shaky legs and went to the washstand. Removing her garments, she cleaned herself, letting the cool water wash away the sensitivity that still lingered. Dressed in a clean pair of trousers and a shirt, she went to the parlour for dinner.

Jenkins opened the door, and Eloise came to a hard

stop as her gaze fell upon Ronan. He had changed back into his clothing, his damp hair slicked back from his forehead, indicating he had washed as well. As he looked at her, a jolt of electricity slithered down her spine and settled between her legs. Shaking off the feeling, she walked into the lion's den.

Eloise sat through dinner, praying Sophie's chatter would make up for the lack of her own. When they removed themselves to the library afterward, Ronan sat across from her. His gaze never wavered, as if he could see through her silence.

Sophie and Niraj played a game of chess in one corner while Eloise pretended interest in the book in her hands. In truth, she had read the same page a dozen times, taking in nary a word. She could have sworn hours passed before the two finally quit their game and left the room. When the cushion next to her dipped and Ronan sat beside her, Eloise forced herself to remain calm.

"You were surprisingly quiet at dinner. Something on your mind?" A smile tugged at his lips.

"I'm perfectly fine. I just didn't have anything of use to say."

Ronan let out a long sigh as he turned towards her, tucking his knee up onto the couch. "Is this how it's going to be now? We can pretend it was an aberration, a one-time event never to be repeated. Although, to be honest, I'd love to kiss you again."

"I thought we agreed not to."

"We did," he said. "I can be attracted to you and not act upon it."

"Most men don't believe that to be true."

"Has anyone acted improperly towards you? Give me their names and I will send Niraj after them."

She laughed, her fingers itching to rake through the scruff at his cheeks.

"I can handle myself," she said. "For as long as I can remember, it's been that way with men. I used to bind my breasts in St. Giles with the hope that, if they thought I was a lad, I would avoid being raped. Even then, some people's tastes don't veer away from the innocent."

"You weren't ..."

She set a hand on his arm, hoping to reassure him. "No. But I knew girls who were. Even pretending to be a courtesan has its dangers. Men assume that because you use your body to make a living, they don't need to treat you as a human, you're free for the taking. Numerous women work the streets and are often taken advantage of. Raped by a man because of their line of work and never paid for the service afterward."

"Doesn't being a courtesan or working in a brothel give some protection?"

"It can, if you have the right servants in place, or the Madame you work for has standards. But oftentimes—" she shook her head. "Knowing what I saw in St. Giles, these women use their bodies to feed themselves and their families, all the while knowing they have very little protections in place. It's one of the reasons I'm so motivated to be the best. The secretary of the Foreign Office has given me a month to prove my worth." She scowled. "Every other agent who works for the Foreign Office has had the same training as me, but when it comes to continuing my career, they give me more obstacles.

Women are strong and powerful. We're intelligent. We deserve to be on an equal level as men, taken seriously for the jobs we do. Paid equally to what men are paid and given the same courtesy."

It was obvious Ronan had never contemplated the matters of being a woman in this line of work. England's political might was wielded by men, leaving no room for the needs or effects on the female half. Eloise knew his mother's only responsibility had been to produce an heir, and the same expectation would be required of his wife.

"If it's any consolation, I believe you can do it. You have proven yourself time and again with me." Ronan wrapped one of her errant curls around his finger, his eyes watching her. Eloise's breath picked up speed, but she could not take her eyes off him.

"You should go," she said, even as her heart pleaded for him to stay.

He blinked, and the spell was broken. "Right then." Ronan stood and took a large step back, his face a hard mask. "I respect your request, Eloise. That isn't to say I don't want you with every fibre of my being, but I shan't act upon it, as you've requested. If you want to further this between us, it will be of your own accord. Just know that I'm here and willing, whatever you wish it to be."

Executing a bow, he turned and left the library.

✧ ✧ ✧

EACH CONVERSATION RONAN had with Eloise left him more fascinated by her than the time before. She was beautiful, of that, there was no doubt, but it was who she was that had become the most stunning thing about her. Her bravery and fortitude in the face of adversity left him wishing he could move mountains for her, if only to make her trials a bit simpler. And the easy smiles and clever quips he had found so enthralling when they had first met still left him mesmerised. This fascinating woman had bewitched him, and each day it appeared he was falling deeper under her spell.

It seemed, however, the same was not true for her.

He would never win her heart. Truly, there was little possibility for a pickpocket from St. Giles and a nobleman. He could, however, ensure she gained what she sought. He wanted to watch her rise through the Foreign Office, to command the place like the leader she was, male-dominated dictates and expectations be damned. And yet, once she had what she came for, she would leave. It might kill him, but he would do anything in his power to make sure she succeeded and solidified her position within the Foreign Office.

Which was why, the next morning, he stood before his father's office, his palms damp with sweat. The door was identical to every other one in the house, and yet Ronan could not help the apprehension that blanketed him as he stood before it. After retrieving the key from Jenkins, the weight of it an unbearable reminder of what he was about to do, he stood before the door for what had to have been an eternity. The key was in the lock, the tumblers already turned. With his hand on the knob, he had frozen, unable to turn it.

Eloise's small hand covered his, her body pressed against his back, her strength seeping into his skin. "I'm right here," she said. "We'll do it together."

Even as his heart thumped frantically, the pulse re-sounding in his ears, Ronan pushed the fear aside. He could do this, especially with her by his side. Ronan swallowed the lump that had formed in his throat and nodded. "On the count of three?"

"One," she said quietly behind him.

"Two," he said, his voice rough.

"Three," they said together, and turned the knob, pushing the door open.

His father's scent of bergamot and lime drifted from the room like a ghost being released from its imprisonment. The smell nearly drove Ronan to his knees, but Eloise's strong presence kept him standing. She hugged him from behind, her arms sliding around his waist and squeezing gently. "You can do this."

"You go in. I need a moment."

"Are you sure?" she asked, sliding around to stand in front of him. Her brows were lowered as her eyes raked over his face.

He nodded, unable to speak. She cupped his face in her hand, her fingers stroking the rough hair on his jaw. Ronan leaned into the caress, his breath returning for a fraction of a second before she drew away and entered his father's office.

Ronan swore she transformed into an agent of the crown before his eyes. Her gaze intensified, taking in every square inch. She checked the windows and doors, reassuring herself the area remained untouched. Eloise walked the length of the room before strolling along the bookshelves that lined the walls of his father's office. She stopped when she reached the estate records, each year listed on the spine of the book. The records dated back hundreds of years, some books nearly as old as the title itself. She withdrew the books from the time his father was marquess, stacking them neatly on the corner of the desk.

"Can you look around and tell me if anything is misplaced or missing?" she asked.

Stepping into the office was a punch to the stomach, his father's familiar scent stronger in the unopened room. As he walked the space, Ronan tried to keep his mind focused on the task, but memories assailed him. Sitting on his father's lap as a young lad while he worked. Returning from Eton and regaling his father with stories of adventures with his friends. His unending irritation with his Latin teacher. His father showing him the ledgers of the estate; how to run it, care for it. Trying to instil the importance of being a lord into his son. And Ronan's intense desire to have nothing to do with any of it.

Pushing aside the memories, Ronan looked the room over, noting nothing odd. "It's exactly as he left it," he said with a croak. At his father's desk, he sat in the chair and stared at the stacks of papers his father had left behind, most likely with the intention of finishing another time.

"Ronan?" Eloise said.

"Christ, this is all too much."

"It's all right if you want to leave. I will look through everything and then close it back up." Ronan nodded but sat staring at the desk. "Is there anything you want from here before you go?" she asked.

"My father had a book of stories he read to Felicity

and me when we were children." Taking a deep breath, he opened the bottom drawer and grabbed the heavy tome. As he stood, a slip of paper fell out of the book. With a groan, he bent down to pick it up, but time seemed to freeze. His name was scrawled across it in his father's handwriting.

Ronan swallowed the lump that had filled his throat.

"What is it?"

"It's a letter." The paper felt like a stone in his hands.

"Ronan?" A soft hand rubbed his back and the impulse to lean into its comfort was tempting. "Are you all right?"

"No," he said, his voice rasping.

"Ronan..."

"Glad to see this door finally open," Niraj said, as he strutted inside, his eyes roaming the space before landing on them. "Everything all right in here?"

"Everything's fine," Ronan said, standing. "If you'll excuse me." He escaped the office, the letter and book clutched in his hand.

Slamming the door to the library closed, he threw the lock before eyeing the decanters lining the bookshelf. Setting the book and letter aside, he poured himself two fingers of scotch. Throwing it back, he poured himself another, and then another.

Dear Christ, he was in over his head.

CHAPTER NINETEEN

A S THE WEEK progressed, Eloise could sense Ronan pulling away. He accompanied her for rides, racing Romeo and Hercules through the park. He still trained with her, showing little reaction if their bodies accidentally brushed against each other. And in the evenings, he sat with her, ignoring Niraj and Sophie's ramblings, choosing instead to read while she played a game of chess against herself.

But it was like a wall had come up between them. He stopped asking her silly questions during their rides, choosing to allow the hustle of London to fill the silence. He excused himself as soon as they returned to the stable, disappearing into his apartments until it was time to spar. If she were honest with herself, she missed him. His laughter had become a brief moment of joy during the unending stress over The Fall of Caesar. His quiet presence and knowing smile gave Eloise the support she had not known she needed.

Unlocking his father's office was the only catalyst she could pinpoint, his endearing openness disappearing as soon as that door had opened, and the letter he had found had never been mentioned again.

While Eloise longed to know its contents, in the dead of night, it was not the letter that filled her thoughts.

Instead, she yearned for Ronan, and cared very little about the rest. She often awoke with worry, her heart aching for him, wanting to console him. After tossing and turning for hours, she threw on her wrapper and made her way to his room, but paused at his door. The fear over what would happen if she did allow herself to care left her terrified, driving away her desire to be with him. She returned to her room, choosing to train mercilessly instead of fantasising about what could have been.

After two days of this behaviour, Eloise was at a loss. Both physically and emotionally, she ached. As they squared off in the training room, she could feel her tension filling every iota of space in the massive ballroom. His attacks were impersonal, lacking any emotion or thought. He practiced a sequence of punches as if he were facing a tree. Her nerves were shot, stripped raw by his distance, so she did the only thing she could. She retaliated.

As he threw his next sequence, she grabbed his punching arm and, using his weight, threw him down to the floor. The look of surprise on his face as he landed on the carpets broke the tension in her chest. She doubled over with laughter while he cursed under his breath and pushed himself to stand. Covering her mouth, she tried to contain her mirth, but the scowl he sent her made her laughter begin anew.

"Knocking my arse to the ground is humourous to you?"

"The look on your face was," she said between chuckles. Taking a stance again, she grinned at him. "I doubt you could do better."

His smug smile was the last thing she saw as her feet

were whipped out from underneath her. Staring at the ceiling, Eloise tried to understand what happened. As Ronan came into view, a cheeky grin on his face, she gasped. "You cheated!"

"I did no such thing! Just because you haven't taught me any foot manoeuvres doesn't mean I haven't watched you and Niraj spar. Beginner's luck," he said, holding out his hand to help her up.

As she grasped it, she allowed him to pull her up before using her weight and toppling them both to the ground. His hands flew out, capturing his weight before he squashed her, his strong arms trapping her to the floor. Laughter shone in his eyes as he looked down at her. With Ronan's body on top of her, heat flew to her sex, and she swallowed as she looked into his eyes. "Good afternoon, sir."

Ronan's eyes widened in surprise before he pushed off of her and stood up, backing away, his hands clenched into fists as if preventing himself from reaching for her. As she rose from the ground, she met his gaze, hypnotised by what she saw there.

Her body ached for him and her heart yearned to regain the connection that she had so carelessly thrown away. Acting on this desire would place everything in peril, including her career, but she was tired of worrying about the future. Tired of the sleepless nights, and the longing for what had been that pulled at her every time he was near. He was under her skin, in her head, and surrounding her heart, until all she could think about was him. It was driving her to madness.

Decision made, Eloise pursued him across the room.

When his back was against the wall, she aligned her body with his and looked into his eyes.

"Will you kiss me?" she asked, as she slid her fingers into his hair. His breath left in a rush as her lips glided over his, but he wrapped his hands around her waist and pushed her back.

"No. You told me you didn't want this, and I'm going to respect your request. If you want me, Eloise, you need to be clear, no uncertainty."

Looking into his eyes, she held out her hand. "Come with me."

His hand folded into hers. She led him out of the ballroom and upstairs to her bedroom. She tried to walk at a sedate pace, but the urge to sprint to her room was great. Once inside, she closed and locked the door before turning to him.

"Take off your clothes," she said, her voice husky to even her own ears.

His Adam's apple bobbed as he swallowed. "Are you sure?"

She nodded. "Please."

His eyes never leaving hers, he ripped off his tunic and pushed his linen pants down to his ankles. He stood in front of her in all his glory, his porcelain skin appearing like cut marble. The training had left his chest and arms corded, even stronger than they had been before. His thighs were muscular and covered in dark hair. Their strength could only have come from his rides on Hercules.

And his sex. She swallowed as she took in his size. His sex jutted away from the dark patch of hair on his body, large and powerful. He was magnificent, her gaze flitted from one part of him to another, greedy to look upon all of him.

Finally, she met his eyes. "Sit." She motioned to the armchair in front of the fireplace.

Her quim clenched with longing. When he sat down, his thick cock jutted straight up against his stomach and she resisted the urge to drop to her knees and lick it. Removing her shirt and pants, she straddled his thighs, pushing her chest against his. They both groaned aloud.

"I want to see you," he said.

"Later." Eloise rubbed her nipples against the smattering of hair on his chest, the wiry texture turning the sensitive tips into hardened points.

Cradling his head, she placed her lips against his. His kiss was light and achingly sweet, but she needed more. She drew her tongue along his bottom lip, then bit down. His mouth opened with a groan and she delved inside, her tongue mating with his. The heat consumed her and her body shook with abject need, but his body remained still beneath hers, denying her his touch.

Pulling back, Eloise found Ronan's hands clenching the arm of the chair, his fingers digging into the fabric, the knuckles white from the force. He truly meant it. It was her decision on how far they took this. The lead was hers. Overcome with power, she met his eyes. "Touch me?"

His hands released the chair and wrapped around her waist, sliding against her skin like velvet. They were merciless as they traced every inch of skin, dancing along her rib cage, swirling at the small of her back, gripping the cheeks of her arse. It was too much. Grabbing one hand, she placed it on her breast and whimpered at the heat. His hand cupped and moulded her, massaging the orb before lightly pinching her already-sensitive nipple. His other hand commenced the same torture on its twin and Eloise groaned as she ground herself against him, dew dripping from her.

She needed him, ached to stroke his naked skin. Her hands started a journey of their own, tracing the dip of his collarbone, her nails raking through the smattering of hair on his chest. She finally slid her hand down, taking his thick cock in her hand, rubbing the moisture that wept from the tip down the length of him. His hips shot off the chair as she stroked him, cupping his balls as her hand moved up and down. When she looked up at him, she paused.

His head was thrown back against the chair, his eyes squeezed closed and his mouth open. He was gorgeous, this gentle giant of a man. She brought his mouth back to hers, sucking his tongue into her mouth as her hands stroked his sex. "I need your hands on me," she whimpered.

He pulled back to look at her. "Where, El? Show me where."

She took his hand from her breast and slid it down her stomach to her sex. His fingers delved into her heat, finding her bud and rubbing it.

"More," she said, rising onto her knees. Two fingers slid inside her core while the heel of his hand pressed against her sex, wrenching a moan from her. He kissed across her chest while his fingers thrust in and out of her, her dew coating his hand. She wanted him, needed him inside her. As her climax crashed over her, she cried his name, his fingers milking out the last of her pleasure.

Collapsing against him, she sucked in air, her chest rising and falling against his.

"Are you all right?" he asked against her hair.

She nodded, aware of his cock still hard against her stomach. Rising onto her knees, Eloise positioned her body over his, rubbing the head of his length against her damp heat, the bulb of his sex only intensifying the ache she felt there.

"El, sweetheart," he said, cupping her cheek.

"I need you," she said, rubbing him harder against her nub. His groan was all the permission she needed, and she gasped as the head of his cock breached her opening. The size of him left her shaking as she shifted, attempting to take all of him inside her. Ronan's hands gripped her hips and he pushed gently each time she swivelled, their motions like waves crashing against the shore. When she was finally seated upon him, her breath came out in short bursts and she held still, waiting for her body to adjust.

"I don't want you to feel any pain." His hand cupped the back of her head as he forced her to look at him.

"This is perfect." She raked her fingers through his hair, bringing his mouth to hers while his hand found her bud, circling the tight nub. After a few strokes, the longing returned, her body acclimating to his size as each second passed. The walls of her sex tightened, ripping a moan from his throat.

"Darling, let me love you." His hands stroked over her back, her thighs, her breasts, as he destroyed her with his kiss.

Coming onto her knees, Eloise lifted and lowered her

body over his, moaning into his mouth at each contact. Ripping her lips from his, she gripped his shoulders as she rode him, her body aching with tension. "I need..." she gasped. "Ronan, I need..."

His fingers returned to where they were joined, rubbing the swollen cleft of her sex with silky, smooth motions. It became too much. Specks of light danced behind her eyelids as she flew, her body exploding into a million pieces, shaking at the onslaught of pleasure.

Ronan thrust into her twice more before pulling out, his release coating her stomach, her name a shout on his lips. As they lay against each other, Eloise sighed, her body depleted. The moment was far too perfect for her to worry. She would examine the consequences tomorrow.

CHAPTER TWENTY

RONAN HELD ELOISE in his arms, her naked body pressing against his. It was the most peace he had found in weeks. Her sighs ruffled the smattering of hairs on his chest, causing gooseflesh to rise on his arms. He smiled, setting his head on top of hers, his arms tightening around her. For however long possible, this phenomenal creature was his. He would shout his joy to all of London if he were not so exhausted.

She chuckled into his shoulder. "I'm not going anywhere."

"I know."

Her head lifted, her green eyes meeting his. "What is it? Are you having regrets?"

"God no." His throat tightened as he took her in. She was stunning. Her curls corkscrewed in every direction, wild and unruly, and her eyes were sleepy while her cheeks remained flushed from pleasure. And her body, well, her body was so magnificent he was doing everything in his power to stop himself from taking her again so soon.

Ronan picked up Eloise in his arms and carried her to the bed, before going to the washstand and cleaning himself off. After performing the same task for her, he discarded the soiled cloth to the floor and joined her beneath the covers, pulling her body in tight along his. He closed his eyes, breathing in her lemony scent, and his muscles melted into her embrace. She shifted next to him. Opening his eyes, he chuckled. "What is going on in that head of yours?"

"Everything," she said with a smile. "My mind never stops."

"Start at the beginning." Ronan kissed her head.

"How are you doing? And don't make light of it, but tell me truthfully. These past two weeks have been a lot."

"I'm working through it," he said with a grimace. "I still haven't wrapped my head around any of it. It happened so quickly, learning the truth about you, the attack. You and your gang of merry men moving into my home. And if what you said about my father is true, I'm not sure what to do. Lord, how would I begin to tell Felicity? She's been through so much already."

"Her husband passed recently?"

"A couple of months ago, yes. She was married to Benedict Knight, the Duke of Harcourt," he said with disgust.

"Lord Knight's older brother? Is that what was between you two at the funeral?"

"Remington Knight is the guardian of Beatrice and George, my niece and nephew. Felicity has struggled to manage the estate and take care of the children since Knight hasn't followed through on his responsibilities. With his brother's passing, he was supposed to look after them."

"I hope I'm not overstepping, but you were angry when you mentioned the duke," she said, cupping his cheek. "Why?"

"The spy in you is quite incredible." He turned his

head and kissed her hand. "Felicity once showed up at my father's home in London with the children. She claimed she only wanted to visit for a few days, but her eyes... I cannot even describe them accurately. She looked frightened. One evening before dinner, I came upon her gently lowering herself into a chair, tears in her eyes. She was in pain. I asked if she was all right, and she claimed to have taken a fall and was merely sore. Like a fool, I believed her. Until I saw the bruise on her chest that looked like the imprint of a man's fist."

"He was beating her?"

"Yes, and as far as I can tell, it wasn't the first time. When I confronted her, she began to cry. She claimed he'd overindulged one evening and she'd displeased him. It was an accident, she said. Begged me not to do anything." He swallowed, looking into her eyes. "And I didn't. I never said a word."

"Did your father know?"

"No. If he did, he would've had words with the duke. Would have ensured Felicity and the children were safe."

"Was Lord Knight aware?"

Ronan frowned. "No. I think, looking at it now, his guilt from not knowing is what drove him away from them."

She nodded. "It would certainly be hard to learn that abuse was happening without your knowledge. The duke never hurt the children, did he?"

"God, I hope not. The day he died, I was thankful. It's shameful, really, but with Benedict dead, Felicity wouldn't have to deal with him. She would be free. Except she's not." He scowled. "That's why Felicity responded the way she did when she saw Remy at the wake. He should be taking care of them. Managing the estates, ensuring George is doing well at Eton and Bea is listening to her governess, but he's left those responsibilities to Felicity. Instead, he's running the Rogue's Den and living the life of a rake while his sister-in-law struggles under the weight of raising a duke."

As she ran her fingers through the light smattering of hair on his chest, he sighed.

"I've known Lord Knight for some time, and he would never shirk his responsibilities. There must be a reason for his actions."

"Maybe," he said, "but all I know is Felicity went from an abusive husband to managing a dukedom. She and the children mean the world to me. They're all I have left. She deserves peace and a life filled with happiness. After what was done to her by the duke, she doesn't deserve to be abandoned."

"I'm sure it will irk you, but Lord Knight probably thought he was protecting them from his business and the potential seedy parts of it. It's all supposition, but knowing Lord Knight as I do, I'm certain he had the best of intentions."

"I hope you're right." Picking up the hand on his chest, he kissed it. "Let's not talk of depressing matters."

"All right," she said, resting her head on his shoulder once more. His hand traced the path of her arm, her skin like silk under his fingertips.

"You feel amazing next to me."

"As do you." As she shifted, her arm brushed against the hardening length of his shaft, and she paused.

"Again?" she asked, looking up at him with a smile.

"This is my normal state around you. It's quite frequent, I'm afraid, but I've become accustomed to it." Brushing her lips with his, he smiled before closing his eyes. Her hand brushed against him again, making his cock jump with anticipation.

Ronan bit back a groan. What kind of animal would force himself on her again?

As she stroked him once more, he opened one eye to peek at her. Her smile was impish as she deliberately ran her hand along his length. "It's too soon," he said between his teeth.

"For you?" she asked, the smile of her lips widening. "Do you need more time to recover?"

Growling, he rolled her over, his body aligning with hers. He devoured her mouth, his tongue seeking hers out as their bodies moved against one another. Drawing back, he looked down at her. Her blonde hair was spread across the pillows, her cheeks pink and her eyes wild. "Are you sure?"

She tugged his head back down and delivered a scorching kiss that left him breathless. "Would you like to make a bet on who comes first?" she asked as she wrapped her legs around his hips.

His moan left her laughing. They were never leaving this bed.

ELOISE AND RONAN lazed about for the rest of the afternoon before Ronan snuck out of her room to change for dinner. They made love twice more, each time with a tenderness that left them both gasping. Afterwards, Eloise soaked in the tub, her sex sore, but she could not keep the smile from her face. Her body was depleted from the pleasure he had wrought, and her heart was considerably lighter. In between their bouts of lovemaking, they had talked, Ronan again asking her childlike questions, each one making her laugh.

A quiet knock on the door had Eloise ducking down in the tub before bidding the person to enter. As Sophie peeked in, Eloise worked hard to contain the blush she was certain lit her cheeks. Focusing on lathering up the washcloth with soap, she found she could not quite meet Sophie's eyes.

"Feeling better?" Sophie asked, sitting on the bed and looking at her.

"Whatever do you mean? I'm not sick," Eloise said, scrubbing her elbow roughly.

"You and Ronan have been circling one another for the past week, then you both disappear for an afternoon? Sister mine, I'm not a fool." Sophie inspected Eloise's neck and smiled. "Plus, given the bruising you have marking your neck, it would appear something, or perhaps some-one, has spent a decent amount of time nibbling on your person."

Eloise bit her lip. "Does Niraj know?" She could al-ready hear his lamentations regarding intimate relationships with one's mark. Given his past experiences, she could not fault him for his worry.

"No, I made your excuses."

"You better not have told him it was my courses."

"Of course not! I'm put out you would think I'd ever bring that up with him unless I wanted to see his face pale." Sophie snorted, then smiled at Eloise. "No, I told him you dealt Ronan a blow to the face during training and it angered him. I said you were in hiding until he calmed down."

"What a wonderful lie, Sophie, except Ronan doesn't have a blow to the face. How exactly am I to explain that?"

"You don't. You need to punch your lover in the face." Sophie said it so carelessly, Eloise was certain she had misheard her. When Sophie only looked at her, Eloise frowned.

"Sophie."

"It's a simple fix."

"Oh yes, I can see how the conversation will go. Thank you so much, my lord, for a delightful afternoon romp. Now if you'll hold still, I need to punch you so my superior doesn't think we were having wild animal sex."

Sophie smiled at her. "Was it wild animal sex?"

Eloise examined her afternoon with Ronan; his caresses, his kisses, the feel of him so deep inside of her, she swore they were joined. "It was mind-blowing and heart-stopping, but also sweet and gentle. And ferocious with need. I didn't know it could be like that."

"It sounds rather tedious," Sophie said, stopping at the ornate vanity. Sitting on the plush bench, Sophie played with several hairpins.

"I'm sure it will be that as well. I don't know what the next steps are. Was it an afternoon of enjoying each other, and we return to the way things were before? Do we continue with the affair while he is here? Does he want more?"

"You didn't set rules? Ellie, you know that's the first thing you do when you start an affair."

Eloise raised a brow at Sophie.

"Besides, you already know the answer. The man was on his way to falling in love with you before he found out who you were, Ellie. And I hate to say it, but it seems like you're using his attraction to your advantage."

"I wasn't intending for the emotional part to go this far."

"But you knew it was there. It's been a constant issue during this entire assignment. Call this afternoon what it truly was, an enjoyable moment to relieve the stress. If it's repeated, wonderful, but it doesn't need to go further. Attachments are dangerous in our line of work. Plus, there is your time limit to contend with."

"I know." She scowled, setting down the cloth and sinking back into the warm water. "I like him, Sophie. I didn't expect that."

"I know, dearest, but it's safest for both of you to keep a distance. Your goals do not include marriage and a nursery full of children, and there's a chance his life is depending on you."

Nodding her head, she sighed. "I believe I just made our mission more complicated."

"You know how to fix it, Ellie. Uncomplicate it. State your intentions to him and then decide where to go from there. It's best if you're both honest with your expectations."

"Right."

Sophie gave her a smile before departing. As the bath-water grew tepid, Eloise sat in contemplation. Ronan was decidedly more invested than she—not that it would take very much to send her heart spiralling into love. In truth, it was nearly there. And yet, their future together was impossible.

Her entire career would be lost in the responsibilities that came with being the wife of a marquess, and he would never let her continue her work with the Foreign Office. He would want children; she could not be pregnant and defend the country.

Eloise grimaced, lifting herself from the water and dry-ing off before stepping out of the tub. Tying back her unruly hair, she dressed in trousers and a linen shirt. She was tempted to avoid dinner and have a tray sent up, but she had never been one to back down from an uncomfort-able situation.

In the hallway, she came to a stop when she spotted Ronan leaning against the wall across from her.

He smiled at her before closing the gap between them and kissing her soundly. "You smell like lemons."

"I bathed," she said, her fingers sliding into his hair to pull him closer.

"You should have notified me immediately. I would have joined you. All for the good of the staff, of course, water conservation and whatnot." His lips trailed down her throat and her head fell back, landing with a thud against the door.

"How is it possible to want you again?" she asked, turning her head to the side to give him greater access.

Ronan stopped his kisses and looked at her. Meeting

his gaze, the heat she saw sent tingles of pleasure coursing through her body. "I want you always, but darling, believe it or not, I can be in your presence without pawing at you."

"Really?" She smiled, looking down at his arms wrapped around her body.

"Well, I think so. You're quite enticing and I can barely resist you, but I will endeavour to try." He kissed her again, groaning against her mouth as their bodies aligned. "Must we go to dinner? We could order trays and spend the evening in bed together."

She laughed as she pushed him away. "You silly man. I'm a bit sore."

"And I told you I can resist your charms. We'll lie in bed and I'll read to you. Or we can play a game of chess, or talk. If none of those options sound appealing, I can hold you. I would rather like that option."

Her heart pounded at his sincerity. His affection for her was so palpable, so bare and apparent, it made her insides quake. "Ronan, what are we doing?"

His brow furrowed in confusion. "What do you mean? I'm trying to convince you to forgo dinner."

"You're being deliberately obtuse. Where do you see this going?"

He sighed as he stepped back from her, rubbing his face with his hands. "Where do you want this to go?"

"I enjoy being with you, Ronan," she said, letting her head fall back against the door, "But marriage isn't for me. My goal is to join the Foreign Office. To work my way up the ranks. I want to leave a mark for women in espionage. I can't do those things as your wife."

He frowned at her. "I know all of this, but it doesn't stop me from wanting you. I'm willing to accept whatever you want to give. So again, I'll ask you, El, what do you want from this?"

"I want you. As much as I can have of you before this has to end."

"Thank God," he said, taking her mouth with his. She wrapped her arms around his neck and stood on her toes, bringing their bodies closer together. Their quiet moans echoed down the hall and Ronan drew back to look at her. "Dinner?"

"We must go," she said breathlessly, speckling kisses along his jaw. "We disappeared all afternoon. They'll wonder what we're up to."

He groaned as he took her mouth again, delivering an exhilarating kiss that left her toes curling. His gaze was hooded, and she swore her knees wobbled at the heat that filled his eyes.

His eyes. Blast.

"Sophie covered for us, but I have to punch you to make it plausible," she said, grimacing at the words that flew from her lips.

Ronan blinked at her. "I beg your pardon?"

"You need to have a black eye."

Worried about his response, she fixated on his cravat instead of making eye contact. His deep-throated laughter brought her head up. He chuckled, tears filling his eyes. "This is humourous to you?" Her mouth pinched in a frown.

"I do enjoy your sister, and damn if her imagination isn't exquisite," he said, wiping the tears from his eyes. As he settled, he kept looking at her, his smile never leaving his face. Standing straight, he wiped the last tears away before taking a large breath. "All right, go for it. Preferably not your right hook, please, as I know the damage it can wreak."

"You want me to punch you?"

"We need to make your sister's story true. Give me your best shot, El."

"I can't hit you on purpose!"

"Whyever not? You know you've been dying to hit me for quite some time."

"That may have been true before, but not anymore."

"Tap into that old frustration," he said, slouching his shoulders and putting on a haughty face. "I'm the king of the castle, lord of the realm. You shall do my bidding. All women want me, and all men want to be me."

Eloise burst out laughing.

"No, no, none of that. Be serious," he said, frowning in disappointment. "You'll bow to me because all women are beneath me."

Eloise scoffed. "As if that were true."

"Ah, there it is!" He took the lavish nobleman stance again. "All women are weak. They should only be mothers and wives and never work. A woman's job is to serve her husband. They're meek and mild creatures, never should they be strong-tempered, never educated. They cannot lead a man, let alone a nation."

Eloise raised a brow at him. "This is ridiculous. I have better control of my emotions than that."

He looked at her before a smile took over his face. "Then I shall try a new tactic." He rushed her, pinning her against the door as his fingers began to dance along her skin, trailing along her stomach. She squirmed against the sensation. When his fingers began to creep towards the undersides of her arms, her body responded without control and she pulled back her fist and punched him in the eye.

"Blast it, Eloise, I said not the right hook!" Ronan doubled over, holding his eye.

"Are you all right?" she asked, rushing to him. Pulling his hands down, she examined his eye. It was an angry red and already beginning to swell. "I'm so sorry!"

"Remind me never to tickle you again." He stood, squinting at her through his right eye. "Well, how do I look?" he asked, posing like a Roman statue.

"Like a fool."

As he drew her close, he placed his lips against hers, tracing the seam with his tongue. "I doubt that. I think I look like a man obsessed with you." Drawing back, he held out his arm to her. "Let's be off to dinner. We wouldn't want to invite speculation, and I'm not sure I am up for another punch in the face just yet."

Eloise slid her arm into his and followed him down the stairs to the drawing room. Niraj and Sophie were seated in the parlour, awaiting them.

"There you two are," Niraj said, a glass of scotch in his hand. "Sophie mentioned you had a bit of a row this afternoon, but I'm glad to see it's all patched up."

Ronan smiled down at her before turning back to Niraj. "She dealt me a rather impressive blow, and I failed to block it. Accidents happen," Ronan said, shrugging. "Thankfully, my cook had an impressive hunk of meat that brought down the swelling quickly." He turned to Eloise. "Would you care for something to drink?"

"Lemonade, please," she said.

"Right," he said, making his way to the sideboard.

Sophie edged up next to her. "His eye looks rather bad."

"I wonder why."

"It was the first thing that came out of my mouth," Sophie said apologetically.

"Perhaps, next time, leave out the physical violence? Be creative. Say we went for a ride."

"Next time?" Sophie asked. "I take it you two figured out where this is heading?"

"We have." She smiled as Ronan made his way back to her and handed her the drink.

"Sophie, you look lovely this evening. The blue of your gown will surely match the bruising of my eye," Ronan said with a wink, and Sophie's cheeks took on a blush. He turned to Niraj. "What did we miss at the meeting?"

"Nothing much," Niraj said. "There have been no leads from the Foreign Office, however, they did mention there've been some whispers in the underworld of a man named The Sparrow, who is leading the Fall of Caesar. Some of the stories are rather graphic. Essentially, the man is not someone to trifle with."

"If he exists at all," Ronan said as the dinner bell sounded. He lowered his gaze to Eloise before holding out his arm. As she slid her arm through his, she could not help but hope the Fall of Caesar and the Sparrow would keep to themselves for a little while longer, if only to give them more time.

CHAPTER TWENTY-ONE

THAT NIGHT, RONAN found his way to her room, waking Eloise with soft kisses along her thighs before his focus turned to the damp spot between her legs. Sleep was long forgotten as they both sank into the desire only they could create. He left her room as dawn broke through the curtains with Eloise fast asleep, a smile on her lips. After a quick wash, Ronan took breakfast in his room before meeting Niraj for a morning spar in the ballroom. By afternoon, he had seen very little of Eloise, the devilish woman having made herself scarce.

Over afternoon tea, as Ronan sat in the library with Niraj and Sophie looking through the estate books, Eloise finally joined them.

Ronan's heart raced as he looked at her. When their eyes met, a jolt of longing slithered down his spine and settled between his legs, creating an unfortunate rise in his trousers. Pushing aside the urge to drag her upstairs and kiss her senseless, he merely smiled at her when she joined them.

"Good, you've already started. What have I missed?" Eloise asked. Sophie's eyes crinkled with mischief as she glanced back and forth between the two of them.

"It looks as if the marquess kept a record of the payments he received from The Fall of Caesar," Sophie said.

"He wrote them all down?" Eloise asked.

"Every last one of them. He had a coded name for the group in his account books. Each deposit was a vastly large sum, and seems to arrive every time the estate coffers are close to empty." Sophie practically vibrated with excitement at what they had found.

"How would the group know when the estate needed money?" Ronan asked as he glanced over another book.

"The estate manager and solicitor are the only people who would know the shape of the accounts," Niraj said. "And you were attacked outside of Miller's office after making inquiries."

"Exactly what I was thinking," Eloise said with a nod. "Someone in Miller's office is in league with The Fall of Caesar, possibly Miller himself. That must be how they're targeting the lords. The agent inside the office informs the group and they arrive with money in exchange for information."

"Noblemen can run their estate on credit for a long time. Why would they betray their country for something so small?" Ronan asked, pulling at any thread he could find that would lead to anything but treason.

"A solicitor tends to know everything, even the affairs of the men he serves. If they have information, they can convince anyone into providing whatever they want," Eloise said, meeting his gaze then looking away. "When was the first deposit made?"

Niraj picked up one of the books from the stack scattered across the desk and scanned it. "July of 1802."

"Before Felicity's debut." Ronan's stomach pitched.

"Blackmail," Eloise said. "She was about to partake in

her first season, which requires a large number of things. She wouldn't have been able to have a prosperous coming out without the funds."

Niraj scanned the book he held in his hand. "The next deposit is dated December of 1804."

"She'd just become betrothed to the Duke of Harcourt," Ronan stated, the pages before him becoming a blur.

"Her dowry was more than likely non-existent. It would have been horrendous if the duke found out and ended the engagement."

"Christ." The book in Ronan's hands fell to the floor.

Niraj stood, heading for the door. "I'll send a missive to the office. I'm sure they'll have someone look into the solicitor's office. It might be the link we're missing."

The room faded to a blur as his mind whirled at the new information. Eloise placed her hand over his. "Ronan?"

He blinked before smiling at her. "I'm fine. I have some matters to attend to," he said, standing and adjusting his coat. "If you'll excuse me." He bowed and exited the room at a quick pace.

Air. He needed air with a desperation that verged upon ridiculous. He rushed to the doors that led to the garden, uncaring as they bounced against the wall from the force with which he opened them. The flowers had begun to die as the cool fall days set in and Ronan stormed his way along the path, winding past the mangled limbs of what was once a lush garden. He stopped at a bench tucked back against what remained of a wall of dried honeysuckle, their brown stalks swaying in the slight breeze. Sitting on the bench, Ronan glanced at the sky, surprised by the speck of blue peeking out between the clouds. The days were beginning to have a cooler bite to them and it would not be long now before snow covered the ground and the sun disappeared altogether.

His father's letter was a weight in Ronan's jacket pocket. In the days since he found it, he had carried it around, praying the right time would eventually arrive that he could open it. Of course, it would be the random deposits made to the estate accounts that brought it about. Ronan took out the letter and held it, his hands trembling.

The wax that sealed the pages mocked him, daring him to rip the letter open and reveal the unspeakable truths that lay inside.

"Fuck." Ronan stood and began to pace, holding the letter in front of him like a feral cat as he took his steps. "Stop being a ninny and open the blasted thing."

With unnecessary force, Ronan ripped the seal apart and opened the pages as invisible hands clenched at his throat. *Dear Ronan, …*

The words sat before him on the page, and the hands around his throat tightened, their long fingers crushing his windpipe with aching slowness. His gaze narrowed, the words filling his vision as the edges blurred. A loud whooshing sound filled his ears; whether it was his heart beating with desperation, or his lungs gulping air in an effort to keep him alive, he did not know. His legs shook and Ronan felt the ground move beneath him, sending him to his knees.

The garden bench sat sardonically before him and Ronan crawled to it, desperate to cling to something sturdy as his world upended. That was how Eloise found him. "Ronan?"

"I'm fine," he said. Even as the words left his lips, his chest tightened and a wave of terror set in.

"I disagree." Her small hand wrapped around his bicep and she directed him to sit. "You seem to be having a nervous attack." Taking his hand, Eloise placed it on her chest, and in turn, placed her hand on his. "Breathe exactly as I do. Inhale, two, three, four. Exhale, two, three, four."

Eloise's chest rose and fell with each breath, and he forced his own to follow even as his brain screamed in agony at the lack of oxygen.

"That's it," she said, her voice a soothing melody to the chaos that danced in his brain. "Nice and slow, just focus on making your breath match my own."

Ronan's eye fell to her lips. He slowly whispered the words she said. Inhale, two, three, four. Exhale, two, three, four. And to his amazement, the noose slowly loosened and the rushing in his ears began to soften until it disappeared.

"Are you all right?" Her jade gaze raked over his face.

"I am," he said, his voice gruff. "Thank you."

"You're welcome." Ronan picked at an errant thread on his trousers. "How did you know it was a nervous attack?"

"Sophie has similar attacks sometimes, especially when she is overwhelmed. I taught her how to count her breaths and the method seems to help." Her hand reached out to rub his thigh. "She said it feels like she is close to death when an attack happens."

Ronan looked at the sky. "Have you ever felt like you were living the wrong life?"

With any other person, such a question would have surely caused an aggrieved response and yet, she sat unmoving, her gaze never leaving his. "I have. Do you think that is what caused the attack?"

"I've been thrust into a position I never wanted, and far sooner than I had planned. I feel inept." He rested his head on her shoulder, closing his eyes and focusing on the feel of her hand in his.

He should be humiliated by the state he was in, and yet, with this woman by his side, he only felt safe. Her power and strength surrounded him, allowing him to be vulnerable. He shook his head, his hair falling across his brow. She pushed the strands aside and cupped his cheek, forcing his eyes to meet hers.

"The letter," he said. "It's a letter from him. I couldn't get past the first words."

Eloise said nothing. She sat next to him and held his hand, occasionally squeezing it to remind him he was not alone. Whether it be due to the woman, the gardens, or his own mental state, he did not know, but he finally accepted the truth. And the truth of it was, he could not bring himself to read the letter.

✧ ✧ ✧

ELOISE SQUEEZED RONAN'S hand, allowing the silence to fill the space around them. He had been trembling so much she was certain he was going to faint from lack of oxygen, but thankfully the tremors had subsided and his breathing had evened out.

Ronan handed her the letter, its creases worn as if he had smoothed the edges a thousand times. He pushed to standing and paced the path, his fingers raking through his hair as he looked wildly around the garden. "I can't read it. Could you..., that is..., would you read it?" He did not wait for her answer, instead turning and striding down the gravel path.

Eloise opened her mouth to call him back, but stopped. Her hands shook as she stared at the letter. Her heart ached to go after him, to comfort him, and yet the agent in her begged her to read the note. With a deep breath, she opened it.

Dear Ronan, By the time you read this, you'll be the new Marquess...

The letter contained a full page of words to Ronan outlining his father's knowledge of the Fall of Caesar, along with a desperate plea that Ronan understand why he had joined the group. It seemed that the previous marquess' love for his children, and longing to give them a life filled with nothing but joy, had led him to be vulnerable to the organization's manipulations.

The paper beneath his letter contained the marquess' contact and the shop where he dropped off his information. Eloise read over the letter several more times, her stomach clenching.

She rushed inside, every nerve ending in her body screaming for her to find Ronan. Hurrying to the library, she spotted Ronan at his desk, staring at the wooden surface before him. Slipping inside the room, she shut the door behind her and rounded the desk.

Propriety dictated she give him a comforting word from a decent distance. Her job would recommend three fingers of scotch, a pat on the back, and then returning to business. Instead, Eloise climbed into his lap and wrapped her arms around him. Ronan's arms encircled her as he buried his face in her neck.

"Don't you need to take the information to Niraj?" He rested his head against her chest and released a choppy breath.

She lifted his chin so his eyes met hers. "No. You need me." She brushed at an errant lock across his forehead.

"You're being nice to me. It must have been bad."

"I do know how to be nice."

He raised a brow at her, then sighed, his breath whispering across her chin. Picking her up off his lap, he set her on her feet. "Take the letter to Niraj."

She cupped his cheek and brushed a kiss across his lips. "Are you sure you don't want me to stay? I don't like the idea of leaving you alone."

"I think I need to be alone right now. I'll see you tonight."

Eloise swallowed the lump that had formed in her throat. She gave him a smile before pressing one last kiss against his lips. A final glance at him from the doorway proved what she had already begun to fear. This man, with his soft words and gentle caresses, could easily topple everything she had worked so hard to procure.

Worse, she could not be certain if that would be such a bad thing.

CHAPTER TWENTY-TWO

H E NEVER CAME. Eloise waited for Ronan for hours before sleep finally overcame her. She spent the remainder of the night tossing and turning, not because she had become used to him beside her. No. It was the case. Surely, it had to be the case.

Walking the hallways of his home the next morning, Eloise could not shake her melancholy mood. Perhaps a novel would distract her. Detouring to the library, she paused, breathless at the sight before her.

Sunlight poured through the wall of windows, sending rays of pale light dancing upon the man who sat at the desk. His dark head was bent over a stack of papers, his pencil tapping rhythmically against the wooden surface, the drumming breaking up the silence. The light grabbed strands of his hair, turning them silver and blue, while dust motes flittered around him like errant fairies.

She stood for quite some time watching him, entranced by the picture he painted, before stepping inside and closing the door behind her. So engrossed in his work, Ronan continued with his rhythmic motions, mumbling under his breath as he read through the pages in front of him. She was a voyeur watching an artist work, and it was exquisite.

After a moment, he set the pencil down and raked his

hands through his hair, sighing. Her heart urged her to go to him, but fear kept her back. Their arrangement was physical only, but her poor heart seemed to have not gotten the message. She must have made a sound because he turned towards her, his blue eyes widening. When they fell on her, they filled with warmth and he smiled. "How long have you been there?"

"Not too long."

He nodded, his eyes falling to his lap. "I decided to read the letter." The words sounded flat, empty.

Eloise's stomach pitched. "You did?"

His brow furrowed and his hands tightened, turning his fingers white. He chuckled, the sounds emotionless, as if pushed from his soul. "It seems you were right all along."

With a sigh, Eloise moved towards him, setting her hand upon his shoulder. "I'm so sorry, Ronan. I was hoping I wouldn't be." Her heart ached at the thought of him pouring over his father's words alone, learning the truth of the man he admired most. "Are you all right?"

He shook his head. "No. I'm not certain I ever will be. My mind is a whirlwind whenever I think on it," he said, chuckling harshly. "Perhaps that's why I'm hiding in my words."

"But you're writing again. That's progress."

"I'm not so certain about progress. This is causing my head to ache."

She came to him and massaged his scalp. His groan of relief sent pleasure to her core as she continued her ministrations. "What seems to be the problem? Perhaps I can help."

Ronan leaned into her hands. "The characters are not cooperating. I'm sure it's due to everything going on, but it's frustrating, nonetheless." He pressed his head against her chest, settling between her breasts. Running her hands down from his neck to his shoulders, she pushed on the muscles, working at the tension.

"Can I ask you a question?" she asked, leaning into him.

"Of course."

"What made you decide to start writing?"

Ronan sighed, his hand grabbing hers. He pulled her around the chair into his lap. She snuggled closer to him.

"When I was on my grand tour, I fell in love with travelling. These other lands, they are so different from the staid mentality of London. They're vibrant and exotic, the smells and tastes, the people. Some cultures celebrate life with decadent food and music. Others have art that cannot be rivalled. It was intoxicating, an addiction I could not bear to part with. But my father made it known that life was not to be mine."

"So, you made it your own in the way you could?"

"Yes, I guess you could say that. I write about the adventures I'll never have. The experiences I longed to enjoy. All in the hopes that maybe for someone else, I'll give them the ability to see the rest of the world. Perhaps, like me, they're trapped in a life that doesn't allow them to leave. Hopefully, maybe, my stories give them a window to a world they'd never have seen otherwise."

"What a very romantic idea," she said, drawing back to look at him.

He smiled softly as his hands spanned her waist. "You

think I'm romantic?"

"I didn't say you were, I said the idea was."

"But I am romantic." He tickled her waist.

"You shouldn't tickle me. It's already led to a bruised eye," she said with a laugh, leaning away from his errant fingers.

"It's a risk I'm willing to take. Tell me I'm romantic and I'll release you." His hands glided along her stomach before brushing the underside of her breast. Eloise's laughter turned to sighs as his hands moulded her curves, his nails scraping the distended tips of her nipples.

"You're a romantic," she said, leaning into his hands.

"I've always thought so."

"So confident." With a sigh, she looked at the door. "I didn't lock the door. Niraj and Sophie could walk in."

Ronan groaned as he pulled his hands back, his eyes never leaving hers. "Have I said recently how much I dislike keeping this a secret?"

"I know, but this is my career. And Niraj frowns upon agents being involved with their target?"

"Involved? What does that mean?"

"You know what it means."

He sat back against the chair, an eyebrow raised. "Do I then?"

Eloise stood from his lap and walked the length of the library. Fiddling with a book, she looked at him. "I'm enjoying our time together, Ronan, but I still have so much to accomplish within the Foreign Office. I don't want it to seem like I've lost focus."

"And having Niraj know we are together does that?"

"No. Yes." She sighed and rubbed at her face. "I don't

know. I'm torn."

"Between what?"

"Between what is expected of me and whatever this is that I feel for you."

"And what do you feel for me?" He searched her face.

Her cheeks heated. "You're a fairly decent man. Obviously attractive."

"Obviously," he said, his voice flat.

"What do you want me to say? That you understand me? My heart leaps when I'm with you?" she said, the admission bursting from her. She looked away, terrified to see his reaction.

"Yes." His voice was a whisper in the room.

"Well, it's true. You do understand me and my heart acts as if I'm racing Romeo each time I'm near you."

"So does mine."

She looked at him then, the sunlight behind him casting his face in shadow. Eloise crossed to him and bent down, her hand caressing his cheek, the coarse hair of his stubble prickling her fingers. Taking his lips in hers, she kissed him, hoping to convey all he meant to her. Her tongue swept along his bottom lip, begging for him to open for her. When he complied, her tongue met his, dancing, stroking, luring. Ronan's groan of satisfaction left her kissing him harder, faster.

His fingers swept into her hair, loosening the ribbon that held the strands back. As her hair fell forward, it created a curtain around them, a hideaway only they could see. His hands stroked the cheeks of her bottom, squeezing and plumping them. Need pooled in her belly. How quickly his kiss sparked a flame within her.

He pulled his lips from hers and whispered, "The door," but she took his mouth again as she dropped to her knees. Her hands tore at the placket of his trousers to free him. When her fingers encountered his length, he groaned into her mouth. Stroking her hands up and down his sex, she marvelled at the strength of him. Liquid gathered at the tip of him and she stroked her palm over it, using the moisture to slicken her hand as she gripped him. His lips ripped from hers as his head fell back, a growl emanating from between his teeth.

As she watched her hand stroke his sex, her quim clenched in response, greedy to feel his strength. Her mouth watered at the image of taking him inside her. Bringing her lips to the head of his cock, she swirled her tongue around the plumpness, licking up the salty liquid. Eloise looked up at him and moaned as he stared at her, his gaze hooded. Opening her lips, she took his length inside her mouth, as deep as she could, his cock hitting the back of her throat.

Ronan's groan was the only sound in the room. Pumping her hand in tandem with her mouth, she slid up and down his sex, swirling her tongue along the tip before she lowered herself again. His hands slid further into her hair, cupping her head as he lifted his hips, driving himself deeper into her mouth.

"Oh my God," he said with a growl as his fingers clasped her head, his release shooting streams into the back of her throat. Eloise swallowed it greedily, licking up every drop.

When his fingers loosened, she released him before resting her head on his thigh. Kissing the soft skin there, she looked up at him. His head was thrown back, his eyes closed, his ecstasy beautiful.

After, he dragged her back into his lap, her head resting on his shoulder. As his hands stroked up and down her body, she closed her eyes and sighed.

No matter what came, she would enjoy the moments she had with him, for who knew what would happen when the Fall of Caesar arrived.

CHAPTER TWENTY-THREE

R ONAN AND ELOISE'S morning ride took on a hint of mischief the next morning as they raced through Hyde Park, their adrenaline high. Even though they had spent the night together, their appetites for each other were merciless.

It did not take very much for Ronan to convince her to seclude themselves behind a row of trees, step out of her trousers, and take him inside her.

They spent the remainder of the morning avoiding one another, but when it came time to train, the tension that sizzled left them greedy for one another. Something about the sweat, exercise, and proximity created a haven for them and her heart was considerably lighter when she returned to her room to bathe and change.

When a note arrived with a footman that afternoon, Eloise smiled at Ronan's flowing script, requesting her presence in the kitchen. A half an hour later, Eloise was walking with Ronan along a gravel path.

Even with her eyes covered, she could feel the pebbles beneath her boots. She gripped his fingers tightly, hoping she stayed sturdy on the uneven ground. "Where are we going?" she asked.

"It's a surprise," Ronan said.

"I assumed that when you tied your cravat over my

eyes," she said. "My question is more in regards to whether you're planning to lure me to a secluded spot in London and murder me."

"Why would I do that? The odds are, you would end me first."

"True." He laughed, and she was certain it was from the surety in her voice.

The October air was crisp, the smell of pine so sharp, she was sure he was leading her into a forest. The clink and scrape of metal had her pulling at his hand. "I'm done with the blindfold now."

"Eloise, trust me."

"Odds are not in your favour, Ronan. I swear, if you lead me into a dungeon and call it an adventure, I'm going to withhold all favours."

"Are you afraid of the dark?"

"No, but I'm not a large fan of spiders."

"You're safe with me," he said, his voice a whisper next to her ear. "I shall protect you."

His hands tugged gently at the knot securing his cravat, the dark material giving way, as the sun hit her eyes. Blinded, she blinked, attempting to focus on her surroundings. A gasp flew from her lips as she took in her environs.

He had brought her to a garden, one surrounded by a large brick wall and an iron gate. The bushes that lined the path were overgrown, trailing their limbs along the cobblestone path. Flowers grew errantly, what was left of their buds twining with one another, creating a cascade of faded colours.

A dilapidated shed sat in one corner, its door hanging from the hinges, ivy clinging to it like a forlorn lover, while an arbour covered in overgrown honeysuckle hid a stone bench. And in the centre of the intimate space sat a shallow pool. What she assumed had once been the crowning glory of the garden now contained green water, the statue in the centre tipped over as if drunk. The effect was stunning. "What is this place?"

"My mother's private garden," Ronan said, walking towards a patch of green. He set down a hamper and blanket. "She never enjoyed the spotlight that came with being the marquess' wife. She preferred the quiet. She would retreat here during the day as if she were stiffening her resolve for the rest of the season."

"She must have loved it dearly."

"Oh, she did. She was here every day, trimming buds, tending the pool. She told our gardener he wasn't allowed to touch the area. Created quite a disagreement." Ronan laughed. "She would bring Felicity and me here once a week for a special luncheon. We would picnic and spend the afternoon playing games, or she would read to us."

"How wonderful."

"It was." His smile turned into a frown. "When she passed, my father couldn't bear to allow anyone to enter this place. And here it has sat, overgrown and in disrepair."

"Why didn't he maintain it? Surely, it would have helped keep her memory alive."

"I think, in a way, by not allowing the gardener to tend it, he felt like he was keeping her memory going."

"That's heartbreaking." Eloise wandered down the abandoned path. A few remaining buds clung to their limbs, resolute in staying their ground, even as the cold weather set in.

"El, this isn't the only surprise I have planned," he said.

"You packed a picnic?" she asked, returning to the blanket he had set out.

"Well, Mrs. Brown, my housekeeper, did, but it was my idea."

"Well then, all credit shall go to you."

Watching him pull items out of the hamper, her eyes widened. Cooked chicken, pasties, bread, and cheese covered the blanket. Strawberry tarts topped with a healthy dollop of cream sat in the middle of the spread. Her heart ached as she looked at the dessert. After everything she had put him through, he still took the time to take care of her.

To see her.

"You remembered," she said.

"Of course," he said, staring at her. "Eloise, are you crying?"

She dabbed at the moisture pooling in her eyes. "No." Eloise wiped at the tear that escaped down her cheek. "I have a speck of dust in my eye."

"You are."

"It's only that I adore strawberry tarts." She bit her bottom lip, willing the pain to stem the tears.

"Oh, darling," he said, cupping her cheek and wiping away the tears. "If I had known this would be your reaction, I would've kept you supplied in them from the beginning."

"To make me cry?"

"No, so you would be eternally grateful."

She laughed, kissing his lips. "Can we eat them first?"

"Unquestionably," he said, handing her one of the confections. Her first was decadent. She finished it quickly, muffling her moan of delight when she saw his smile.

"Whatever are you looking at? Do I have anything on my face?" Eloise brushed at her mouth, searching for crumbs.

His eyes crinkled as he smiled. "I'm only looking at you."

"All right."

"Tell me about the tarts?"

"The tarts? That's not an exciting story at all."

"No?" He set his hand on hers. "But it is a story about you."

Eloise bit her lip as she squeezed his hand. "There was a tea parlour I used to hang about. The pickings were ripe, and if you knocked on the backdoor, the chef would give you a piece of bread. Sometimes it was my only meal of the day. Once, when I knocked, he let me inside and told me I would have to wait a moment while he finished his task. As I watched, he covered these small tarts with thick cream. They smelled heavenly." She laughed as her stomach rumbled in agreement. Reaching for another tart, she nibbled on it.

"He saw me watching, most likely saw the desperation in my eyes, and offered me one. I cannot describe how it tasted. It was wonderful. Pure joy inside a treat. I started to set aside some of the money I picked to purchase a tart, a spot of happiness in a rather dreary world. I never told Sophie about it. When I started my work with the Foreign

Office, I gorged myself on them. The result was a terrible stomachache and the understanding that too much of something, even joy, can be painful."

"I'm not so certain there is such a thing as too much joy."

"I worry when there is this much happiness, the universe becomes unbalanced. Something catastrophic always happens to even it out."

"The universe is not a scale, Eloise."

"Perhaps." What she would not give to end the topic. Perhaps it was because he had not seen the bad parts of life growing up as she had. Ronan, in his pristine townhouse in Grosvenor Square, would have very little understanding about the evil that lurked in the world outside of Mayfair. Whatever the reason, nothing he could say would change her mind.

Ronan's eyes followed her as she filled her plate with the other offerings. She wondered at the image he had of a young Eloise, scared and hungry on the streets of London.

"Eloise, look at me," he said. When she finally convinced herself to meet his gaze, he said, "There is such a thing as being happy. It won't be that way all the time, but for the most part, it remains. Such as right now. I'm the happiest I've been in quite some time. Yes, things could be better, but right now, I'm happy, sitting here, having a picnic with you."

Her throat tightened, and she swallowed against the feeling. He was beautiful in the autumn sun, his skin cast in the golden light. Their time together was limited. No matter what awaited them beyond the horizon, she had to be honest with him. "I'm happy as well."

After dinner ended that night, everyone retreated to their own entertainment. Ronan excused himself from the dining room, murmuring something about his manuscript, while Eloise and Sophie headed to the library to look over the account books. After an hour had passed, her neck began to ache from leaning over the books, but she reached for the next volume in the stack they had collected, setting her spectacles back on her nose. As she scanned through the itemized lists, she could feel Sophie's gaze upon her.

With a sigh, she lowered her glasses and looked at Sophie. "What?"

Sophie grinned broadly before taking one of the other volumes and placing it on her lap. "You and Ronan are rather friendly these days."

"Ask whatever it is you're working your way towards so we can get back to work." Setting her glasses on the book before her, Eloise leaned back and crossed her arms across her chest.

"You seem happy. And so does he, for that matter."

"We are." Eloise rubbed at her brow. "I'm not sure where you're going with this."

Sophie fidgeted with the pages of the book she held. "I just want to make sure you know what you're doing."

Eloise snorted. "What do you mean by that?"

"Come now, Ellie. We both know how important this investigation is for you. You've done nothing but natter on about how it is necessary to solidify your career, how you want to make a place for women in the Foreign Office. I only want to make sure you know what you want, be it in espionage or in love. I don't want to see you lose something you've been working so hard for if he isn't the one."

Heat rose to Eloise's cheeks, and she pressed her hands against them. "Sophie, I'm here with you right now, going through his father's finances. I got him to open the bloody office door so we could look inside. So what if I enjoy spending time with him? I have a clear understanding of where this is going."

"Does he?" Eloise scoffed, but Sophie waved her off. "Your relationship with Ronan aside, think about the case. What have you done to move this investigation forward? You haven't left this house since he was injured. You haven't been to a single societal event, we have no leads, beyond the previous marquess' confession, and you've done nothing to start pursuing the other names on the list. You've both hid yourselves away in this house in some sort of honeymoon daze."

Eloise's jaw dropped. Sophie's words were a sharp burst to the haze she and Ronan had surrounded themselves in. Sophie slid an invitation across the table before leaning back in her chair.

"What is this?" Eloise asked.

"An invitation to a ball being thrown by the Duke and Duchess of Westmead. From what we've learned, there are several individuals from the list that will be in attendance."

Eloise swallowed the lump in her throat.

"The choice is yours, Ellie. Just be sure you follow your heart. No one would blame you for picking Ronan. I can see how happy he makes you. I just don't want to see you live with regret."

"Right."

Flicking the corner of the invitation, Eloise frowned. Sophie's observation shook her out of her reverie, whether that had been her intent or not.

She could lose everything if she did not redirect this investigation. Her throat tightened as if an invisible hand clenched it in its grasp. The years she had spent working to escape St. Giles, trying to save Sophie from a life of poverty, it would all go to waste.

"Excuse me a moment," Eloise said, taking the invitation with her as she stood. Sophie frowned as Eloise passed. It would seem her sister was displeased by her decision.

Eloise found Ronan in his apartments, his head bent over a piece of paper as he wrote with a fervour. She stood, watching him, the invitation a lump of hot coal in her hand. Clearing her throat, she waited for him to look at her before sitting in the chair across from him. "You seemed engrossed."

"I know." He rubbed the back of his neck. "Something clicked and the words have been flowing again." He sounded almost relieved at the admission.

"I'm glad." Eloise looked down at the invitation in her hands and counted her breaths silently.

"What is it?" He reached for her hand and squeezed it reassuringly.

"The Duke and Duchess of Westmead are throwing a masquerade ball tomorrow evening. You received an invitation. I wish to attend."

"Eloise, I'm not sure how I feel gallivanting about the ton, not so soon after my father's passing."

She frowned at him. "We both know society is much

kinder to men when it comes to impropriety. I'm sure they'll forgive you for the infraction."

"El, you're asking too much of me."

Firming her resolve, she played the one card she had. "This isn't a request, Ronan. We had a deal. You'll attend the ball, introduce yourself to the individuals I require, and you will do so with the demeanour of a regal aristocrat, as we agreed."

His eyes searched hers, shock written all over his face. "El…" His brow furrowed and his mouth set to a frown. "Right." He looked down at the page before him. "Was there anything else you needed?"

"No," she said, looking away from him. "Nothing at all, my lord."

CHAPTER TWENTY-FOUR

TURNER PREENED AS he dressed Ronan that evening, sighing with delight as he sculpted the errant curls on Ronan's head. The valet nearly danced with glee as he removed the heavy scruff from Ronan's face with a few tufts of cream and some deft flicks of his wrist, leaving Ronan's cheeks naked, and frankly, cold in the October air. When Turner began to trim and buff his nails, Ronan nearly stormed from the room at the pointlessness of it all. He was a stallion being led to the auction block and even as he was being fawned over, he was still that much closer to being made into glue. Not literally, of course. However, if forced to choose between a night surrounded by society or being led to slaughter, he would prefer the glue.

When he was trussed up like a turkey in a midnight blue coat and black breeches, his shoes polished to a shine, Turner tied an intricate knot at his throat before sending Ronan on his way.

Tapping his foot on the marble floor of his foyer, Ronan swallowed his impatience as he glanced at his timepiece. He was going to be late, and to an event he had little interest in attending, no less. Eloise's tenacity for her profession had once again led him into a path he never intended to take. The betrayal was a bitter pill to swallow.

He smirked as Niraj sighed in frustration. The agent

cum bodyguard stood across from him awaiting Eloise's arrival as well so they could discuss the noblemen she would need to speak to. Ronan smiled, eyeing the man.

If Eloise was intent upon making him late, at least he could aggravate the bastard who stood across from him. After all, Niraj had been the one to hit him over the head outside the Rogue's Den, and it would certainly help ease his mind from the heavy emotions swirling about in there. Tapping his shoe louder on the floor, Ronan hummed a ditty he had learned at a pub in Versailles.

"You're being a right bastard," Niraj said, and Ronan fought back another smile.

"Pardon? Did you say something?"

"You're attempting to pick a fight, but I'm afraid I'll have to take away your fun. I won't let you ruin Eloise's future." Ronan's stomach dropped at the words, the accusations ringing a bit too close to the truth.

He was miserable, and the prospect of spending his evening surrounded by the ton only amplified his misery, but Niraj was right. The clearing of a throat sent his head turning to the staircase.

"I'm so sorry. The hem of my gown tore and I had to decide whether to fix it or exchange it for another," Eloise said. She descended the stairs with ethereal grace and Ronan swore the world stopped. The peach gown she wore would have been demure, if not for the low-cut bodice displaying her décolletage. A collection of gems was sewn in an intricate design along the hem, glimmering with each movement she made. Her pale blonde curls seemed to defy gravity atop her head and a black feathered mask covered her eyes, only enhancing her alure.

"You look lovely," he said, hoping she did not detect the breathlessness of his tone. Even as he simmered with irritation at her unreasonable request, his body still responded to her.

Eloise's stride faltered when she saw him. "You shaved your beard." She frowned, her hand rising toward his cheek before catching herself. "You look very handsome," she said, before turning to Niraj.

The pair spoke in whispers, neither of them looking at him, and he could only stand there as her statement resounded in his ears. Eloise nodded before accepting her cloak and handbag from Jenkins.

Inside the carriage, he sat across from her, staring as she adjusted her skirts. The interior of his carriage filled with the scent of lemons and the notion that she had bathed in made his chest tighten. The image was exquisite torture. For a moment, he wished he had joined her in the tub, that he had convinced her to remain with him instead of venturing out.

"Thank you," she said, her eyes still focused on her skirts.

"For what?"

"For agreeing to the ball."

"You didn't give me much of a choice, Eloise. You forced me to attend tonight with little regard for my father's passing, nor his memory, so your gratitude rings hollow."

She looked at him but in the darkened carriage he could not discern her reaction. But he could see her hands as they wrung the gloves in her lap, twisting the fabric with her jerky movements. Before he could open his lips to speak, to beg her to change her mind, the carriage began to slow. A peek out the window confirmed they were in the long queue in front of Westmead's home.

"We're here," he said, his voice flat. "Have you ever been to a ball?"

"I haven't. The closest I've come was a wedding celebration for a friend, but that was years ago. And most certainly nothing like the formal affair we're headed to."

"Are you nervous?" When she glanced at him, he smiled. "I only ask because you're wreaking havoc on your gloves and if you continue, they'll be in a rather poor state."

She sighed and pulled the soft lacy confections on, covering her pale skin up to her elbows. "I'm fine. It's just another task, a chance to play pretend."

"I've seen your acting skills and they're rather remarkable. You'll do phenomenally."

He heard her swallow at his words. If she played pretend so easily with others, what were the chances she was doing the same with him? Who was to say that what they had found was even real and not some elaborate scheme she had concocted to get her way? Uneasiness ate at him.

When it was their turn to depart, Ronan jumped out and handed her down before escorting her up the steps of the glistening Grosvenor Square home. The assembly was slow and overwhelmingly hot, and the glances he received from other members of society made his stomach twist with anxiety. He could only assume their speculations on his sudden appearance which would no doubt make the gossip pages by morning.

After greeting the duke and duchess, they made their

way into the ballroom. The din of the crowd, mingled with the accompaniment of the musicians, rose to a deafening roar as he entered, driving home how unaccustomed he was to these types of gatherings. The longing looks he received from debutantes sent his skin crawling, but he forced a smile on his face. He shook hands with the gentlemen and fawned over the ladies, keenly aware that Eloise had slipped away from his side and was somewhere in the ballroom. With his receptions complete, he was in need of a stiff drink and a secluded balcony.

Instead, his eyes were drawn to the goddess in peach making her way around the ballroom in a black feathered mask. The men stared at her with near glee, their lust evident. Their eyes followed her every move, and yet, she took it all in stride, talking with those who greeted her and brushing off those who ignored her.

His stomach churned as she was approached by a young lord, the wretch intent on getting to know Eloise. Pushing through the crowd, he murmured his apologies as he made his way to her, itching to stake his claim, but stopped when Eloise smiled at the bastard. She laughed as they chatted, her demeaour and mannerisms so similar to how she had spoken to him that it made his heart ache.

"Lord Vaughn, I'm surprised to see you out and about," someone said, startling him from his possessive thoughts.

"Lord Strathmore," Ronan said with a bow. "I must say I am surprised to find myself here as well."

Strathmore followed Ronan's gaze as he watched Eloise and Lord Cole talking across the room. "It seems you're as enthralled with that beauty as the rest of the young bucks." Strathmore chuckled, slapping Ronan on the shoulder. The blow sent him forward a few steps before he caught himself.

"Enthralled, right."

Strathmore chuckled once more, the sound a grating beat in the already overly-loud ballroom. "Well, it seems fate intervened in having you here this evening as you were just the man I had hoped to see. I've been meaning to stop by and check up on you and your sister. See how you both are faring."

Ronan's eyes returned to the young lord and Eloise and he clenched his jaw as the youth brushed against Eloise's arm. "Word has not gotten around yet, but Felicity and the children departed for Yorkshire some time ago. There were estate details she needed to attend to that could not be put on hold a moment longer."

Strathmore snorted and Ronan shot him a glance. The old lord smiled in return, although the motion seemed forced. The man's paper-thin skin stretched to accommodate what appeared to be an uncommon gesture. "She always was such a curious girl, interested in learning this and that. I'm not at all surprised she has taken an interest in estate affairs, but I'm sure the previous Duke, God rest his soul, had a more than competent manager to assume such trivial manners. It is a shame she left you to bear the burden of your father's mourning."

Ronan frowned. "It was I who insisted she return when she informed me of the matters with which she was dealing. It seems the previous Duke left the estate in a rather unkempt manner. The Duchess has taken extraordinary measures to ensure that it becomes a profitable seat for her son."

Strathmore's smile fell at Ronan's words. "Right. What an admirable thing for the Duchess to do." Strathmore cleared his throat and looked about the room before meeting Ronan's eyes. "Perhaps there is a time you would be available to talk in the coming days? I was hoping to discuss whether you would be interested in taking over your father's seat in our weekly game of vingt-et-un. It would be a delight to have you join us. The group has been playing weekly matches for decades and I know there were several acquaintances of your father's that would enjoy the opportunity to meet you."

Ronan opened his mouth to respond, only to freeze as the young lord reached for Eloise's hand and drew it to his mouth for a kiss. "We can meet later this week," Ronan said, his hand balling into a fist at his side. "Stop by anytime and I'll be happy to discuss it with you."

"Wonderful." Strathmore clapped his hands together. "Well, I will leave you to enjoy the evening, Lord Vaughn." Strathmore clapped Ronan on the shoulders one more time before taking his leave, yet Ronan could only focus on the scene before him.

A drink. He would get a drink, take a stroll about the terrace. Eloise would be fine. After all, this was what she wanted. His eyes met hers and Ronan could only nod at her before turning away. They were at this ball by her request, and whatever goal she had in mind she would do alone. He would not be helping her. Eloise was the spy. Let her figure a way out of this herself.

CHAPTER TWENTY-FIVE

"**M**Y LORD, YOU such a charming devil," Eloise said, forcing her voice into a breathy croon. "Didn't your wife accompany you this evening? I wouldn't want to see you in get trouble for speaking so familiarly with me."

Lord Cole's cheeks blew out in bluster but his eyes darted around the crowded ballroom. "There is nothing sinister in talking to a beautiful woman at a ball. Isn't that the fun of a masquerade?"

"It surely is, and yet you've not questioned whether or not I am here with my husband."

"If you were attached, he would be here at this very moment escorting you around the room."

Eloise smiled at the man even as her blood seethed. "I don't need a man to escort me about a ballroom."

"Well, perhaps I can persuade you to dance with me?"

Her skin crawled where Cole still held her arm but she kept her smile in place. "I'm so sorry, but I must decline." Praying her firm set down would keep him from pushing the issue, Eloise stepped back, removing his hand. Curtsying to him, she turned and walked to the punch table instead of sprinting like she wanted to. Taking a glass from a footman, and whispering her thanks, Eloise swallowed the watered-down concoction.

"You're the belle of the ball," a voice said at her shoulder, and Eloise refrained from punching the man in his other eye.

"This would be far simpler if you would simply provide my introduction," she said under her breath. While a serene smile graced her face, she was sorely tempted to dig her heel into his shoe.

"You asked me to bring you. There was never a discussion about playing your lapdog." Ronan sipped the scotch he held in his hand. Grabbing the glass, Eloise poured it into the potted palm that stood next to her, cringing at its scent. "Why the devil did you do that?"

"Because the only way I'm going to get through this evening is if you are sober and follow directions."

"And tossing out my very lovely glass of scotch does that?"

"Since I cannot throw it in your face without making a scene, yes." She turned to him, touching him on his arm. "I don't want you to play my lapdog. I had hoped you would see yourself more as my partner. I've several individuals to investigate and it would mean a lot if you would do me the honours of introduction. But first," she said as the notes of a waltz began, "will you dance with me?"

His brows furrowed. She sensed he was on the verge of declining. Taking his arm, she pulled him along until they were at the edge of the dance floor. "Ronan, please?"

Ronan sighed. Her spine shivered at the sound. He dragged her out onto the floor and after a brief bow, they began to dance. Eloise's breath caught in her throat as he guided her effortlessly across the floor. Couples flew past and Ronan navigated them with precision. Each turn was calculated, each step pushing them away from danger even as it drew them closer to it and she was enamoured by the thrill of it all.

"This is remarkable," she said.

His eyes fell to hers, his ice blue gaze wide as he took in her face. She no doubt had the look of an entranced child, but she could not bring herself to care. The dance was marvellous. It was as close as she would ever come to flying.

"Have you never danced at an event before?"

"Not like this. Sophie and I practised when I was in training. After all, a courtesan must be able to fill all needs, but now, my ballroom is where I train. There's little space for dancing and I'm not sure the last time it saw a night like tonight," she said, hearing the remorse in her voice.

"Well then, let's do something about it," he said, pulling her closer. His motions became smoother, lighter. The air rushed by them at exquisite speed and Eloise was filled with exhilaration. She was a bird, a cloud, soaring through space. Graceful. Free.

It was addictive, dancing.

The moment crashed around her as she caught sight of young women lining the dancefloor, their intense gazes focused on Ronan as he steered her around the ballroom. Those women were his counterparts. One of them could be his eventual bride.

She was a fool if she allowed herself to imagine a life with him that spanned beyond this assignment.

Eloise closed her eyes, forcing the depressing thoughts

from her mind. All too soon the music ended and Ronan was escorting her to the edge of the dancefloor once more. "Who would you like to speak with?" he asked, his grip on her elbow gentle.

"The Earl of Bellgrave should be a good place to start."

"Right. Well then, let's get this over with."

"You sound as if you're preparing for battle."

The smile that had overtaken his lips while they danced hardened to a grim line. Ronan walked through the crowd towards a heavy-set man with an extraordinary moustache, while Eloise followed a few paces behind. The earl glanced at her as Ronan made his approach, but his gaze returned to Ronan, dismissing her. Interesting.

While Ronan made introductions to the earl, Eloise watched the earl as he conversed with the group.

"Lord Vaughn, I do hope you'll be joining us in Parliament soon and taking up the issues your father so valiantly fought for," Bellgrave said. "And I'm sure Strathmore has already begun his attempt to recruit you to our weekly card night."

Ronan smiled but it did not reach his eyes. "He has. I can't be doing either anytime soon, I'm afraid. I plan to continue my mourning for a bit longer before stepping fully into his role, but I look forward to your guidance when I do attend."

"I'm sure my guidance is the last thing you need. Knowing your father, I'll bet he raised you to carry the same beliefs that he did. It will be a smooth transition having you take his place."

Ronan's smile thinned, his lips all but disappearing as

his mouth pinched. "While that is true, I'm afraid I do have some ideas that do not follow along with my father's, but I am sure that will be understood when I join a session."

As Ronan talked with Bellgrave about the Corn Laws currently being debated as well as the man's upcoming plans for the holiday season, Eloise watched the stout man respond, his movements relaxed, the ease of a man who had done nothing wrong.

And yet, his name had been on the list.

Meeting Ronan's eyes and motioning to the terrace, she plastered a smile on her lips and headed out the ballroom doors as he made his excuses and followed her outside. The air was cool against her overheated skin. Eloise welcomed the reprieve from the crush.

"Well?"

Eloise was sore to admit it, but the earl did not seem to have nefarious designs. "Have you heard anything about Bellgrave recently? Any rumours?"

"There was something about him intending to find his current heir. It seems the earl has lost several family members to one ailment or accident after another and is now pulling at the slim threads of family ties to find the next one." Ronan pulled a flask from his coat pocket and took a heavy swig. When the pungent scent of gin reached her nose, her stomach pitched. Clutching the bannister, she leaned forward, certain she would spill the contents of her stomach.

"What the devil? Are you all right?"

"I'm fine." She gasped as the smell heightened when he neared her, her stomach rolling at the scent.

Ronan pocketed the flask, his arms wrapping about her waist. "You're pale. What the blazes is going on?"

"Just a reaction to the smell," she said, leaning against him. Thankfully, his person still retained his clean scent. "I'll be fine in a moment."

"You look faint. I'm taking you home."

Eloise opened her mouth to protest but her words were silenced as Ronan lifted her in his arms and carried her around the side of the manor to a separate set of doors. "I'm all right," she said, grasping his arms as he attempted to navigate the darkened room they had entered. "Ronan, please, I'm fine."

"I'm taking you home. Whether you're fine or not, you have done enough sleuthing for the evening."

"Don't be ridiculous. We cannot leave so soon."

"We can, and we will. Now, am I carrying you out of here like a babe or will you walk?"

Pursing her lips, Eloise was tempted to argue once more, but he was right. Her stomach was still unsettled from the smell of gin. "I'll walk."

He placed her down on wobbly legs and she leaned into his embrace for only a moment before regaining her balance. Following after him, she kept her head high and her pace sedate as she walked past guests milling about in the hallways. Once inside the carriage, Eloise laid her head back against the seat, the gentle rocking aggravated her already sour stomach.

"Do you want to tell me what that was about?" he asked.

"Not particularly."

"Shall I tell your superior you nearly fainted?" His

attempt at lightening the mood only served to heighten her embarrassment.

Eloise swallowed as she squeezed her eyes closed. "My father's vice was gin."

"I'm sorry, I didn't know."

"How could you? I've never told you every detail of my life in St. Giles. I've never told anyone."

"You know you can tell me all of it."

Eloise pursed her lips at his words. "It's the exact opposite of what your life is, Ronan. How could you possibly understand? You're surrounded by opulence and glamour, as much as you long to escape it. You had tutors and nurses as a child. An education. My education as a girl was learning that if my father made out poorly in a pick, we'd get beaten. And if he succeeded, well, then he'd buy gin with the money he got, become soused, and then he'd beat us."

"Eloise…"

"Please, save your pity. Besides an occasional ill response to the smell of gin, I do believe I've turned out all right. I have a decent career, food in my belly, and a roof over my head that not only holds heat but doesn't leak." She smiled, determined to keep up appearances. "If all goes according to plan, I'll secure my position within the Foreign Office and never have to think about that place again."

As the conveyance slowed, Eloise was thankful for the short trip and the knowledge her bed was within reach. When it stopped, she grabbed her things and moved to descend, but Ronan's hand on her arm stopped her.

"Are you sure you're all right?"

"I'm fine. Thank you for tonight."

He nodded before releasing her arm. Pursing her lips, she pushed open the door of the carriage and climbed out.

She was tired. Not just from the day, but from the year. From her life. And if tonight had brought to light a single thing, it was that outside of the haven they had created in his house, there were far too many differences threatening to pull them apart. As she climbed up the steps to his home, she feared they could never go back to the way things were before.

CHAPTER TWENTY-SIX

R ONAN SAT BEFORE the fire in his room, his journal next to him. He had intended to write, going so far as to even open the notebook to its most recent page, his pencil sitting in the crease of the spine. But he could not bring himself to work.

His mind kept replaying Eloise's smile as she stood with Cole, the feel of her in his arms as they danced, and the fragility she had shown from the smell of gin. The events of the night circled in his head like a kaleidoscope, each twist showing a different facet of the woman he had begun to care for.

He would have enjoyed going to an event like tonight's with Eloise if the circumstances had been different, but her blackmail soured any joy he might have found in the moments with her. During training sessions and rides through the park, their agreement taunted him like a spectre, and at night as he held her, depleted from their lovemaking, it danced in the back of his mind, reminding him that their time together was tenuous.

They stood on a precipice, teetering back and forth, and he had begun to fear the ending would decimate them both.

His bedroom door clicked open, his body sensing her before she even entered. Their days had taken on a pattern, a battle of wills as they each sought to prove the other wrong, but at night, they joined together in a dance of heavy breaths and longing bodies. It seemed that even as the seams of what they had built had begun to pull apart, the strands that held them together were determined to remain bound.

She sat behind him, her arms wrapped around his waist as she rested her cheek against his back. Her scent filled the room. His body responded as it always would, with a need only she could slake. "I'm sorry," she said, her voice a whisper. "Tonight was a mistake and I should not have coerced you into attending the ball." She released a heavy breath. "It would seem my occupation trickled in once again and I cared very little about who got in the way."

He remained silent, unable to find the words to describe how deeply she had wounded him. It was more than her incessant reminder of his father's treachery. It was the fact that she knew what she was doing to him, forcing him into a world he did not want, all for her own gain. His affection for her was a chess piece that she played easily, ultimately leading him to his ruin.

"I'm so sorry I hurt you." She hugged him, her hands stroking his stomach. "I should have never put this before you, never made you sacrifice your comfort for my gain." Her forehead rested against his shoulder, and he could almost imagine her chastising herself. "The damage I've done is no doubt irreparable, but I will still do everything I can to make it right."

"Why the sudden change of heart?" he asked, forcing his hands to remain in his lap even as he longed to comfort her.

"The only moment I truly saw you tonight was when we were dancing, but after that, you retreated into a cold shell. I despise myself for doing that to you." She sighed as she held him. "I couldn't let the night pass without apologising. Without making amends."

Ronan sighed, his eyes drifting to where her hands lay wrapped around his waist. In spite of everything, he understood why events had unfolded in the way they had. The immense pressure she was under was certainly something that would force anyone to their absolute extremes, making demands regardless of the harm they caused, but it still stung nonetheless. He wrapped his fingers around her wrist, pulling her into his lap. The weight of her body settled against him, and he kissed her forehead, stroking the blond streaks out of her face. "Thank you for apologising."

She nodded, her arms still wrapped around his waist like a small child. "You had Turner shave your beard. I'll never forgive myself for that."

Ronan chuckled at her words. "We're counting my beard as a loss?"

"Huge. Enormous loss. Biggest mistake of my life," she said against his chest.

"I'll grow it back for you," he said, sliding his hands between the edge of the fabric of her wrapper. "Will that make you happy?"

She stopped his hands from their exploration and looked at him, frowning. "Don't say things like that. You make it sound like I'll be here in the future to see you with it."

Ronan kissed her neck, and she shivered in his arms. "Not tonight. We can examine things tomorrow, El, but please, not tonight." He whispered the words against her skin, biting the spot where neck and shoulder met as his hands renewed their journey up her thighs. Her core was wet with need and Ronan swirled a finger in her heat, growling at how her body responded to him. He may not ever have her heart, but at least he had this. At least there was a part of her that needed him.

She whimpered as he rubbed the spot between her legs and spread herself wide for his roaming hands. Pushing her wrapper off her, Ronan sat back and stared. Each time he got her naked he was struck by how achingly beautiful she was. These memories of her would stay with him until he died.

Ronan laid her on the carpet and kissed each inch of skin he could find. His teeth worried her nipples before moving down to trace the indentation of her belly button. Pushing down his trousers, he climbed up her body and, with aching slowness, slid his cock into her swollen heat. Her sex clenched around him and light exploded behind his eyelids as her fingers dug into his thighs. Eloise tightened around his length, and he stilled, trying to find some semblance of control while her hand stroked through his hair.

Ronan wrapped her legs around his hips and reached for her hands, pinning them to the carpet. His eyes open, he pulled his cock back a small inch and watched as she undulated beneath him, soft gasps escaping her lips.

"Ronan," she said, attempting to thrust her hips to meet his.

Ronan kept her hips pinned with his and thrust inside her, angling himself to rub against her bud as pelvis met pelvis. The whimper Eloise released let him know he was on the right track. Rubbing his nose against hers, he waited as her eyes opened to meet his before thrusting again, repeating the same motion as before. Her eyes nearly rolled into the back of her head as she gasped.

Ronan was resolute, craving to wring out every ounce of pleasure from her that he could, even as his balls tightened and his cock begged for him to fuck her into oblivion. Three more strokes and Eloise was frantic beneath him, her hands squeezing his as she begged for her pleasure. She whispered things she would do to him, each one filthier than the next, if he would only give her what she wanted, but Ronan kept up his pace. Slow thrusts and a swirl of pressure against her clitoris until she screamed, her sex squeezing his shaft in a fist of pure bliss. Ronan's growl filled the air as she shouted his name to the sky. He pulled himself out of her body before thrusting once, twice more, and spilling on her stomach. Rolling to his side, he pulled her to him, both of their breaths harsh in the quiet room.

When his body quieted, he kissed the top of her head, then went to the bed and retrieved a blanket. They lay on the floor next to the fire until the flames became embers, but Ronan could not bear to leave the small cocoon he had built.

Her soft snores met his ear and he smiled but could feel his heart breaking a bit more. Determined not to fall asleep, he stayed awake the rest of the night, holding her close to him, whispering all the words of love he could never say out loud.

✧ ✧ ✧

THE NEXT AFTERNOON, Ronan and Eloise sat in the library playing a game of chess. The fire roared in the hearth, filling the room with a snug heat. Sophie and Niraj had made themselves scarce, Sophie claiming a headache, while Niraj checked in with the two agents he had brought in to keep watch on the exterior of the home.

Sitting in the armchairs near the fire, Eloise gazed at Ronan. His evening attire was reserved. He had eschewed a cravat and jacket, instead choosing to lounge in his shirtsleeves, a black waistcoat, and a pair of trousers, his dark hair raked out of his eyes.

With a sigh, she sipped at her coffee and waited for Ronan to make his move. At the noise, he looked up at her and raised a brow. "Are you all right?"

"I'm fine. I only wish I knew what to do next with this case."

"That sigh was more than just the case," he said. "What is truly going on in that head of yours?"

"A lot."

"Start at the beginning."

Eloise loved when he said that. It made her feel valued as an equal. He never mocked her ambitions, nor stated that she should focus on more mundane tasks. "You look like an ordinary gentleman, someone I used to imagine marrying, having a family with. And this," she said, waving her hand at the room, "this is comfortable. We have our daily schedule, we spend so much time in each other's company that I'm not sure what my day would look like without you in it. All that's missing is the children and a few hounds. Perhaps a cat." The chuckle that followed the omission was swallowed quickly.

"It's making you anxious."

"Yes. It's not that I'm not enjoying this time with you, because I am. It's just that this isn't the life I would choose. And I hate it because this is the life that has you in it."

"Do you want me in it?"

She closed her eyes before answering. "More than anything."

Ronan stood and rounded the table. He picked her up in his arms and sat in the chair she occupied. As he held her close, she took a deep breath, her body releasing the tension it held as his scent wrapped around her. "For what it is worth," he said, clearing his throat, "I want you to remain in my life as well."

Drawing back, she took his face in her hands and brought his mouth to hers. Her kiss was gentle, and she poured all the love she had for him into it, all of the words she had left unspoken and would probably never say. They were both on a path that would soon fork, taking them in opposite directions.

"You could stay with me. You could continue your career, and I could come with you on assignments, if necessary," he said, grasping for a way to keep her.

"You need a proper wife." She shook her head. "You need children, you deserve them. And you cannot say you'd allow me to head off into danger with every assignment, risking my life, and potentially the life of our child." The shock on his face was the confirmation she needed. The lives they wished to lead were two pieces of a puzzle that would never fit together. Eloise swallowed the knot of emotion that crowded her throat. "We'll stay this way until the assignment is over. There's no need to end it now, to deny ourselves time together." Eloise fiddled with the buttons of his waistcoat. "And, honestly, I'm not ready to let you go yet."

"Me neither," he said. "Until the end of the assignment." He drew her close and kissed her forehead.

The door to the library burst open as Niraj ran through, but he pulled to an abrupt stop he saw the position they were in. His usually tan skin was pale, and his breathing was heavy as his eyes darted back and forth between them.

"One of the agents covering the house has been found stabbed in the mews," Niraj said, swallowing. "The Fall of Caesar is near."

CHAPTER TWENTY-SEVEN

E LOISE'S BODY FROZE at Niraj's announcement. Ronan could practically hear the wheels turning in her head as she calculated her next move. Standing from his lap, she adjusted her shirt and trousers before looking at Niraj.

"Have there been any other developments?" she asked.

"No," Niraj said, his eyes darting back and forth between the two of them. "I beg pardon, but did I interrupt something?"

A blush blossomed on Eloise's cheeks, but she shook her head.

Before Eloise could question the man further, Remington Knight, former best friend and now sworn enemy, followed into the room behind Niraj. "Remy, what in the blazes are you doing here?" Ronan asked.

When the blond giant did not respond, but glanced at Eloise instead, Ronan frowned at her. "You never mentioned how exactly you came to know Remington Knight," he said.

"You never asked."

Awareness dawned as Ronan took in Remy's exasperated face. "Wait, you're the superior officer Eloise spoke of? The one who caught her picking his pocket?" His jaw dropped as he looked at Eloise. "This arsehole?"

Remy shook his head, his eyes lowered in frustration.

"You think I find joy in your involvement in this? You're lucky I don't mention every detail of it to your sister," Remy said.

"I would love to watch that encounter," Ronan said with a smile he was certain was not all that kind.

Eloise grabbed Ronan's upper arm, squeezing hard until he gasped. "It would be best for everyone if you kept your mouth shut," she said. "Can we set aside whatever this is and focus for a moment, please? Whatever nonsense you have with one another is sorely deficient when compared to what we are up against. Knight, why are you here?"

"I had a meeting scheduled with Niraj since this assignment has stalled. Now I see why," Remy said, gesturing to Ronan. "Any other brilliant ideas in that head of yours as to what we do next?"

"Someone should stay with Ronan while the others cover all the entrances to the house," Eloise said. "If we can get whoever attacked the agent to approach Ronan on our terms, we'll have the upper hand."

"You plan to use him as bait?" Niraj asked, a smile on his face.

"Yes," she said, her eyes on Ronan's. "If we can guide them to a chose spot in the house, we can catch them."

Her eyes seemed to plead with him, begging him to go along with her plan. Even as his heart urged him to heed her every desire, his mind argued against the notion. No. It was time to ignore his heart and use common sense. "And then what?" Ronan asked.

She swallowed and looked away. "Then we arrest whoever this is and take them to the Foreign Office. We'll interrogate them, then try them before the House of Lords. Between their crimes and the marquess' letter of admission, we'll have everything we need to give to the secretary."

As she confirmed his fate, Ronan's stomach dropped and he swore he could hear his heart breaking. "You cannot mean to use my father's letter in a court of law. He'd be found guilty of treason. I would lose my title, my lands. You wouldn't only ruin the legacy of the Marquess of Vaughn, you'd ruin me."

Eloise looked at him, her mouth turned down with sorrow. "Ronan, we need his letter. It's proof of this organisation and all it entails. He wrote down details and we know of the other lords involved."

"You'd use the letter, even knowing the result it would have? You'd devastate my family? Damage me all for the sake of your career?"

Niraj cleared his throat, bringing both of their attention back to him and Remy. "We'll get Sophie and the rest of the staff working on closing down the house," he said. "If you'll excuse us," Niraj said, backing out of the room.

"Yes, we'll leave you two to your lover's quarrel," Remy said, shutting the door behind him.

Eloise walked towards him, taking his hand and squeezing it gently. "Ronan, I'm not doing this to hurt you. You must know that."

Ronan shook his hand from hers and stepped back, putting a sizeable distance between them. "I know this isn't being done to hurt me, but it's certainly not being done with care for me either. It's a chance to secure your spot, isn't it? That's what it all comes down to. You won't stay with me because of your profession, and you'll destroy my family in pursuit of it."

"That's not fair," she said. "Ronan, this is how the law works. Those who do wrong, who harm, should be tried for their crimes."

"And the fact that it will accelerate your position has nothing to do with this?" His heart prayed silently that she would lie, tell him that she only sought justice, but he knew it was not true.

"I won't lie to you and say it doesn't help my cause. You know how precarious my position is. Yes, this will help me with the path I'm on, but it's not the motivation behind my decision. The agents who have lost their lives deserve justice. The Fall of Caesar needs to be stopped, and their leader should be hung for his crimes."

"At the cost of me and my family." He pinched his lips together. "And what of our relationship?"

"This doesn't have to end because of this. I love you, Ronan."

He shook his head at her admission. "Eloise, please, you have to find another way."

Her eyes opened wide, scanning his face as she shook her head. "I can't do that, not with everything that's on the line. You're asking me to forfeit my career, everything I've worked for," she said, with a frown. "This is about more than me. This is about women being taken seriously in a line of work we've been told we're incapable of. This is about women rising up and showing men we can be more than just a wife and a mother. You would ask me to give that up? To let down all those women who deserve the same chance I got?"

"This is about more than those women. This is about you and your need to find validation."

"What are you talking about?" She took a step away from him, her hand clutching her chest.

"I'm talking about the fact that everything you do is not for the greater good of some unknown female with an urge to be a spy. You are choosing this path because you are willing to do anything to avoid returning to St. Giles. You're afraid this is all you're good for."

"How dare you? How dare you make assumptions of me while you sit in your ivory tower and whine about the rich and flourishing life that has been handed to you."

"Eloise, please." He took a step towards her, his hands reaching out, but stopped when he saw the firm look of determination on her face. "This will ruin Felicity and the children. If you love me, like you say you do, you'd find another way to do this without crushing everything they have left."

"It seems you know nothing of love, then," she said, her eyes shimmering from held back tears. "I thought you saw me. I thought you believed in me and what I was trying to accomplish. It looks as if I was wrong."

He swallowed, the lump in his throat refusing to leave. "It seems we both were."

She nodded her head before turning and walking towards the door. "Please stay inside the library until Niraj can return to stand guard. You might not believe it, but it would kill me to lose you." The door closed with a whisper behind her, a deafening click that set Ronan's stomach rolling.

Retaking his seat in front of the fireplace, he glanced at

the chessboard next to him. Much like their relationship, each move had been calculated. Pieces were sacrificed, and unfortunately, the game would remain unfinished. Ronan growled, upturning the board. The black and white bits flew through the air.

A gentle rap at the door took his attention. Perhaps it was Eloise coming back to apologise. He scoffed at the idea. It was most likely Niraj come to guard him against whatever evil Eloise had concocted. He was certain the blighter would find great joy in Ronan's torture. He bid them enter. Eloise came in first, eyes begging for him to see something he could not understand, though her lips were silent. She held herself stiffly, almost unnaturally. "What do you want?" he asked. "I thought we both made our sentiments perfectly clear."

"Oh, you did, my boy," a male voice said, the familiar tenor sliding over his skin with a chill. "But Mrs. Delacroix, and her delicious lady's maid, beg you to reconsider, seeing as how their lives are on the line."

Ronan froze as the door swung open, revealing Eloise, and Sophie, who had a ghastly knife held to the soft tissue of her neck. Holding the knife was Lord Strathmore, a sickening smile upon his face. He pushed the pair into the library, closing the door with a resounding click.

CHAPTER TWENTY-EIGHT

"STRATHMORE? WHAT IS the meaning of this?" Ronan asked, standing from his chair. Strathmore clucked his tongue as he pulled Sophie to his side, his knife tracing the veins of her neck with a delicate motion. Ronan's gaze slid to Eloise, and she shook her head. There was nothing she could do, not while Strathmore held Sophie at knife point.

"Ronan, my boy, I think it's very clear what this is. I've come to negotiate," Strathmore said with a smile, his hand stroking up Sophie's side. The girl grimaced as the lord's hand grazed her breast, and Eloise's hands clenched into fists at her side.

"Let her go," Ronan said, his voice hoarse. Blinking, he stared at the man he had known for decades, his mind reeling at yet another deception. Suddenly, his ever-constant presence began to make sense.

"I'll let this delectable pair go as soon as you agree to do what The Fall of Caesar asks of you."

The words were a punch to the throat, confirming his worst fear. "How do you know about The Fall of Caesar?"

Strathmore winked at Ronan. "Dear boy, who do you think introduced your father to them?"

Ronan frowned. "You're a fool. There are agents positioned all over the house. You're insane if you thought you could walk in here unnoticed."

"Surely you don't mean this weak woman?" Strathmore said with a laugh, motioning to Eloise with his free hand. "As for Remington Knight, I had no idea he was working with the Foreign Office, at least not until I overheard him instructing Mrs. Delacroix's bodyguard to alert the agents around the home. A pity really. The fool's club had the makings of a brilliant influx of information for our group, but it seems we were beat out in that matter."

"How did you get in the house?" Eloise asked, her eyes pinned on Strathmore's knife.

"I was stopped by some crude individual in the alleyway, but he was easily dispatched. Then I walked to the front door like any regular individual of the aristocracy." Strathmore looked at Ronan. "I told you last night at the ball I planned to stop by. Your idiot of a butler let me in and left me waiting in the sitting room for a half an hour," Strathmore said, his brow furrowed. "I finally decided to search for you on my own and had the fortunate timing to overhear Lord Knight. I must say, I'm disappointed in you. Getting the Foreign Office involved," he tsked, "so cowardly. Did they tell you they would protect you?"

"I don't need protection and I'm not afraid of the group you work for."

"You sound so much like your father. He too thought he was stronger than the Fall of Caesar. A pity he decided to find his conscience."

"That's enough."

"Ronan, you must understand that what your father

did was necessary. As long as he provided the informat
required, his coffers were kept full," Strathmore s;
"The man had everything he could want and you, my (
boy, you could take his place and reap the reward.

"And what is it exactly that you get from working
them?"

"Me?" Strathmore scoffed. "I have an unending su
of funds at my disposal. Even if this country went t
devil, I'll still be rich as Midas. The true power ir
world is money, my boy." Sophie's soft gasp
Ronan's gaze to her. Strathmore's knife had nicke
neck and a small trail of blood trickled down he
skin. A glance at Eloise showed her lips were pinch
she met his eyes, her hand motioning towards th
place.

The only weapon within reach was the fire p(t
would have to do. His mind reeled as he replayet
Eloise had taught him. People love to boast abou-
selves, she had said. If he was ever cornered, held
keep the assailant talking, and bide his time whileng
for a weapon.

Edging slowly towards the fireplace, he looked at
Strathmore. "I fear you've underestimated the s."
With his hand behind his back, Ronan grabbed tldle
of the fire poker and clutched it tightly.

"Those men are nothing but a small complicand
are much too busy keeping the evil criminals ore's
really no other option for you, Ronan. The Fallesar
will succeed in their reign of horror and Nap will
take his rightful place as emperor. You do g by
siding against him and his followers. Think you

ould gain with the funds they provide. You could follow
our true dream and disappear to Heathermore. Write
our books and let the seat manage itself."

Ronan went still, his eyes finding Strathmore's. "How
id you know about that?"

"Your father told me about your dreams, my boy.
old me how much you disliked the notion of taking over
s position. He could never understand why you would
int to throw away your rightful place in the aristocracy,
t I understand, Ronan. And the Fall of Caesar can help
u do that." Strathmore took a step closer towards him,
face soft as he spoke. "So now, you decide. Will you
tinue the work your father started and live the life
've always dreamed of, or will you die, as he did?"

"Neither," Ronan said, brandishing the weapon like a
e.

trathmore's grasp on the knife faltered, and Eloise
advantage. In a series of moves, she rushed forward,
ing the blade towards the ceiling with her left hand,
punching Strathmore in the stomach with her right.
man stumbled back at the onslaught, gasping for
, his grasp on Sophie loosened.

ise bent down to retrieve her daggers, only to pause
ror as Strathmore recovered, his gaze pinned on
. The bastard wasted little time training the knife on
. Eloise ran towards Sophie as the blade flew
h the air. In a matter of moments, both women lay
ground, unmoving. Strathmore turned to Ronan
mile. "Now it seems it is just you and me, Ronan."
an could not take his eyes off Eloise. Her body lay
ess, and blood began to drip onto the carpet.

"I did you a favour, truly," Strathmore said, following his gaze. He smiled at Ronan. "Now you can marry a girl that is a match for you instead of wasting your time with a whore who has been used by the ton."

Ronan looked back at his father's oldest friend, blood roaring through his ears. "You miscalculated."

"How so?"

"You assumed I would join you. I've no intention of doing so and will gladly take you with me to hell." Ronan attacked Strathmore with vigour. The man stumbled back as Ronan hit him with strike after strike. Ronan circled his weapon and the pointed edge nicked Strathmore's face, causing him to scream as blood poured from his cheek.

He pivoted the weapon back for another attack but paused with the iron in the air as Strathmore removed a pistol and pointed it at him. "I believe it was you who miscalculated," the lord said, cocking the pistol and aiming for Ronan's heart.

Ronan closed his eyes, his thoughts returning to Eloise. Perhaps in death, they would be together.

Yet, instead of a gunshot, Strathmore screamed. Opening his eyes, he was stunned to find Strathmore on the ground, Eloise's knife protruding from his thigh.

CHAPTER TWENTY-NINE

THE DOOR TO the library burst open as Niraj and Remy ran in. "He's there," Ronan said, pointing to Strathmore, who lay on the ground. While they dealt with the man, Ronan hurried to Eloise's side. Sophie was already huddled over her, examining the horrendous knife protruding from Eloise's shoulder, her face taut with worry. Eloise's green eyes were open but her mouth twisted in pain, her forehead lined.

"You're alive," he said.

"Of course, I'm alive," she said, annoyance lacing her voice. "Did you think I'd go out of this world so simply? I plan on being pinned with several medals and having tea with Prinny before I meet my maker."

Ronan laughed, before noticing Sophie's furrowed brow out of the corner of his eye. "How bad is it?"

Sophie frowned as she stared at the gash. "It's bad. She hasn't lost a lot of blood, but who knows the damage the knife wrought when it entered. It could've nicked an artery and we have no way of knowing."

"Stop clucking about me like mother hens. It's obnoxious," Eloise said with a grimace, her eyes losing focus.

"You're in a bit of a bad way," Sophie said.

"I'll be fine. Stitch me up and I shall be back in the training room within a week." She said with a laugh, then gasped at the pain it caused. "Where's Strathmore?"

"He's down. You got him in the leg," Ronan said, stroking her hair, frantic as her skin took on a deathly pallor.

"I missed."

"No, my love," Ronan said, kissing her forehead, "You got him."

"No." She shook her head. "I was aiming for his neck," she said, before losing consciousness.

Ronan's stomach dropped and he looked at Sophie. "We need to get her upstairs," she said.

"And then, what?"

"I don't know," Sophie said, covering her face. "I don't know, but I'll think of something. She can't stay here."

Ronan slid his arms under Eloise's shoulders and legs, cradling her to his chest. He stood, taking care that her wound did not get jostled. Even with that care, her shoulder shifted, causing her to moan. He waited for Remy to look up from where they had trussed Strathmore like a pig.

Remy's gaze went from Eloise to Ronan. "I'll get Strathmore patched up and sent to the Foreign Office. I'll return as soon as I can," he said.

Ronan nodded, then turned and walked up the stairs, Sophie trailing a few steps behind him. Hurrying to the bed, he lowered Eloise to the sheets. His heart raced as he pushed a blonde lock out of her face.

Her brow was furrowed and her breathing shallow. "We should call a doctor."

Sophie shook her head. "They'll only want to bleed

her, or worse, they'll believe the injury fatal and let her die."

"She'll die either way," Ronan said, his stomach clenching at the statement.

"I can't let that happen," Sophie said, tears tracking down her cheeks. "She did this to save me."

"This isn't your fault, Sophie," Ronan said, resting his hand on her shoulder. "She would never blame you for this, you must know that."

Sophie nodded tersely before going to the washstand and cleaning her hands. Once the task was completed, she gathered as many towels as she could, creating a stack on the bed. She pulled on the bell, then looked to Ronan. "You'll need to wash your hands as well. We can't risk anything."

As Ronan scrubbed at his hands, a maid appeared at the door. Sophie requested more towels and the kit she kept in her room for injuries. When the door closed behind her, she went to the bureau that sat against the wall and began pushing it towards the side of the bed. Ronan rushed to help, and together they manoeuvred it to run along the side Eloise laid upon. When the maid returned, Sophie assembled the newly acquired items on top of the bureau.

"What are you planning to do?" Ronan asked, coming up beside her.

"I'm going to pull the knife out."

"You just said there could be damage inside that we don't know about," Ronan said.

Sophie looked at him before grabbing the stack of towels and handing them to him. "We can't leave it in there forever," she said, walking towards the bed.

Ronan followed her, standing beside the bed where Eloise lay motionless. "You're right. How can I help?"

"I need you to hold her down while I extract the blade. She's going to fight you, so be ready."

He nodded. "Should we dose her?"

"No. She hates laudanum, and for good reason." At his chuckle, she looked at him. "She told you about the dosing?"

"She did."

"As soon as the knife is out, we're going to use the towels to apply pressure. Hopefully, the bleeding will subside and we'll be able to clean the wound and stitch it up."

"Hopefully?" Ronan asked. "What happens if it doesn't?"

"Then she bleeds out," Sophie said, avoiding his gaze.

Ronan nodded. "Let's begin."

Ronan moved the pillows aside to make room at the head of the bed while Sophie tied off her skirts. She hiked them up and straddled Eloise's legs. With a pair of shears, Sophie cut away at Eloise's linen shirt, leaving the upper half of Eloise's body bare. Grabbing the handle of the knife, Sophie looked at him. "Ready?"

Ronan looked at Eloise. Her eyes remained closed, her breathing shallow. "Yes."

"On the count of three," Sophie said, before slowly counting. When she said three, Ronan held down Eloise's shoulders as Sophie withdrew the knife. Eloise's eyes shot open and a scream left her throat as she thrashed around, but Ronan held tight, trying to meet her eyes.

"El," he said, waiting for her gaze to catch his. "Eloise, it's all right, you're safe." When his words seemed to penetrate the pain, she settled down, the fight leaving her body. Sophie threw the knife to the bed and grabbed the towels. Placing them on the wound, she pressed down as hard as she could. Eloise screamed once more before the pain overtook her and she lost consciousness.

"Is she all right?"

"It's better that she not be aware of this part," Sophie said. "Can you take over so I can get the needle ready?"

"Of course." As he bore down on the towels, Sophie got up and rifled through the items she had placed on the bureau. Wet liquid began to cover his palms. Blood soaked the towels, the pieces of cloth barely withstanding the onslaught. "Sophie?"

She looked up. "Push as hard as you can. You need to get the bleeding to stop."

Ronan pushed down harder on Eloise's shoulder and a whimper escaped her mouth. "I'm hurting her."

"I know."

He remained crouched over her, pushing hard for several moments until it seemed the towels had collected every drop of life. He was certain that, if he were to remove the pressure, he would be the death of her. He looked to Sophie for guidance.

"Let's change out the towels." She grabbed a stack of fresh linens and exchanged them for the used ones.

After several torturous minutes of pressure, the towels in his hands remained somewhat dry. Relief filled his chest as he looked down at Eloise. She remained so still, her breath choppy and her skin almost grey. Why was she not waking up? "It's stopped."

Sophie nodded at him before walking towards the bed with a bowl of water and soap. As she deftly cleaned the laceration, Ronan kept his eyes fixed on Eloise.

Nothing changed. She remained still, as if death had already come for her. When the tasks were complete, Sophie grabbed a needle and began to stitch the injury. Even though Eloise whimpered at each poke of the needle and tug of the thread, her eyes remained closed. Sophie tied off the end and stepped back with a sigh.

"Why won't she wake up?"

"She lost a lot of blood. We might as well give her a small dose of laudanum. She'll hate it, but it's more tolerable than dealing with the pain."

Ronan nodded at her directive. Looking down at his hands, he could only see that they were covered in blood. Her blood. Hurrying to the washstand, he dunked his hands in the bowl. The water turned pink, making his stomach roll.

Together, they changed the bedding and got Eloise into a nightgown. Eloise hated sleeping in them, complaining that they made her feel confined, but he kept the comment to himself. Once Sophie administered the tonic for her pain, she left the room.

Eloise looked so close to death, lying in the bed. Her blond hair was fanned out, the sheets lying loosely at her hips. His mother had looked that way in her casket. Shaking off the maudlin thoughts, he lay down on the bed next to her, taking one of her small hands in his.

She would survive this, she would prevail. She had to, because he did not know how he would continue without her.

CHAPTER THIRTY

E LOISE LAY IN bed in a daze for the rest of the day.
They awakened her often to have her drink broth and
continued to administer laudanum. Ronan sat by her side
as night turned to morning.

As the next day progressed, Eloise never regained consciousness. Sophie relieved him of his duty at luncheon,
her anxious demeanour worsening as she checked on the
wound.

On the second morning, after his ablutions and a quick
breakfast, he went to Eloise's bedchamber. Sophie sat next
to Eloise's bed, tears coursing down her cheeks. Fear filled
his heart as he rushed to her side, looking down at Eloise.
Her skin was flushed and her breathing erratic while wet
strands of hair stuck to her skin. In her fitful sleep, she had
kicked the sheets to the end of the bed, her nightgown
hiking around her thighs.

"What is it?" Ronan asked, even as he recognised the
signs.

"She has a fever," Sophie said, wiping away the tears.
"It started last night. I bathed her in cool water, and I
woke her to feed her some broth." She shook her head.
"None of it helped. It keeps climbing, and she's become
restless. We're losing her."

"It'll come down, Sophie, we have to believe that."

"I can't lose her," she whispered, her gaze never leaving Eloise.

"When did you last sleep?"

Her hysterical laugh answered his question. Walking towards the door, he asked a footman to fetch his housekeeper. Helping Sophie to stand, he handed her off to the housekeeper who guided Sophie to the door even as she protested.

"I'll send for you the moment something changes," he said. "You must rest, Sophie. She'd be livid if she knew you weren't taking care of yourself."

She nodded her head and followed the woman out of the room, and Ronan closed the door behind her. At Eloise's bedside, Ronan stared down at her. Sweat covered her brow, yet her fever raged. Ronan cupped her cheek, whispering soothing words as he smoothed back her hair. He pulled back his hand, stunned by the heat she emanated. Worry tugged at him as he laid his hand back over her brow, and she quieted at his touch, leaning into his hand.

"It will be all right, El. Everything will be all right."

But as the sun began to set in the sky and night took its place, Eloise's fever only rose. She became frantic in her movements and incoherent in her ramblings. He helped a maid cover her body in cool cloths, but with her agitated motions, the fabric never stayed in place. Hating to wake Sophie, but needing her expertise, he sent the maid to get her.

Moments later, Sophie hurried into the room, her hair unbound and dress haphazardly buttoned. "What's going on?"

"She's burning up and we can't get it back down."

Sophie rushed to Eloise's side, her hand pressing to Eloise's forehead. "This isn't right," she said. "Have you looked at the wound?"

"No, she'll barely let us touch her without pulling away."

"I need to check it, just to be sure."

Ronan held Eloise in place while Sophie unbuttoned the gown and pushed it down over her right shoulder, revealing the injury, and they both gasped. The wound was bright red and inflamed, the stitches stretched tight from the swelling as pus seeped out between the threads.

"Oh my God," Sophie said.

"You need to remove the stitches so we can clean out the gash."

"Have you ever seen a wound fester this badly when you travelled?" Sophie asked as Ronan set to the task of pushing down Eloise's nightgown.

Ronan nodded his head. "Once. They didn't survive." Ronan swallowed as he looked down at Eloise. He could not lose her now.

Sophie called for a maid and requested boiling water and a stack of towels. When she returned to his side, she gently cut away the threads at Eloise's shoulder with a pair of scissors, opening the wound. Discharge escaped, seeping down Eloise's arm and onto the bed. Sophie reached for the towels the maid had brought, handing them to Ronan. "We have to get as much of it out as we can. Press as hard as you can on it. Use the towels to soak it up."

Ronan took it and pressed on the laceration. Eloise awoke with a piercing scream, fighting against the pressure.

"Eloise!" She paused in her movements to look at him. At her whimper, he placed his forehead against hers. The fire that raged in her body seeped into his skin, making him break out in a sweat. "I know, love. I know it hurts, but you have to let us do this. Please."

At her brief nod, he reapplied pressure to the injury. She closed her eyes, squeezing them tightly. While she bit back her screams, whimpers occasionally escaped her lips, the sound heartbreaking. Ronan spoke soothingly to her, telling her she was strong and brave. After ten minutes, he pulled the towel back to look at the wound, and Eloise's breath left in a sigh as she sagged against the pillow.

Sophie peeked over his shoulder and looked at the wound. Pus still oozed from the gash, now tinted with blood. "What's next?" he asked.

"We wash it again." Coming to stand next to Eloise, she bent down and pushed Eloise's hair away from her face. "Ellie, the water is very hot. It should kill the infection, but it won't feel pleasant. Can we give you a dose of laudanum for this?"

"I hate being dosed," Eloise said, her eyes closed.

"I know, dearest, but it will hurt less."

Eloise swallowed, then shook her head. "No," she said through dry lips.

Ronan handed Sophie back the laudanum. "I want you to drink something."

"I can't," she said.

"Please. Just a bit?" He lifted a cup to her lips.

She took a small sip and sighed as she swallowed. "More." As he brought the cup back to her lips, she drank the liquid greedily.

"Not too much. I don't want you to make yourself sick." Ronan helped her lie back down, and when she scowled at him, Ronan could not help but chuckle. It was the first time in three days he caught a glimpse of the true Eloise. Lord, how he missed her.

Sophie returned with the water and soap and the remaining stack of towels. "This will be messy." She set the bowl of water down on the table beside the bed.

Ronan rolled up the sleeves of his shirt. "I'm not afraid."

Together, they set about cleaning the wound. Flushing it with the scalding water, they cleaned the area with soap, then washed it again. Blood mixed with water. The waterlogged bedlinens squelched with their movements. Eloise remained lucid through it all, swallowing her screams as they scoured the area repeatedly, all the while, Ronan continued to whisper to her, murmuring words of encouragement. He was not sure if she understood any of it, but it helped his heart to say them.

When the entire kettle was empty, Sophie and Ronan changed the sheets on the bed. Forgoing a nightgown, Sophie had Eloise lay naked beneath the sheets, her wound exposed to the cool air of the room. Her fever still raged, pulling her into sleep as soon as they covered her up.

"We'll need to do that every few hours."

"Must we?" Ronan asked. "We're torturing her."

"I know, but it should keep the area clean."

"Then it's what we will continue to do until she is better." He nodded. There was no other choice, and he refused to think there would be any other outcome.

CHAPTER THIRTY-ONE

R ONAN BARELY SLEPT as he sat by Eloise's side. She was dying, of that he was certain. She did not need the laudanum; she never regained consciousness. Her fever threw her into a world where he could not reach her, where monsters lurked and pain smothered her. And he could do nothing to save her.

As the night passed into morning, and daylight turned to night once more, Sophie attempted to relieve him of his bedside duty several times, but her efforts were fruitless.

Eloise tossed and turned restlessly, crying out as she slept. As time passed, Ronan became certain this was his fault. Strathmore might have lured his father into the Fall of Caesar, and he might have thrown the knife that injured Eloise, but the true villain was himself. If he had only agreed to her plan, the courses of that evening might have turned out entirely different.

Remy arrived the next morning and strode into Eloise's room. "How is she?"

"Not well. The fever won't break and her injury is infected. She hasn't woken since we first cleaned out the wound." With a frown, Ronan realised his words held little venom. He did not have the strength to battle against Remy.

"She'll pull through this."

"How can you be so certain?"

"I'm not," Remy said, "But I can be hopeful."

"I'm afraid I've lost all hope."

"Eloise is a force to be reckoned with. She'd only leave this world in a blaze of glory, guns firing, knives flying. You know her, with all her great plans. You can't believe she would allow this to be how it ends."

"Did you not hear me? Her fever hasn't lowered and she won't wake up. You can't believe her will can change any of this."

"The mind is a very strong thing, Ro. You'd be surprised how much it can control. Let me ask you this," Remy said, looking at him. "How does Eloise calm herself when agitated?"

"She breathes."

"Yes, but how does she breathe?"

"She counts her breaths. Inhales, holds, exhales, holds. Four counts each."

"Her mind is controlling that. Her mind is telling her body to be calm, that all is well. A mind is a powerful tool we all have, but few seem to use." He glanced at Eloise, then back at Ronan. "Even though she's not lucid, she's aware of everything going on around her. She can hear our conversation, your conversations with Sophie, the maid, even the conversation you have with yourself."

"I'm supposed to converse with her? And do what? Beg her to fight? Beg her to come back to us? Tell her Sophie loves her? That she has so much work to do at the Foreign Office?"

"I believe you've answered your question," Remy said, walking towards the door. "I know now is not the time, but I want you to know I am sorry for abandoning Felicity and the children." He motioned to Eloise who lay prone on the bed. "I'm sure now you understand why I had to distance myself. I can't risk something like this happening to any of them." The blond giant rubbed at the back of his neck. "And I'm sorry for the way our friendship ended. It was never my intention to lose you as well."

Ronan glared at the man's back, allowing his silence to speak for itself.

"Right then," Remy said with a sigh. "When you're finished, I'll update you on Strathmore."

"When I'm finished doing what?" Ronan asked, but the door closed behind Remy.

Ronan walked to Eloise's side and retook his seat next to the bed. He stared at her, her blonde curls scattered across the pillow. The sheet was twisted around her hips. A bright pink flush covered her face and chest and the gash, while still red, gleamed from its cleaning a few hours before. Even on death's door, she was stunning.

Reaching over, he grasped her hand in his, stroking between her knuckles. She sighed, her body shifting towards his touch.

"El, I don't know if you can hear me, but Remy seems to think so," he said. "I need you to fight, my love. I need you to put all the power and energy you have into making yourself better because we need you. Sophie, Niraj, Remy, and me. I need you. Hell, the fate of women in espionage depends solely upon you."

Kissing her hand, he rested his head against it. He told her stories of his childhood. Growing up with Felicity, their romps through the fields of Heathermore and games they would play with their nanny.

He talked about his travels. The map he had pinned in his room as a young man, plotting his next adventure, foolishly believing his father would be around forever. He talked until his throat was parched, his eyes itchy from his tears. Until his back ached from leaning over her hand and his head throbbed from trying to find something new to say.

Ronan brushed a kiss across her forehead and whispered, "I love you," then left the room. Stopping a maid in the hallway, he requested Mrs. Brown sit with Eloise, but told her to fetch him as quickly as possible should anything change.

Sophie, Niraj, and Remy were waiting for him in the library. Ronan cleared his throat, aware of the puffiness around his eyes. He looked to Niraj. "Well?"

"There was a bit of an altercation on the way to the Foreign Office," Niraj said sheepishly.

"What does that mean?" Ronan asked.

"Strathmore didn't make it there."

"He escaped?" Ronan asked.

Niraj dared to look offended. "Do I look like the type of agent that would allow a man to escape?" he asked. "He tried to escape, I prevented it, and in the course of things, he wound up dead."

"What does this mean for the Foreign Office?"

"It means we're back at square one with only your father's letter to lead us and that blasted list of names," Remy said. "I'm rather put out that we weren't able to interrogate him, but he did give us some information."

"He did? Did he confess his sins to you before he died?

Did he ask for atonement?" Ronan sneered.

"I'm going to forgive your attitude, Ronan, as I understand it's an emotional time. No, he did not confess. He took responsibility for the death of Nigel Loge, as well as the attack on you and Eloise at the solicitor's office. The man was determined to bring you into the group no matter the consequences. There were letters and such in his office that hint to a location for the Fall of Caesar's headquarters in London and we believe Lord Bellgrave might be privy to that. It's not a lot, but it's more than we had originally." Niraj paused and looked at him. "He must have said something to you to give us a clue how the group operates."

"You're relying upon my memory alone to investigate how the Fall of Caesar is conducting its schemes?" Ronan asked. "I barely recall the past few days of Eloise's decline."

"Think back, Ronan. You were in that room for longer than it takes to kill a man. He must have said something. Men like that always love to talk."

Ronan tried to think back on the night of the attack. With Eloise's deterioration, it seemed ages ago. His brain was sluggish, making it difficult to recall anything. Sophie walked to his side and placed her hand on his shoulder. "Perhaps you should rest. You've been by Eloise's side for two days. Some sleep should help you remember."

Ronan nodded. "I'll see what I can do." Closing the door behind him, Ronan leaned against it. His body trembled with exhaustion, but his mind raced as he tried to remember any nonsense Strathmore had spewed. Raking his hands through his hair, he fought against the temptation to drop to the floor and give in to the chaos.

Dragging himself upstairs, he paused in front of Eloise's room. The door was closed, but he could hear her mumbling, her voice loud enough to reach through the portal. Turning the knob, he pushed the door open. Mrs. Brown sat at the chair beside Eloise, mopping her brow.

"How is she?" he asked.

"The same, my lord," Mrs. Brown said, replacing the cloth in the bowl.

"I'll take over, Mrs. Brown, thank you." Standing at the foot of Eloise's bed, he took her in. The sheet had been readjusted, covering her, but her legs moved restlessly, disturbing the fabric.

Recognising the dismissal, the housekeeper left the room, closing the door behind her.

Ronan walked to the opposite side of the bed where Eloise lay. Stripping the clothes from his body, he pulled the sheet back and slid down next to her. Enfolding his hand in hers, he kissed her brow, her fever heating his lips. Closing his eyes, he allowed the fatigue to claim him.

CHAPTER THIRTY-TWO

I NVISIBLE HANDS TUGGED at Ronan's clothes as he walked a dark hallway. Voices whispered, their words indecipherable murmurs as he stumbled along, banging on each door he came across, begging for their help, but none would open. He was frantic for someone to answer him, to find him.

The danger was coming. He could feel it looming and he needed to warn them, but they would not answer his calls. A hand on his shoulder ripped a silent scream from his throat as he turned to fight.

Ronan awoke with a start, his heart racing and perspiration dotting his brow, yet the pressure on his shoulder remained, stroking him in the shadowed room. Turning his head, he found Eloise looking at him, her eyes clear but tired. Her hand continued to caress his shoulder as she smiled at him. "You were having a nightmare," she said.

He smiled at her, sleep trying to lure him back under its heavy caress even as his brain screamed for him to recognise what she was doing. His heart picked up its pace as recollection dawned, and he rolled to his side, his hand cupping her cheek as his eyes looked over every bit of her, certain he was still dreaming.

"You're awake," he said, stroking her hair, the tangled blonde strands catching on his fingers. Her skin was cool against his hand, all signs of the fever gone. He blinked back the tears of relief that threatened to spill. "How are you feeling? What do you need?" he asked, pushing himself up to sit.

Eloise smiled. "I'm just tired."

"I imagine you would be, fighting for your life and all," he said, holding back the urge to kiss her. Her skin was pale in the candlelight, her lips dry and cracked. He left her side for a moment to get her a cold cup of tea, helping her to take slow sips.

"How long have I been ill?" she asked, after finishing the brew.

"Nearly a week. The wound became infected."

"I feel like I've been in a fight and lost." She laughed softly, then hissed in pain.

"Sleep," he said, pulling himself towards her. "I've got you, just rest."

"Your dream."

"It's all right," he said, stroking her hair. "We can talk about it in the morning. Sleep, El."

As she rested her head on the pillow beside his and her breath evened out, Ronan could barely contain his relief. She would recover, he would see to it himself. And even as his body begged him to fall into the same slumber as Eloise, he removed himself from the bed to search for Niraj. Not only because he wanted to share the good news of Eloise's recovery, but because he remembered what Strathmore had said. The Reign of Horror was coming.

✧ ✧ ✧

"REIGN OF HORROR?" Niraj asked, when Ronan joined him and Sophie in the library. "You're sure that's what he said?"

"It is. I don't know what they have planned, but it doesn't sound good. They currently have any number of Parliament members being blackmailed for information. Napoleon is on St. Helena, and even though he is guarded, these people seem able to blend into any environment. Who knows how many members of their group are already in place for what is coming? They're determined to see him as Emperor."

Niraj looked at Sophie, who was sitting next to him. The sun had started to rise, and the servants in the house had begun to stir, the quiet sound filling the home.

Ronan's body ached and his eyes burned from his lack of sleep. He longed to go back to Eloise, to lay by her side and reassure himself she truly was on the mend, but Niraj needed to know this information. Sitting on an overstuffed armchair, Ronan let his body sink into its warm embrace while Niraj and Sophie planned.

"We'll need to look at the list again," Niraj said to Sophie. "Each individual most likely has someone close to them keeping an account, as Ronan's father did."

"Well, then, we need to place our agents in their home as well. The first one to come back with information is who we follow more closely," Sophie said.

Niraj nodded and stood from the couch. "We can't do much more tonight."

"I think you mean this morning," Ronan said with a smile.

"Bloody hell, I'm exhausted. Let's all get some sleep

and we'll begin again once we're rested," Niraj said, helping Sophie to her feet.

Standing, Ronan groaned. Leaving Sophie and Niraj in the library, he hurried up the stairs to Eloise's bedroom. Opening the door, he paused. She was still asleep, the sheet covering her body. Her soft breathing was like music, hypnotising his body into a sleepy lull. Closing the door behind him, he stripped off his clothes and joined her. She sighed as her body relaxed against his.

"Is everything all right?" she asked.

"Everything is fine." Rolling onto his side, he faced Eloise. Taking her hand in his, he allowed his eyes to trace her face, etching into his brain every line, every detail. "El, you scared the devil out of me."

"To be truthful," she said, looking into his eyes, "I scared myself as well."

"Seeing you on the floor after Strathmore's knife hit you. The blood and the fever," he paused, clearing his throat, "I need to hold you. I need to reassure myself you're here and you're all right."

She nodded, the fingers of her good arm stroking his.

"How close can you possibly get without hurting yourself?" he asked. When she aligned her body with his, he sighed. "I plan on staying like this for the next month."

She groaned in exasperation. "I cannot lay naked with you for a month."

He smiled as he pulled her closer. "I'm sure we'll find something to do after the first week or two." She laughed against his chest, her breath soft.

In the week that followed, Ronan spoiled Eloise in every way possible. Lavish meals were brought to her bed where they ate side by side. He read her *First Impressions*, adopting voices for each of the characters, which made her laugh. And at night, they lay next to each other, longing for the intimacy the other could bring but refraining from anything more than holding one another.

In little time, Eloise's strength was back. She was making trips around the bedroom and chomping at the bit to do something other than play the invalid. She convinced him that she be allowed to train, and after getting permission from Sophie, began to strengthen her arm with small exercises.

Her rapier shook as she attempted to hold it at length, causing her to respond with adequate frustration. Each attempt to strike the beam sent her into complaints of a tingling numbness that overtook her arm.

But each day, she trained with the hope her strength would be restored, and each evening, she left the room disconsolate and ill-tempered at her slow progress. Yet, Ronan remained by her side, training with her, reminding her it would take time. And slowly it did.

CHAPTER THIRTY-THREE

A S HER STRENGTH returned, so did Eloise's resolve to bring The Fall of Caesar to justice. A month after her confrontation with Strathmore, she was fully on the mend. During the day, she locked herself in the library with Niraj and Sophie, formulating plans, sending missives to Knight, and avoiding Ronan.

At night, she lay beside him in bed, her body longing for his, but her heart aching as it replayed the words he had said that fateful night. Although they were right next to each other, he seemed an ocean away.

He stood beside her as day by day she gained her strength back. She trained like the devil, determined to recover faster so she could dismiss Ronan and the ache he wrought. She made sure they never spoke about their relationship, avoiding all attempts made to delve further into their future. The stronger she became, the less she would need him, and the sooner she could do that, the sooner she could return to her work in the Foreign Office.

As she sat in the library with Niraj and Sophie to discuss the next lord they would target, Ronan walked in. Niraj and Sophie both paused as he entered the room, guilt etched on their faces, but Eloise only felt numb at his presence. As Sophie and Niraj excused themselves and made a hasty exit, Ronan seemed to be unable to take his eyes from her.

Looking down to ensure nothing was amiss, she assessed her clothing. Her dark trousers and soft white linen shirt hung off of her loosely. She had yet to gain back the muscle she had lost while recovering and her clothes draped on her frame awkwardly. Running a hand over her hair, she made sure each strand was in place, before checking the ribbon she had used to tie it back.

"You're planning to start this charade again," he said quietly.

"Yes. I've almost fully recovered and am well enough to resume my occupation. We shall be out of here soon enough and your home should return to normal."

Ronan walked towards the table that sat beneath a window. He set the book he had been carrying down on the glistening surface. "This is how you are choosing to end this?" he asked, unable to meet her eyes.

"We had already come to an understanding of what our ending shall be."

"Remind me again what that was?" He walked to her and knelt.

"Your father's letter was needed to bring Strathmore to justice. How lucky for you that Strathmore is no longer a problem. I shall return the letter to you as soon as possible and none will be the wiser to your father's treason. And since there are no more leads here, I see no further need to continue our—" she paused, unable to meet his gaze.

"Affair? Arrangement?" he asked. "Are those the words you're looking for? Because I would use relationship or partnership, but it would seem we do not agree on that as well."

She recoiled, the words acting like a blow. "How can you call this a relationship when you called me a liar as I told you of my affections? When you informed me I couldn't possibly love you if I was willing to put your father's legacy in the hangman's noose?"

"This is a relationship. I've done nothing but stand by your side through your illness and as you gained your strength back."

"You only did that because you thought I was dying!"

Ronan froze, staring at her. She pushed her shoulders back and crossed her arms in defiance. Her body trembled as she held her stance, unwilling to show the slightest sign of the fear and pain that threatened to consume her.

"I did it because I love you. Because I was wrong to ever ask you to sacrifice your dream for me. Just so we are clear." Bowing in her presence, he held her hands as he looked at her. "I'm sorry for the things I said. For diminishing the love you so easily gave. I was a bastard for pushing you away. You are more important than any legacy, more important than any title. I love you, Eloise. And it did not take a knife wound for me to realise it. It has always been there. It was there when you stood by me as I dealt with my father's death. It was there each morning when you raced me on Romeo, and it was there when we made love each night."

"You're only saying this because I cannot use the letter."

"The hell I am. Use the letter, give it to Prinny, I don't care. I only want you," he said, closing his eyes. "You once told me what you knew of me. Let me tell you what I know of you. I know you drink tea, but wish it were coffee. You're quick with a dagger and, although you excel at it, you hate to use a gun. You count your breaths when you're overwhelmed. You never let anyone close, including your sister, and you act as if the fate of womankind is upon your shoulders. You adore strawberry tarts, hate alcohol," he paused, swallowing, "and love me."

"Choose your career, but please, Eloise, choose me as well," he said, kissing her knuckles. "I love you. No conditions, no restrictions. If you want to be the greatest spy England has ever seen, I'll stand by your side through it all. Cavort around the continent if you must, but come home to me afterward. I'll wear disguises, I'll dress like your bloody maid if I have to."

Her eyes scanned his face, but she could not find any words to say. As the moment stretched on, she finally broke the silence with a laugh.

Ronan's eyes fell to her hands. When she finally settled, she lowered herself down to her knees. "I'm sorry, it's only that I pictured you dressed as a woman." She cupped his cheek, then broke into laughter again.

He joined her, leaning into her hand. "It's a rather ghastly thought."

"Niraj might be better equipped to pull it off."

"He does have that luxurious head of hair," he said, smiling at her. Leaning down, he pressed his mouth to hers, and her laughter ceased.

She slid her fingers into his hair, pulling him down to her. Her lips found his, her tongue licking at the seam, begging for entrance. When he submitted, she sighed in delight as her tongue met his, sliding and thrusting, a demonstration of how she needed him. He pulled back to look at her, "Are you sure?"

"Take me upstairs, Ronan. Please."

Lifting her into his arms, he carried her out of the library and up the stairs to her room. She laughed as he gained speed, heading towards the bedroom. Ronan entered her room, and then kicked the door shut behind them before setting her down. She began tugging her shirt loose, but his hand on her made her stop.

"May I?" he asked.

She nodded, her hands moving away from her clothing. Ronan walked towards her, and her heart picked up its rhythm in her chest. He lifted the hem of her shirt, and slowly brought it up over her head, letting it fall from his fingertips as he took her in.

He kissed his way down her neck, pausing where her neck and shoulder met to run his tongue along the groove before nibbling the flesh.

She whimpered, longing for the pressure of him. He could not keep his hands still as they spanned her waist, traipsing lightly over the skin. Her nipples tightened, even more, the buds pressing against his chest.

Pausing at her wound, he kissed her softly on the healing skin. "I almost lost you," he said, his voice aching in agony.

She brought her hands to his cheeks, forcing him to look at her. "I'm right here." She took his mouth with hers, pushing at his jacket until the heavy material fell to the floor. She untied his cravat and unbuttoned his waistcoat, flinging the items to meet his discarded coat. Leaning back, she said, "I want to see you."

Ronan wasted no time taking off his shirt. Her sigh had him smiling at her as if he could read her mind. Eloise stepped close to him, rubbing her breasts against his chest. The friction caused them both to moan, as his mouth took hers with urgent need. Ronan pulled away and she mewled in frustration.

"I know," he said with a small smile. Undoing the placket of her pants, Ronan picked her up and walked her to the bed. He divested her of her boots, stockings, and trousers, leaving her bare to his gaze. He drank in the sight of her against the pillows.

Shifting her leg, she used it to shield her sex. Surprised by her sudden covering, he gave her a questioning look. "Equality," she said, waving her hand at his clothing.

He rid himself of his remaining garments before joining her on the bed. She laughed at his haste before she leaned her body into his. "Slowly."

Ronan took her mouth again in a kiss as his hands skimmed their way down her side. His fingers brushed over the curve of one breast, causing her breath to hitch as she anticipated more. When the devilish fingers brushed her nipples, she shuddered in his arms. She thrust her breast into his hand as she bit down on his bottom lip.

Lazily circling the tight bud with his fingers, Ronan slicked his tongue against hers in a soft kiss, lingering on the corners of her mouth. His fingers danced along her flesh, taking their time reaching their destination.

Eloise groaned with want.

"Slowly," he said.

"Any slower and I am going to perish," she said against his mouth.

He took the bud, pinching it, and Eloise moaned as she thrust her sex against his. Ronan lavished the other nipple with his attention and Eloise writhed against him as he tormented the buds with mouth and fingers. Her hips lifted towards him, begging for his weight, but he ignored it as his hand slithered down the inside of her thigh. He slid his fingers against her sex, her need dampening his hand, and when he swirled his fingers in her heat while his mouth took her nipple, Eloise's sex clenched, her climax so close she could barely stand it.

Ronan worked himself down her body, his shoulders separating her legs as he gazed at her quim. She was beyond care as she lifted her hips, all but begging him to take her in his mouth. The puffs of air from his chuckle had the walls of her sex throbbing, and she lifted her hips higher.

"Slowly," he repeated, kissing the inside of her thigh.

She whimpered, her hips gyrating of their own volition. Her hand strayed toward her quim, willing to do anything to ease the pressure he had built there. Ronan grabbed her wrist, kissing the fingers, before setting it to her side. "No cheating," he said, his lips trailing down to the outer lips of her sex.

Eloise became desperate as his hot breath danced upon the sensitive skin. "Ronan, please."

"Please what?" he asked, switching his attention to her opposite thigh.

"Please, I need you."

"Where, El? Where do you need me? Tell me what you want."

"I want your mouth on me."

"Where?" he asked, his tongue tracing her hip. "Here?"

"On my quim," she said, her fingers sliding into his hair. "I want your mouth on my quim. I want you to suck me, make me come. Please."

He lowered his head, his mouth capturing the lips of her sex as his tongue sought out the tight bud at the top. Eloise screamed as he scraped his teeth against the swollen flesh, his fingers entering her core. Ronan took her bud between his lips and sucked as his fingers brushed against a spot that sent light dancing behind her eyelids, and Eloise flew, her pleasure claiming her as she screamed his name. Her sex milked his fingers while his mouth stayed firm, coaxing every last pulse from her.

Barely giving her a moment to recover, he pulled his hand away and rose over her. He slid his hard cock inside of her, the last of her orgasm clenching his length, his groan one of ecstasy. "Slowly," she said.

He held still against her as he kissed her. Her body begged her to move, but she could feel his pleasure was close, his muscles shaking under her hands. He was holding on for her. She squeezed the walls of her sex around his cock, working the hardened length, and he shuddered before pulling his hips back. "I won't last long if you do that."

"That's the point." Pushing him on the shoulder, she held on as he rolled them over until she was on top, impaled on his length.

"I've fantasised about this."

"What?" she asked, looking down at them.

"You riding me like you do my horse. Taking charge,

using my body for your pleasure."

His hands came up to her hips as he nudged his sex into her and her eyes crossed, the sensation so exquisite it sent tingles of pleasure through her core. He chuckled as he lifted her before slowly lowering her back down on his cock. She leaned forward and grabbed his hands, pinning them above his head. Lifting her hips, she rode him, adjusting to find the right pressure. His cock rubbed against her with each return and she shivered, her body beginning to climb again. Ronan lifted his hips to meet hers, the force creating more friction as she rode him.

"I need ...," she stuttered as she searched for the missing piece to send her off the cliff.

"I know, love," he said, rolling her back onto her back. He pulled her legs over his arms, the angle creating a delicious sensation as he thrust his cock into her. With each movement, her body shuddered.

"Oh God, Ronan," she said as she was thrown from the cliff, her body exploding in ecstasy as he pumped inside her.

His strokes became harder and faster as he held her close, looking into her eyes. "Eloise," he said, seating himself fully inside her once more before he pulled himself from her and spilled on her stomach.

Her legs slid down his arms as he lowered himself over her, kissing the side of her neck. She stroked his back, loving the feel of him in her arms. She had missed this.

He leaned back to look down on her and Eloise smiled as she met his gaze. "I love you," she said, kissing his mouth.

Ronan paused above her, his body shuddering at her

words. He drew back, looking into her eyes. "And I love you," he said, taking her mouth with his and kissing her again.

In the dim firelight, she lay upon Ronan's chest, his arm wrapped around her while he twirled a strand of her hair with his fingers. "What's next for us?" She could hear the worry in his voice.

"What do you see?"

"Promise not to laugh?" he asked. When she nodded, he said, "In a perfect world—," Exhaling deeply, he pulled her closer. "In a perfect world, I would marry you tomorrow. I would throw caution to the wind because no matter your occupation or my station, we love each other."

"That does sound like a perfect world," she said, her heart aching. "What about this moment? Where are we then?"

Ronan scooted down to lay on his side so he could face her. "Why cannot this one be the same as that?"

"Because of my occupation. Because of your station," she said. "You cannot have a wife gallivanting across the country, putting her life on the line, when she should be here hosting parties."

Ronan rolled her over onto her back, peppering her face with kisses before he pulled back. "You're a confounding woman. Did you hear what I said earlier? I love you, Eloise Dempsey, and I will follow you to the ends of the earth, to every mission, every assignment, every challenge. I love you, and I'm willing to make this work through anything, as long as we do it together."

Tears sprang to her eyes, flowing down her cheeks as

she looked at him in the firelight. "Are you sure you'll be all right, being with a spy?"

"Madame Delacroix, I would like nothing more."

Eloise wrapped her arms around him, pulling him down upon her. Relief spread through her as she held the man she loved, kissing his shoulder, his neck, anywhere she could reach. "I love you, Ronan."

"I love you," he said back to her, tucking her into his side. "Well, what is the next assignment? Does Remy have you hunting for another member of the Fall of Caesar? Are you to protect the Prince Regent? The bounder better keep his hands to himself."

She laughed as she looked up at him, "I do believe my next assignment is mistress to the Marquess of Vaughn."

"Wonderful," he said, "We'll start tomorrow. But first, I need to make love to London's greatest spy." She laughed into his chest before he began to kiss her senseless. This might be her most complicated mission yet. She could not wait.

EPILOGUE

THE CRIES OF gulls and the scent of saltwater permeated the air around Eloise. The docks bustled with travellers and sailors, making their way to their destinations without a care for those around them. The spy within her wanted to remain, intrigued by the potential of each individual's story. A matron edged along the worn planks, her companion next to her, holding her arm against the rush of civilisation.

Eloise bit her lip as she watched the slight woman walk, her gait weary. When the porter made to grab for the woman's valise, she whipped her cane about like a sword and sent the man scurrying away. Swallowing a giggle, Eloise turned to the large ship that loomed ahead.

"Mrs. Delacroix, how are you this fine morning?" a voice said.

Her stomach flipped as the gentleman said her name. In the past months that voice had crooned at her, argued with her, and whispered naughty words while the body it belonged to took her to new heights of pleasure.

All the same, he should have met her thirty minutes ago.

"You sir, are late," she said, forcing her face into a scowl as she turned to Ronan.

"My apologies, madame. I was delayed by a last-minute errand." He winked at her before nodding to a black carriage behind him.

Eloise strolled towards the conveyance even as her heart begged her to sprint. She had an image to maintain after all. Opening the door, she nearly squealed when she spied Sophie and Niraj. "Whatever are you two doing here?"

"We've come to see you off," Sophie said. "It's not every day your sister departs for Italy."

"But I bid you both farewell this morning."

"Yes, well I didn't quite have my fill of hugs yet." Sophie wiped at the moisture gathering in her eyes. Eloise fought to contain the tears that threatened.

"Blast. Come here." Stepping inside, Eloise plopped down next to Sophie and pulled her into a deep hug, certain she was squeezing too tightly. Tears gathered at the corner of her eyes and she allowed them to flow. Perhaps, Eloise Delacroix could disappear for a small moment.

"I'm so sorry to be a watering pot," Sophie said, her voice husky. "It's only we've never been apart and I don't quite know what I am going to do without you."

"You'll have Niraj and Knight. You'll train and learn and by the time I return you will be a better agent than I."

Sophie nodded and briskly wiped at her eyes before attempting a smile. Eloise mopped up her tears, then turned to the man sitting across from her.

"And what of you?" Eloise asked the man across from her.

Niraj raised a dark eyebrow at her, but his lips tugged into a small smile. "I am merely accompanying Sophie on this excursion. I hadn't any idea where we were headed in the first place."

"Of course. I wouldn't have guessed otherwise," she said, smiling at him in return.

"Bloody hell, Eloise, hug me and then get your arse on that ship. Knight will have my head if you miss it."

Eloise hugged him quickly, then exited the coach.

"Lord Vaughn," Sophie said, smiling at the large man next to Eloise. "If any harm comes to my sister, I will break every bone in your body."

"Completely understood, Miss Dempsey." Ronan bowed deeply to Sophie before shooting her a quick wink.

Giving them both a final smile, Eloise blew a kiss to Sophie and closed the door. Ronan extended his arm and she slipped her hand inside. "Did you plan that?" she asked.

"I did not. Sophie knew you would want to be seen off at the docks but that you wouldn't risk your cover. I merely told them our direction and ensured that they made it on time."

"Well, whether you had a hand in it or not, it meant the world to me."

"I'm glad," he said, picking up her hand and kissing her knuckles. "Let's get aboard this ship and start our adventure, shall we?"

"Are you sure you're all right with this?"

"A trip to Italy with the woman I love? Of course."

"Ronan..."

"So, you'll also be on assignment. It's nothing we haven't handled before. I'll write and you'll pursue your career."

"And the fact that I'll be Eloise Delacroix, courtesan,

and not Lady Vaughn, doesn't bother you in the slight-est?"

"Marriage can wait. Hell, if it never comes, I shall be fine, as long as I am by your side."

After meeting with the captain and storing their items in their cabin, Eloise and Ronan headed to the bow of the ship. Leaning against the wooden railing, she was soothed by the rise and fall of the boards beneath her. The fact that she was embraced by two solid arms made it all the better.

"Ready for our adventure, El?" Ronan asked, the whiskers of his beard rough against her cheek.

"Absolutely."

Coming 2024

Seasonal Habits of Husbands and Honeybees
Genus of Gentlemen
Book II

Harrison and Phee's story

ABOUT THE AUTHOR

Emmaline Warden lives in Colorado with her four kids and an ungodly number of animals. Her love of romance began with an accidental copy of Susan Elizabeth Phillips and a trip to D.C. She's been reading and writing romance ever since.

emmalinewarden@gmail.com
Instagram: authoremmalinewarden
Twitter: @emmalinewarden
Facebook: emmalinewarden
Goodreads:
goodreads.com/author/show/18507128.Emmaline_Warden

Sign up for her newsletter and receive, **HEART OF STONE**, a historical paranormal short, as a special gift! www.emmalinewarden.com

Made in United States
Troutdale, OR
12/02/2023

15237843R00179